He crossed ~~...~~ **teasing in his eyes.**

"Am I to understand you are both asking permission and waiting for approval? Are you quite sure you're Ida Landway?"

Something fell away between them. The carefully tended wall of employer and employee slipped down to reveal a timid, fresh partnership that went beyond children, medicine or education. When she heard him say her name, her view of him shifted from Dr. Parker the institution and took a small step toward Daniel Parker the man. The man who had just brought her paint to bring beauty into this tiny world they shared.

"Quite sure," she said, wishing the words did not sound so breathless. "Thank you. Thank you more than you can ever know."

"The sky blue is my favorite," he said in the tone of a secret. "What's yours?"

"All of them. Every single one of them."

There was a moment of powerful silence, as if the air itself had changed between them. Ida wanted to look anywhere but into his eyes, but at the same time couldn't pull her gaze away from their intensity. He seemed both bothered and more comfortable, which made no sense at all.

Allie Pleiter, an award-winning author and RITA® Award finalist, writes both fiction and nonfiction. Her passion for knitting shows up in many of her books and all over her life. Entirely too fond of French *macarons* and lemon meringue pie, Allie spends her days writing books and avoiding housework. Allie grew up in Connecticut, holds a BS in speech from Northwestern University and lives near Chicago, Illinois.

Books by Allie Pleiter

Love Inspired Historical

Love Inspired

Gordon Falls Series

Visit the Author Profile page at Harlequin.com for more titles

ALLIE PLEITER

The Doctor's Undoing

HARLEQUIN® LOVE INSPIRED® HISTORICAL

Recycling programs
for this product may
not exist in your area.

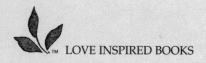

TM LOVE INSPIRED BOOKS

ISBN-13: 978-0-373-28309-5

The Doctor's Undoing

Copyright © 2015 by Alyse Stanko Pleiter

www.Harlequin.com

Printed in U.S.A.

Whenever the rainbow appears in the clouds,
I will see it and remember the everlasting covenant
between God and all living creatures
of every kind on the earth.
—*Genesis* 9:16

To clever, long-suffering,
much-needed school nurses everywhere

Chapter One

July 1919
Charleston, South Carolina

Brr. Cold.

For July in Charleston, South Carolina, that was quite a feat. The shiver that ran down Ida Lee Landway's back had nothing to do with the afternoon's heat—which was oppressive—but everything to do with the frosty feeling coming from the imposing iron gates of the Parker Home for Orphans. One didn't have to know children to know those looming cement walls and thick black iron grating were just plain wrong. Charleston homes boasted many beautiful wrought iron gates and graceful stone walls, but this entrance was large, clunky and downright unwelcoming. *Oh, Father*, Ida gulped toward Heaven, *have I made a wrong choice?*

She checked the notice in her hands one more time, hoping somehow she'd gotten the address wrong. The multibuilding compound—what she could see of it through the gates—looked more like a factory than an orphanage to her color-loving artistic eye. Many of the buildings had the city's classic red brick and black shutters, but somehow the place still looked as if someone had doused the whole affair with a bucket of gray paint. Even Charleston's red-clay soil seemed to have more vibrancy to it.

A small face popped into her vision. "Who're you?"

An artist by nature, Ida was a student of faces. She collected a dozen details of this tiny countenance in a matter of seconds. Clean, but pale, with powder blue eyes. Her blond hair hung in utilitarian braids down each side of her head—again, neat but without any bows or ribbons. She looked about seven, with a pair of her front teeth missing to show the tiny white buds of their adult counterparts poking through pink gums. She looked like a child who existed, but not one who thrived.

The girl stuffed her hands into the worn pockets of her faded white pinafore and stubbed a scuffed black shoe against the gate's lower rung. With the large vertical iron bars between them, Ida couldn't shake the notion that it felt as if she was at the zoo—and that was an awful thought for a place where children lived.

Ida applied her friendliest smile. "I'm Nurse Landway. Who are you?"

"Gitch."

Ida raised her brow at the odd name. "Gitch?"

Gitch shrugged. "Gwendolyn Martin, actually, 'cept nobody should bother with that name. I've been Gitch since I been here."

"Gwendolyn's a pretty name." When the child obviously didn't agree, Ida added, "But Gitch is definitely memorable. And rather fun." She reached a hand through the gates to the girl. "Pleased to meet you, Gitch. How about you let me in?"

Gitch looked as if that were a ridiculous request. "Everybody knows I can't do that."

"Really." It made perfect sense why a child of her age couldn't simply unlatch the orphanage gate, but Gitch seemed so ready with a more involved explanation that Ida found herself eager to hear it.

"Dr. Parker's the only one what's can open this gate. Well, he and Mrs. Leonard, but she died. Mr. MacNeil can, too, but he's not here." She ran her pink tongue along her bottom lip before adding, "You're a nurse?"

"I am."

"This gate's for visitors." She narrowed her eyes at Ida's valises as if to declare, *You sure don't look like a visitor to me.*

It felt as if the world was daring her to declare herself a visitor and simply walk away to somewhere that didn't feel even drearier than the war hospital Ida had just left. "No," she replied, hiding the heavy sigh she felt in her chest. "I'm not a visitor." Out of the corner of her eye, Ida spied two other sets of curious eyes peering at her from over a stone bench just behind Gitch. "I'm your new nurse."

"Not mine." Gitch's thin chin jutted out. "I'm never sick."

"A fact I take great pride in, Miss Martin." The deep, crisp voice from her left startled Ida. "I work very hard to keep you well and healthy."

Ida studied the man's face. Dark, almost black eyes assessed her with a clinical precision. The doctor. Equally dark hair, combed to precision, framed a pleasant face—save for the utter lack of a smile. He was tall, very official looking in his crisp brown suit and starched shirt. That he was wearing a suit *and* vest in Charleston's July signaled a man committed to decorum and order. General Barnes back at Camp Jackson had offered a less intimidating countenance, and he was not known as a friendly man. The man ran a home for children, for goodness' sake. Shouldn't he be a mite friendlier than the imposing gentleman in front of her?

"Dr. Parker?" It would have been wiser to keep the astonishment out of her voice.

"Indeed." He nodded at the paper she was holding. "I take it the instructions to use the side gate were not to your liking?"

"Oh. I...well, I suppose I didn't read that far." Ida peered down at the set of detailed instructions that filled the bottom of her paper. *All employees should use the side gate located on the south side rather than the Home's front entrance.* "Well, I'm not technically an employee yet now, am I?" She offered an even friendlier smile than the one she'd offered Gitch. "You could say I'm a guest...still."

The attempt at humor fell far short. Rather than reply, Dr. Parker made a noise entirely too close to a *harrumph* and produced a set of keys to swiftly work the lock. Ida tried not to hear the hinge's groan as an omen of doom. To think she'd considered this the least gloomy of possible postings available to postwar army nurses! Children shouldn't be kept behind locked doors as if the place were a jail. She tried to regard the wrought iron fencing that ran around the outside of the compound as ornate, but failed. It couldn't have been more than five feet tall, but it felt much taller.

Dr. Parker stepped out onto the walk and picked up

Ida's two valises as though proper Charleston gentlemen hefted luggage every day—which, as far as she knew, they most certainly did not. Maybe he wasn't such a stickler for propriety, despite his tailored appearance. He looked around. "No trunk or other cases, Nurse Landway?"

And there it was. Ida had spent the past years on Camp Jackson, an army encampment where fine frocks and other such things hardly made an appearance. As such, she'd almost forgotten her "low station," as Mama surely would have put it. Those who came from the backwoods of West Virginia were not counted among society's "young ladies of quality." The truth was she didn't have trunks of dresses as one might expect of a Charleston lady. She'd gone on scholarship to nursing school, which meant she'd done very well for herself by West Virginia standards, but still fell far short of South Carolina's social elite.

Ida shrugged. "No, just these." She forced confidence into her voice, although the answer felt woefully insufficient.

"Excellent." Dr. Parker nodded and turned through the gate.

Excellent? Dr. Parker, of the impeccable suit and starched collar, found her paltry wardrobe excellent? "I beg your pardon?"

Dr. Parker set the cases down inside the compound, then pulled the gate shut with a resolute *thunk* and twisted the key. "I requested an army nurse for a specific reason, Miss Landway." He picked up the cases and began walking on ahead at a brisk pace, clearly expecting her to follow. "We've our fill of finery with the ladies' guilds and other such volunteers." Ida had to nearly trot—and Gitch had to practically run—to keep up with the tall man's stride. "I attend more philanthropic balls and charity socials than I can stand—for the good of the Home, of course," he said over his shoulder as he made his way down the cracked sidewalk toward the largest of the buildings. "But I assure you what this institution needs more than anything else is good, practical help. I need a nurse more preoccupied with basic health than the state of her petticoat."

He went on speaking, but Ida found herself staring at the saddest little collection of hydrangea she had ever seen. She wasn't much of a gardener—although she loved to paint flowers almost as much as she loved to sketch faces—but even Ida knew the plants to be capable of stunning colors when tended correctly. The balls of blossoms looked to Ida like the rest of the orphan home compound: capable of color yet sadly lacking.

"Nurse Landway?" The doctor's irritated tone pulled Ida from her thoughts. She looked up to find him staring at her from a good ten paces away. Gitch stood baffled in the middle of them, her blue eyes darting back and forth between the two adults. She had a "don't mess with Dr. Parker" warning in her eyes that was far too old for her tender years.

"My apologies, Dr. Parker." Ida quickened her steps to catch up with the doctor. As she reached Gitch, the girl grabbed Ida's hand and tugged her along as if it were Ida who needed supervision rather than the orphan girl. "I was merely wondering who tends your gardens here at the Home."

"You'll meet our groundsman, Mr. MacNeil, later.

The facilities are his charge, and it is no small task, I assure you."

Gitch tugged on Ida's arm. "Mrs. Leonard kept the flowers, only not so much as she got sick. Mr. MacNeil fixes things, but he ain't much for flowers and such."

"*Isn't* much," Dr. Parker corrected as he walked on. "Mind your grammar."

Gitch rolled her eyes with such classic childhood weariness that Ida could only chuckle. She leaned down to the girl. "I ain't much for grammar, neither."

Gitch's formerly narrowed eyes popped wide in shock, then she swallowed a giggle. Ida held a finger to her lips, smiled and offered Gitch a wide, wild wink. Well, at least she seemed to have one young ally at the Parker Home for Orphans. As for Dr. Parker, only God knew if he was friend or foe.

Daniel placed the two—thankfully light—cases down at the entrance of his office, genuinely puzzled. Camp Jackson had assured him Nurse Landway was practical, hearty and generally well suited for the end-less job of keeping so many children fit. "Hearty and practical" suggested a stout, older female much like the late Mrs. Leonard. What stood before him was a slender, curvy peacock of a woman with wide, brilliant eyes, unruly hair and evidently not much focus.

He watched Miss Landway say goodbye to the Mar-tin girl as if the child was Queen of England. Holding out a formal hand, Nurse Landway dropped a curtsy worthy of the stage and declared, "Fare thee well, Lady Gwendolyn. I look forward to our next meeting—gram-mar and all."

Fare thee well, Lady Gwendolyn? Daniel shut his

open mouth and waited for little Miss Martin to explode in protest to the use of her full name. She always did. Why the child hated her given name so, he could never work out. Nor could he bring himself to refer to her as anything so crass sounding as "Gitch," keeping to "Miss Martin," or avoiding calling her by name altogether. To his shock, the child only smiled and—most surprising of all—attempted a curtsy of her own. Nearly falling over, she erupted in a flurry of giggles and a "Bye, y'all" called over her tiny shoulder as she tumbled from the room.

Miss Landway stared after her, laughing. "Oh, she's delightful." She turned to look at Daniel. "Are they all like that?"

Daniel tucked his astonishment back down inside as he motioned her to take a seat at the chair in front of his desk. "Like what, exactly?"

She cocked her head so far to one side that a curl bobbed over her raised brows. "Such contradictions—pale, sullen, then suddenly friendly. I was worried they'd all be grim, given the troubles they've had."

"They're children, Miss Landway, not soldiers. Many of them are sullen, as you put it. Withdrawn. Others are cheerful, despite coming from some dreadful situations. Many of them haven't had a dependable home or meal until they came here."

"That's just wrong, if you don't mind my saying so." He'd forgotten a grown woman could pout as easily as any youngster. "Children shouldn't know so much sadness. Children ought to have mamas and papas, don't you think?"

A wiggling tendril of doubt over this recent hiring grew stronger in Daniel's chest. He steepled his hands.

"Children ought to have a lot of things the war took from them. Surely your work at Camp Jackson gave you some preparation for situations like theirs."

She looked out the door that Gwendolyn—he used the name in his head now that she'd permitted it—had exited. "I'm no stranger to a sorry tale, Dr. Parker. I've seen some sad, lost souls come back from the war inside bodies that barely held their skin on." She returned her gaze to Daniel, pointedly meeting his eyes. "Only it seems a double sorrow to bear so much at a young age." Miss Landway made a dramatic gesture of clasping her hands and planting them in her lap. Miss Landway was fond of dramatic gestures, it seemed. "I want to help."

Daniel couldn't decide if her enthusiasm stood any chance of holding. There were days when the demands of the Home nearly drowned his spirits. So much was out of reach for these youngsters. Starting life with so many strikes against them sometimes loomed like the largest of hurdles; a burden that pressed against his ribs so hard some nights, he had trouble catching his breath. "Excellent." The last two nurses had left after a handful of weeks, and Daniel needed this one to stay.

Donna Forley, one of the oldest girls in the Home who often helped out around the office, poked her head into the door. "You asked for me, Dr. Parker?"

"Miss Forley, I'd like you to meet Nurse Landway. Can you show her to her rooms?"

Miss Landway stopped midhandshake to blink at Daniel. "Rooms?"

"You were expecting an army pup tent?" Daniel could not remember the last time he'd cracked anything close to a joke. Why had he chosen such an inappropriate time to start?

"Well, I'm just astonished, that's all. It's been a long time since I've had room*s*. As in plural—to mind my grammar. The army's not known for generosity in lodgings, you understand."

Daniel tucked his hands in his vest pockets. "You have a suite of three rooms on the first floor of the girls' dormitory."

Her hand swept grandly to her chest, and the wiggling in Daniel's own chest returned. "Three!" she pronounced. "A veritable embarrassment of riches. I'll get lost."

Donna launched a wave of teenage giggles at the jest. Giggling. Was he to be surrounded by giggling from here on in? "I highly doubt that. They are small rooms, I assure you. But I can promise you the luxury of a private bath."

"A private bath. I swoon at the very thought." She struck a pose that sent Donna into another round of tittering.

Daniel swallowed his sigh. "All the same, dinner is at five thirty in the dining hall. You can meet the rest of the children then, although I suspect Miss Martin will have told half of them about you already."

"Gitch has a big mouth," Donna confided.

"Well then, she's my kind of gal. I like conversation, and lots of it."

Daniel took a breath to ask Donna to help with Miss Landway's cases, but the nurse had already plucked the pair of them off the floor. She squared her shoulders at the teen before he could get a word out and commanded, "Lead on, my dear Miss Forley." The pair of them marched from the room, bright as sunshine and chattering already.

However had the army managed the likes of Ida Lee Landway? More to the point, how would he?

Chapter Two

Ida took a small bit of time to explore the Home as she made her way to the dining hall for her first dinner. Her few visits to Charleston had shown her that the Home's buildings were ordinary by the city's standards: three stories high with a few of the requisite columns and shutters framing the windows. Still, the compound held none of the ornamental grace for which Charleston's buildings and residences were famous.

The front entrance led into the center wing of the U-shaped main building. This segment housed a half-dozen classrooms on the upper floors, while what few offices there were shared the main floor with the dining hall. On one end of the main wing sat Dr. Parker's office and a small receiving parlor. Ida presumed his living quarters sat beyond the French doors at the far end of that parlor, but didn't dare investigate. On the other end of the wing sat a library and a common study room. Her infirmary was just around the corner from the library, at the beginning of the girls' residential wing. The boys' wing sat sensibly on the other side of the main building.

It was the thing that struck her most: the sheer *sensibility* of the place. The overwhelming practical, even institutional feeling of the whole structure. It felt off, wrong somehow. *Too* sensible. For someone coming from an atmosphere of the highly practical US Army, well, that was saying something.

She ventured out to explore the courtyard formed by the U of the buildings. A tidy, functional little play yard sat with swings, a teeter-totter, groups of benches and other diversions shaded by a large tree. True to Gitch's word, there were also small plots that looked as if they had once been flower beds. She'd enjoy having flowers to look at again if the gardens could be coaxed back into life—sandy, scraggly Camp Jackson wasn't ever known for its pleasant landscaping.

Knowing all the children were gathering for supper, Ida crossed the courtyard into the boys' wing, which was a predictable mirror of the girls' wing. She found an outward-facing window, and peering through it, found the side gate she should have used this morning. To her left, at the boys' end of the common buildings, she saw what was likely the kitchen, for there were pots and shelving and washtubs outside as well as another neglected garden—this one looking more as if it had hosted vegetables rather than flowers. The clang of pots and pans and the smell of what might have been bread met her senses and reminded her she'd not had much of a lunch.

To her right was the back of the compound, where several outbuildings of various sizes stood. A garden shed, a storage shed and a third building Ida guessed to be the bathhouses. A friend had told her about the Home's most unusual "luxury": a set of small square bathing pools under gazebo-like roofs. Given that the children couldn't easily be shipped off to the cooler beach or up into the dryer mountains, they seemed an unusual but practical way to battle the hot, humid days that made a low-country summer such torture.

Beyond all these lay the wrought iron fence that enclosed the entire Home. Simply put, Ida didn't like it. Wrought iron fences could be beautiful—delicate, even—but this was hardly either of those things. It was a useful fence. Actually, if Ida were to put an adjective on the thing, she'd have chosen *mean*.

Not that the Parker Home for Orphans was an unpleasant place. Ida found she could be thankful for the small comforts and luxurious sense of space her quarters now had. Compared with the army, it was downright palatial. Three rooms, all to herself!

Still, the place wasn't what she had been expecting. The feel of the whole compound simply stumped her, and she couldn't work out why. All she could put a name to was a low, constant thrum in her stomach that it could be so much *more*.

A clue to her impression came to her as she came up on what had to be the dining room by sheer virtue of location, though definitely not by atmosphere. It was the quiet of the place that unnerved her.

Ida had found army mess halls to be loud affairs, and had expected dinner at the Home to be just as earsplitting, if not more. These were children, after all, and even her limited experience had taught her that young ones were noisy critters. Right now, the only thing that met her ears as she walked down the hallway toward the dining hall was an unnatural quiet. Children? Over fifty of them? This quiet? Ida had never known such a thing in all her days.

She turned the corner to view row upon row of noiseless children hunched over tin plates. A young boy gasped out a "Huh?" at her appearance, followed by a wave of swiveling heads. One would have thought these children had never seen a nurse before. Some of their mouths gaped, midchew, the youngsters astonished beyond whatever meager manners they possessed. Fond as she was of attention, Ida wasn't accustomed to being such a cause of amazement. Whatever friendly greeting she'd rehearsed to give upon entering left her mind with the "whoosh" of pivoting heads.

"It's her!" Gitch chirped, standing so quickly to shoot a waving hand in the air that it knocked a fork to the ground. The clatter rang like a fire bell in the quiet hall. Ida waved back, glad for a friendly face, only to watch an older child yank Gitch back down onto the bench and produce a "Shh!" nearly as blaring as the fork.

"Nurse Landway." Dr. Parker's voice came from where he'd obviously been waiting at the other end of the room, producing an equally massive wave of turning heads in his direction. Ida had the ludicrous thought that, were they to attempt a conversation like this, someone might end up seasick. "Children, please say hello to our new nurse."

The "Hello" Ida received rang so hollow and obligatory that her insides echoed like an empty canyon. A gulp fought its way up her throat, and she stifled the urge to turn right around and repack her bags. It was the one voice, Gitch's delightfully loud "Howdy!"— resulting in another yank back down onto the bench— that tugged Ida farther into the room instead.

They *were* like little soldiers. Sad, drab little soldiers lined up in unhappy rows too much like the rows of beds in Camp Jackson's rehabilitation wards. Ida had expected sadness, had anticipated unhappy little frowns, but nothing on the order that faced her at this moment. She folded her hands in front of her, suddenly wishing she had a chair or railing beside her to clasp. "Hello, children." She hated the lifelessness in her voice, but it was as if the room tamped down joy upon contact.

"Please come and join us in the staff dining room," Dr. Parker said, motioning to the door behind him. They didn't eat with the children? That made some sense if the children were noisy, but they clearly weren't.

As she walked down the dining hall's center aisle, Ida's feet seemed to grow shoes of stone as every eye followed her. At Camp Jackson, such an entrance—a nearly bridal-aisle walk down the center of a room—would produce a flurry of whispered commentary. As a woman amid hundreds of lonely soldiers, Ida was no stranger to turning heads and loud, often ill-mannered commentary. Truth be told, she rather enjoyed such attention. It showed that the men were aware of and engaged in the world around them, a far preferable outcome to soldiers who closed themselves off after the horror of battle. Here, the quiet settled hard and hollow in Ida's stomach.

Dr. Parker shut the French doors of the staff dining room behind him and pulled a chair out for her at a small oval table. Three other adults were already seated, but the two men rose at her entrance. "May I present Mr. Arthur MacNeil, who keeps things in running order around here."

"It's a pleasure to see a new face around here, lassie."

A red-haired man bulging out of his suspenders offered a friendly nod. His congenial features arranged themselves around a bushy ginger mustache. Narrow gray eyes framed in wrinkles gave him the look of an overworked but kindhearted soul. He looked to Ida like a man who would offer assistance in a tight spot but grumble about it endlessly afterward.

"Pleased to make your acquaintance, Mr. MacNeil." Ida hoped her wide smile would gain her access to whatever gardening information the man had accumulated over the years.

"And this is Mrs. Jane Smiley, who serves as our girls' schoolmistress." Dr. Parker gestured toward a lady with a surprisingly angled face. How Mrs. Smiley, who had such a happy name and such a jolly plump build, managed to have such pinched, hard features was beyond Ida's reckoning. She looked as though she ruled her classrooms with an iron fist.

"Good evening," Mrs. Smiley said, allowing Ida to discover the woman's voice was as sharp as her nose.

"Hello, Mrs. Smiley. How do you do?"

The woman offered no answer—and certainly no smile. Ida made an immediate mental note never to cross the fierce Mrs. Smiley.

"And finally, may I present Fritz Grimshaw, who serves as the boys' schoolmaster."

"Miss Landway, welcome to our facility." Ida craned her head to meet an astoundingly tall man's eyes. Long and thin, he resembled a tree with large, blinking eyes that peered over bottle-glass spectacles. She couldn't hope to guess his age, for he seemed both young and old at the same time. While he didn't seem to possess the authority Ida thought his position might require, she couldn't help but wonder if Mr. Grimshaw's sheer height allowed him to keep a large group of rambunctious boys in line. One could never hope to outrun legs so long.

"Thank you," Ida said, feeling as though she were addressing the chandelier. While she was pleased Grimshaw had said "welcome," she was equally displeased that he referred to the place as "our facility." *Facility?* The clinical term matched the clinical decor. Even coming from the monochromatic army world, Ida found the lack of color in the Parker Home for Orphans nearly suffocating. First thing tomorrow she was going to write her dear friend Leanne and beg her assistance in finding some cheery curtains for her "suite" of rooms.

Parker took his place at the head of the table, at which point everyone sat. "Let us give thanks."

Ida gave a sigh of relief. Table grace had always been a particular comfort to her, and she was glad to know the practice was in place at the Parker Home. She folded her hands and lowered her head, curious to hear the doctor's deep voice in prayer.

"Bless us, O Lord, for these Thy gifts, which we are about to receive from Thy bounty, through Christ our Lord. Amen."

Ida had never heard such dear words uttered with such a complete lack of emotion. In truth, the doctor's grace was as hollow as the children's greeting. He did *mean* the words—there was no doubt about that—but she could hardly guess if he *felt* them at all.

"There were times at Camp Jackson when table grace was a test of faith," she offered, smiling at her new colleagues as she draped the dull gray napkin on her lap. "Army food isn't always worthy of much thanks, you can imagine."

No one laughed.

It was going to be a long meal. Gracious, it was likely to be a long year.

Daniel watched his mother's ringed finger tap against the rim of her tea glass. He'd learned it as a sure sign of her irritation. It was a suffocating Tuesday afternoon, and she blamed her slow movements on the season's wretched heat. He could hardly blame her for that. As immune as he often was to the humidity, today it bothered even him.

"How are you feeling?" he asked as gently as he could. "That ache bothering you again?"

She shooed away the question with a flap of her hand and a muttered, "Pshaw, Daniel, don't you start. I am old and it's a steam bath out this afternoon. I should be in the mountains."

He refused to reengage in that battle. He'd given Mother endless permission to go, but had been just as persistent in his unwillingness to go with her. He was needed here. Instead, Daniel changed the subject. "The new nurse arrived yesterday."

Mother's eyebrows shot up. "Did she? The one from Camp Jackson?"

"Yes. Miss Ida Lee Landway." The sight of Miss Landway peering through the Home's front gate came back from his memory. He'd expected someone so much more sensible looking. Ida Landway struck him as a barely contained whirlwind.

"A war nurse." Mother waved her hand in front of her face as if to fend off the unpleasant thought. "To tend to children. Whatever got into your head?"

Daniel sipped his coffee rather than reply.

"Why do you drink that dreadful coffee in this heat?" His mother had always accused him of preferring coffee simply to irritate her tea service. He could never truly dispute the theory.

"You know I dislike tea. Hot coffee makes me feel cooler by comparison." It was a trick told to him by a schoolmate who had summered in Turkey. While it had some scientific basis, today it sounded like a childish prank when repeated to his mother. How had Ida Lee Landway become the least unpleasant choice of conversation topics? "And as for Miss Landway, we needed someone sensible and…stout hearted." It was a terrible choice of phrase. *Sensible* and *stout hearted* were the last adjectives he felt could apply to Miss Landway— though he hoped and prayed he was wrong. The orphanage couldn't bear a third vacancy lightly.

"Heavens, Daniel, you sound as if you were buying a mule, not hiring a nurse for children." He watched her shift weight gingerly off one hip.

"With the war over, Camp Jackson is the best source of experienced nurses. We tried hiring ones fresh out of school, and you know what happened."

Mother snapped her fan open. "I can't believe Charleston has no other fine nurses."

"There are plenty of fine nurses, Mother." Daniel set his cup back down on the rattan table between them. "Just not many willing to work for what the orphanage can pay. I stand by my choice."

"March over and tell Buxton Eckersall you need more donations." Mother threw a scowl in the direction of the Eckersalls' impressive house just down the street. According to Mother, she'd been over there yesterday pleading the orphanage's case. "They lost no boys in the war. I'd expect them to show a little more gratitude."

"I take it the Eckersalls didn't…"

"They did, but not nearly what they ought to have," she said, cutting him off. "It was all I could do not to be offended. And now we're resorting to army nurses." She made it sound like the most drastic of choices, sniffing a final proclamation of annoyance in the Eckersalls' direction. "I'd expected more of Lydia Eckersall, really."

Mother expected more of everyone. She had good reason. There was a time—back before the war changed so much—when a single direct glare from Amelia Parker could move societal mountains. "The Parkers are a force to be reckoned with," Father would always say when Mother had achieved one of her social victories. The name still commanded—and demanded—respect, but not on the scale it once had.

"The war has ground down many fortunes." Daniel sighed. It was what he always told himself to ease the sting of shrinking donations. All while the mountain of need continued to grow.

"Well, not *his*," Mother nearly hissed. "All the more reason to show some kindness to the unfortunate, I said." Daniel huffed, and she turned to look at him, her eyes softening. He held her gaze until she backed down. "Well, of course I didn't actually *say* that, but I tell you the thought hung in my mind. You should go over there and make him see why he of all people should contribute more."

Difficult as she was, it was hard to stay annoyed with his mother. For years, Amelia Parker had nearly single-handedly funded the causes of her choice, bending the pockets of Charleston society to her will in the name of any number of philanthropies. His father had been named chairman of the war-bond effort not so much for his persuasive skills as for his wife's. But the orphanage had always been their special project—the one to which they had given their name, and their direct supervision. Daniel's mother felt charity to be her God-given gift, and she wielded it with a boldness the Lord Himself surely admired. Her stories from after the War Between the States, her tales of generosity to friend and foe alike, were the foundation of his faith, shaky as it was.

Only it seemed as if those rules of Southern culture were shifting without this generation's permission. Mother couldn't fathom that the playing field had so shifted, and every time her application of social pressure failed to achieve desired results, she would command, "You go over there and make him see."

"I will," Daniel conceded, returning to his coffee. And he likely would. He could leave no stone unturned, no pocket unbeseeched, in the name of the Home. For the Home was his "gift," a yoke settled on his shoulders by both earthly and heavenly fathers. His earthly father had since joined his heavenly one, leaving Daniel to run the Home and its ever-growing operations. "Only I doubt I'll have better results."

Mother folded the fan shut and pointed it at Daniel. "A Parker prevails, always." She invoked the family motto whenever Daniel expressed doubts as to his ability to call forth charity out of thin air as his parents once did.

He had begun to wonder if the adage had crumbled with Charleston's other traditions.

Chapter Three

By Wednesday morning, Ida had settled in sufficiently to launch a thorough examination of her new infirmary. It was a small, tidy place, brighter than the rest of the facility thanks to the traditional white of the furnishings. A wall of cabinets and a small desk, as well as three chairs and a meager examining table, completed the room. Ida had spent the past hour peering into cabinets and opening drawers, stopping far too often to wrangle her hair back into place.

She'd been here not even two full days and already the humidity had wound her curls into a bird's nest. Wasn't it supposed to be cooler by the sea? Either it was the humidity or the closed-in feeling of these buildings, but Charleston seemed to be poaching her composure. Not to mention the woeful lack of supplies—if there was one thing the army had been, it was well stocked. Not so here. Counting far too few rolls of bandages, Ida blew out an irritated breath.

"Something not to your liking, Miss Landway?"

She startled, banging her head on the cabinet. Hard.

The blow sent her backward into her desk chair, nearly toppling furniture and nurse over in an undignified heap.

"Don't you knock?" she snapped, head stinging. Ida looked up, cringing in recognition as her eyes met the owner of that voice. "Pardon me, Dr. Parker, I hadn't meant to be so direct. You startled me."

"The door was already ajar. And somehow I think you *always* mean to be so direct."

Ida grabbed the chair arm, seeing stars. "It seems I can't find enough open doors and windows in this heat. And what's that supposed to mean about being direct?"

Dr. Parker pushed the infirmary door farther ajar and peered at her. "You're bleeding."

Ida reached a hand up to her hairline only to feel a wet warmth that confirmed the doctor's diagnosis. "Your cabinet has teeth." She went to walk toward the cabinet, but found rising to be a rather painful enterprise.

"Sit back down," Dr. Parker ordered, motioning her into the chair. "I am a doctor, you know."

"Why Dr. Parker, that could almost be called a joke." Ida sucked in a breath as a change of expression sent a stinging pain through her forehead.

"Despite what you may have heard, I do possess a minute portion of bedside manner." He reached into the predatory cabinet and handed back a bottle of disinfectant and a roll of bandages.

Ida took them gingerly. "I'd have preferred to discover your lighter side under more dignified circumstances."

He turned and narrowed his eyes at her forehead. "Let's hope you don't need to discover my skill with sutures, shall we?" He made an odd motion toward his own head with his hands.

She cocked her head at the gesture, an unfortunate choice since it sent sparks of pain flying across her hairline. Furrowing her brow against the ache only made things worse.

Dr. Parker made the motion again, then finally rolled his eyes. "Your hair, Miss Landway. You'll need to move it out of the way."

"Well, why didn't you say so?" Ida slipped off her nurse's cap and went to smooth her hair back—only to be rewarded with bloody fingers and an additional stab of pain. "My stars, but that smarts."

Dr. Parker unrolled a swath of bandage, snipped it from the roll and handed it to her. "I'm sure I don't have to tell you to apply gentle pressure."

"No need to tell me to be nice to my own noggin. Not when it hurts like this." She gave the cabinet an angry look. "What in blazes bit me in there?"

Dr. Parker must have been wondering the same thing, for he was already running his hand around the corner of the shelf. "This. There's a nail that's come loose from the hinge." He returned his gaze to her. "I don't think it's cut too deep or you'd be bleeding more than you are. You'll be spared my stitchery, I suspect, but I'll send MacNeil in here immediately to take care of this cabinet." He leaned against the small desk. "Let's have a look."

Looking up at him, Ida felt small. She'd tended everything from sergeants to generals and never felt ill at ease, but Daniel Parker made her jittery. Yes, he was her superior, but that didn't explain the discomfort that always walked into a room ahead of him. "I'm sure I'm fine."

"Did you know," Dr. Parker said as he peeled her hand away from the bandage and lifted it himself, "one of the first things they told me in medical school was that when a patient insists he's fine, he seldom is."

"I'm not a patient, I'm a nurse." He was close enough that she could smell the soap on his hands. She could see the spot on his cheek where he'd nicked himself shaving this morning. She closed her eyes, mentally putting a dozen miles between them before her head chose to resume swimming.

"At present, you're a patient. And a difficult one, were I asked to categorize."

Ida heard him unscrew the top of the disinfectant bottle. "You're about to douse me with that horrid stinging stuff and *I'm* the difficult one?"

He gave a low laugh. The sound surprised her, popping her eyes open despite her best intentions. He was way too close. She squinted them shut again. "Chin up, Miss Landway." He'd applied his "doctor voice," the one she knew every medical professional employed when about to do something that would cause pain. "This will only hurt for a moment."

"If you think I—" A hiss of pain cut off the rest of her thought as the disinfectant found its target. If she hadn't been seeing stars before, she saw a whole constellation now. "Genesis, Exodus, Leviticus, Numbers… I'd forgotten how much that smarts."

She felt Dr. Parker's hand take hers and guide it up to hold the gauze in place. He had a doctor's touch— precise, firm and yet a bit tentative. Theirs wasn't the classic doctor-patient relationship—at least not in this case—and his touch told her he felt as uncomfortable as she did. In a moment or two she opened her eyes to see him leaning against the table, putting the cap back on the disinfectant, wearing the echo of a grin. Not a full smile, mind you, just the echo of one.

Ida lowered her good brow. "You enjoyed that."

"On the contrary. I'm merely glad you didn't cry. A good many of my patients end up in tears around here, so I'm grateful when I get the chance to tend to an adult." He set the bottle down. "Genesis?"

"A trick I learned at Camp Jackson. Keeping a patient speaking helps prevent them from tensing up in pain. Some of those boys had to endure me pulling up bandages day after day, so I'd cue them if they didn't know their books of the Bible. Opened up a lot of conversation about the topic, too."

"Are you in the habit of conversing on the nature of your patients' souls?"

Ida couldn't tell if Dr. Parker considered that a good thing. "Only when the Good Lord opens the door. I'd understood this to be a Christian institution."

"It is, but the army is not."

"Dr. Parker, you'd be amazed how much a man wants to talk about his soul if he thinks he's dying. Or ought to have died. I'll tell you, God is more in that army hospital than lots of churches." Parker shook his head as if he didn't know how to respond. Now that her head felt a tad clearer, Ida thought it might be time to stand her ground. "*Is* this a Christian institution, Dr. Parker? Does God live here at the Parker Home for Orphans?"

She took some comfort in the fact that Dr. Parker thought for a moment before answering. She didn't want some rote response to a question like that. Finally, he

said, "I'd like to think He does, yes." After a second
he added, "That's a rather bold question for someone
who has been here two days. Why did you feel the need
to ask it?"

*You've opened the door, Lord, I'm walking through
it.* "Because—" she dabbed one last time before taking
the bandage from her brow "—were that the case, I'd
think this place would have more joy in it."

That brought a gruff laugh from the doctor. "You're
expecting joy—from displaced orphans?"

"Dr. Parker, I expect joy from everyone. I believe
in joy. I thrive on it. And yes, I've only been here two
days, but I tell you this place is more dull gray than the
army was drab green. Seems to me children are natu-
rally happy, noisy, joyful creatures. I know they've seen
hard times, but that ought not to knock all that happiness out of them. And if that *has* happened, I think
maybe it's our job to give that joy back to them. So far
I haven't seen that. I hope you don't mind my saying
you could knock me over with the quiet in this place."

Dr. Parker tugged on his vest. "You are not shy with
your opinions, are you?"

Ida shrugged. "I'm not shy, period. If I've got something to say, I'm going to say it—provided it's worth
saying, that is."

She waited for him to reprimand her for her tongue—
it had happened often enough at Camp Jackson—but he
stroked his chin with eyes narrowed in consideration. "I
think you have much to learn about troubled children.
And I suspect your assessment of what's 'worth saying' might differ greatly from mine."

Ida folded her hands in her lap. Mama always said
she let her mouth run ahead of her sense.

"But I do wonder if we couldn't use a dose of positive thinking around here."

Ida looked up, feeling the first sparkles of hope light in her chest.

"You're welcome to share your opinions, but I will ask that you do me the courtesy of sharing them with me and not with the other staff. I should like to temper your…shall we say, enthusiasm…with a bit of experience and practicality. I'd like to think I am in charge for a good reason."

Ida nodded. "You *are* in charge, Doctor. If the army's taught me anything, it's how to take orders." It wasn't really a fib, though it was unquestionably an exaggeration. She'd been written up for doing just the opposite more times than she cared to count. But she'd been working on it—and praying on it—and would continue to do so.

"See you mind that cut for the next day or two. And stay away from Louie Oberman until you're sure it won't bleed again. The poor child vomits at even a drop of blood."

MacNeil knocked on Daniel's study door that afternoon. "I fixed the infirmary cabinet like you asked. Found one or two other loose nails and fixed them, too." The groundskeeper wiped his hands on his trousers. "You mind telling me what she was doing poking her head into that cabinet?"

It had been an amusing scene to walk past the infirmary and see the profile of Miss Landway bent over with her head in the cabinets. "I expect our new nurse likes to poke her head into everything." He chose his description carefully. "She seems more…enthusiastic than I was expecting."

MacNeil smiled. "She's a bit of life in her, to be sure. Not a bad thing, all around. Different from the others, though."

"That's what I'm hoping. We need this one to stay."

MacNeil nodded. "Aye, we do. I wasn't much for the last one, if you don't mind my saying. She looked afraid of everything, and little ones pick right up on such things."

The last nurse had indeed been a disaster. A frail, delicate woman who seemed astonished by every bump and bruise. She looked far more suited to a nanny's job than to nursing fifty-eight children's daily scrapes and ill stomachs. It's exactly why he had turned to the army, thinking an army nurse would have the stalwart constitution to take on whatever harm the children encountered. "Miss Landway doesn't strike me as afraid of anything."

"We're no battlefield. It can't be that hard for her to tend to this lot."

"I'd say we have a rather good safety record for the number of children and the age of our facilities. I owe a lot of that to you." He did. MacNeil was a master of repairs, cobbling together old parts and generally working wonders with precious little funding. "I can't think of anyone we depend on more than you."

MacNeil flushed. "Don't let Grimshaw be hearing you say that. Or worse yet, Mrs. Smiley." He leaned in. "It's my opinion Smiley thinks she's second in command."

"Nonsense," Daniel replied with a smile, "you are."

This sent MacNeil into a gush of laughter. "I don't

know why everyone says you're such a serious lot. I find you funny. Smart, yes, but you can make your share of jokes when it suits you."

"Only with you."

"Well, I'll be making no jokes with the kitchen drains this afternoon. We got one working fine enough, but the other one's giving me fits. I might need to buy some new parts." He delivered that last line with the air of bad news. It was—the Home had endured a run of failing equipment in the past month, and the budgets were stretched already.

"Parkers prevail, MacNeil. We'll find a way to make it work."

MacNeil nodded as he turned toward the door. "You always do, sir. You always do."

Chapter Four

Ida sat on the side of her precious private bathtub Friday evening and gingerly toweled her hair. My, but a cool bath did wonders to ease the tightness of a hot Charleston day. She'd been at the Home all of five days, and had discovered that by supper she felt so sticky and tired it was a challenge to converse with the other staff at all. Maybe that's why the children were so quiet at supper—perhaps the days sapped their energy, as well. But they were hardly more boisterous at breakfast. No matter what the reason, Ida just hated to think that life had beaten the joy out of so many children all at once.

She walked into her bedroom, glad again to catch sight of the cheery yellow curtains her friend Leanne had delivered this morning. Leanne Gallows had been her roommate at Camp Jackson, and the two had fast become dear friends as well as colleagues. Leanne had met her new husband, Captain John Gallows, at the camp in a whirlwind wartime romance with the happiest of endings. John and Leanne lived in Charleston for now, but would soon be heading up to Washington, DC to John's new post in the diplomatic corps. It seemed a special grace that even when Leanne left, these bright yellow curtains would remain as a daily reminder. They brightened the room the same way Leanne's friendship brightened Ida's service in the long, difficult war.

The old curtains had been a horrid dark green, nearly as lifeless as the endless gray of every building wall. Today even the old red brick of the building exteriors seemed to boast more life than the dull walls inside. Where were the paintings? The drawings? The happy fixtures of a joyful home? How could children grow and thrive without color and light?

Ida let her hand run along the frilly yellow ruffles that now skimmed her windowsill. She couldn't wait to watch the sunlight catch them tomorrow morning. Braiding her hair, Ida toured her three-room suite again, giddy at the luxury of so much space. Walking over to the bureau in her parlor—her heart bubbling *Look at me, I have a parlor!* for the tenth time as she did—Ida opened the bottom drawer, where she'd stowed her paints and charcoals. These new days at the Parker Home were like a feast for the quantity of fresh faces to draw. Even now her hand hovered over a set of sketching pencils, eager to capture that skeptical look in Donna Forley's brown eyes or the sharp angles of Fritz Grimshaw's brows.

Only one thing stopped her: the charcoal's gray color. She couldn't bear to bring one more drop of gray into this world—even with something as harmless as a sketching pencil. *I've simply got to paint.* Certainly there were a dozen tasks clamoring for her attention on her first free afternoon tomorrow, but none of them would be more satisfying than to paint. Just the thought of filling any blank canvas she could find with a festival of color lightened her spirits. Ida wanted to capture the gentle blue of Gitch's mischievous gaze or the particular pink of Jane Smiley's ears when she got mad.

Or the curious puzzle that was the color of Dr. Parker's eyes. She'd never thought of a set of eyes as colorless before. Not that they were without hue, but they seemed to have no distinct shade. They were dark, surely, but even the darkest brown eyes had flecks of warmer tones in them. Dr. Parker's seemed neither brown nor gray, and yet Ida knew they couldn't be a true black, either. The artist in her longed to stare at them hard in good sunlight, to unlock the mystery of why she couldn't see colors in those eyes.

Restless, Ida closed the drawer and returned to her bedroom windows. She opened them as wide as they would go, hoping to catch Charleston's famed off-the-water evening breeze, but the night's stillness prevailed. The heat was like a living thing here, pressing against one's chest, pulling a soul down. Ida found she had to deliberately fight it, the same way a war nurse deliberately fought against sadness and despair. "Not even a foothold," her nursing teacher would always say. "Mind your thoughts as much as you mind your sanitation, for both can infect with equal power."

Guard my heart, Lord, Ida prayed as she slipped into bed, thinking even the thin sheet too much tonight. Already her night shift felt as if it were cementing itself to her arms. *And if it's not too much trouble, send a breeze.*

An hour later, Ida turned over yet again, unable to get comfortable in the thick night air. No matter how much she needed sleep, it was nowhere to be found tonight. Her ability to nod off in even the worst of conditions had been a blessing at Camp Jackson—Ida couldn't remember the last time she had trouble catching winks. "Fine!" she declared to the dark room, sitting up and reaching for the light. "Now what?"

She didn't feel like reading. She'd already organized most of her things, and that sounded as if it would make too much noise anyhow. There wasn't enough light to paint properly, and the black and white of sketching sounded entirely unappealing.

It wasn't a breeze that the Good Lord sent, but an idea with just as much refreshment. Dashing to the bottom drawer of her bureau, Ida found her knitting needles. Leanne had taught her the craft at Camp Jackson, where many of the nurses worked in their free time to make socks for the thousands of soldiers who fought for freedom on tired, cold feet. Ida had become a competent knitter, even if the required soldier colors of navy, black and olive left much to be desired.

Now that the war was over, colored yarn had become one of life's everyday luxuries. As a matter of fact, Ida was pretty sure she had just enough… "Aha!" she cried, as her hand found the small ball of bright pink yarn. It had been a gift from Leanne. A cheery bright pink was just the thing to lift her spirits.

Trouble was, the only thing Ida really knew how to make from memory were socks, and this ball wasn't enough for a full-size pair, nor was it the proper thickness.

Unless the feet were very small. Surely, somewhere in all those children in all those sizes was a pair of feet tiny enough to fit whatever socks emerged from this yarn.

Grinning and wide awake, Ida peered at the ball and her needles, calculating if her memorized sock pattern could be adapted just enough to create a pair of small pink socks. "There's only one way to find out," Ida told the yarn in her hands. "I'm ready if you are, and it surely beats staring at the ceiling."

Adjusting her lamp, Ida tucked herself into the chair by the window and began to knit.

Saturday morning had brought a drenching rain, a sweet relief to the choking heat that had pushed children and staff to the limits of their manners. While Daniel could always do without the mud puddles and the leak that invariably sprung in one roof or another, he was always grateful for the way a good "gully washer" could rinse the world fresh and clean. A smile found its way across his face as he walked in the welcome shade of the afternoon. Midsummer like this, rain perked up the plants around the grounds, coaxing out a few of the blooms that still graced the yards from the years when the property had been a grand estate. "The Home still has the bones of a great lady," Mother was fond of saying, even though both women were showing their age. Time hadn't been kind to either of them, and Daniel felt that sting more fiercely with every passing month.

"See how that makes a circle right there? How it meets that line from the other side?" He caught Miss Landway's voice as he turned a corner toward the front of the compound.

"It's just shapes?" a child's voice, full of wonder, came in reply. Daniel slowed his steps, not wanting to intrude but still curious. He peered to his left to see Miss Landway seated on the stone bench by the front gate. She had a pair of girls on each side of her, more at her feet and a large pad of paper perched upright on her lap.

"Shapes and color. That's how an artist sees the world." She moved her hand over the paper, and Daniel shifted closer to improve his view. "Look at the gate and tell me what shape it is."

"A rectangle," one girl said. Miss Landway's laugh chimed across the courtyard in reply.

"A rec*tangle*, yes. Very good." He watched her sketch out the shape in the center of her page. "But not just any old rectangle. What's special about this one?"

"It's got a moon on top," Gwendolyn Martin, on the bench right next to Miss Landway, piped up as she pointed to the gate's rounded arch.

The nurse's smile was warm and bright as she nodded toward her seatmate. "Right you are, Gitch. The moon is also a shape, called an arch or a crescent, and if you plop that big old moon sideways on top of our rectangle—" she added the curve to the top of the drawing "—you get our gate." Miss Landway spun the drawing around so that the girls at her feet could see, and a chorus of wide-eyed *oooh*s met her display. The part of him that worried how long the Parker Home could retain a nurse was happy to note she used the word *our* when she referred to the gate. *Lord, You know I was looking for someone entirely different, but I'd still be grateful if this one actually stays.* He could try to learn to see the world in colors and shapes if it meant she stayed here where she was most definitely needed.

As if she'd heard his thoughts, Miss Landway opened a tray of watercolors on her lap with a flourish and announced, "Now we've got to add the colors. Call out the ones you see."

"The gate is black," young Miss Martin offered.

"Only it's got red and orange around the hinges and in spots on the side," added another girl.

"The dirt is brown but the leaves are green," another girl spoke up, pointing to the objects she named.

"But not the same color as those leaves over there," came another comment. "Those are a different green."

The children called out half a dozen colors and a few more shapes as they peered hard at the landscape before them. Miss Landway held up her pigments and had each girl match the color she saw with a color from the tray. For a woman who continually bemoaned the lack of color at the Home, she was wasting no time in digging up a palette right here. He stood and watched, fascinated, as she used each color to create a painting of the gate and the plants around it. Miss Landway had skill; the image was pleasant enough to hang in the staff dining room.

If only she had stopped there.

"The best thing about art," she said once she'd finished with each child's color, "is that we don't just have to leave the world the way we found it. We can have more fun than that."

Daniel felt his jaw go slack as Miss Landway dove into her palette and created a riot of hues around the gate. Under her enthusiastic brush, a full and wild garden sprung up around the gate on her paper. In a matter of minutes, two outrageously colored birds perched on the wall under a blinding yellow sun. A bright red house rose up beyond the gate whereas in real life only a dull gray shed stood on the other side of the street. Before she was finished, every inch of the paper was filled with motion and color until the canvas looked more like a tropical circus than the scene Daniel saw before her. When Miss Landway flipped the painting around to show the children, giggles and applause echoed across the courtyard along with her loud and musical laugh.

How had she done that? Daniel's gaze flicked back and forth between the real-life gate and Miss Landway's fantastical painting. It irked him that suddenly the Home's serviceable but pleasant front gate now looked dull and dreary, even to him. He'd liked the gate just fine before, and ought to still like it now. He didn't care for the funny, poke-in-the-ribs feeling Miss Landway's artwork produced, nor did he care one bit for the sad dissatisfaction that filled the eyes of some of the children after a moment.

She didn't realize what she had done. It would probably never occur to the plucky Miss Landway that she had just shown them a world they could never have, and left reality that much worse for the visit to a fantasy. How on earth was he to explain such a thing to the likes of Ida Lee Landway?

He walked over to the group, flipping his watch open as he came closer. Gwendolyn saw him first and stood up, a streak of fear in her eyes. They all looked as if he'd caught them doing something naughty, and that bothered him immensely. He took pains to soften his voice when he asked, "An art lesson, Miss Landway?"

"The girls wanted to watch me paint."

"Our gate is a rectangle with a moon," Gwendolyn pronounced. It bothered him that the little girl offered it like the grandest of compliments.

Miss Landway raised one eyebrow, a "what are you going to do with that?" gesture that made Daniel feel as if he were being tested. It should have been the other way around. Even ten minutes later, Daniel still hadn't quite figured out how Miss Landway had turned the tables on him so that he walked away without uttering one word of the lecture on appropriate reality he had planned. An hour earlier, he had thought his biggest fear in regards to Miss Landway was the possibility that she would leave. Now he had a new fear entirely—that she would stay, and fill the children's heads with dreams that were out of their reach.

His mother's admonition echoed in his brain as he made his way back to his office, stumped and more than a little worried. "Be careful what you pray for— the Good Lord just might give it to you."

Chapter Five

Daniel was just sitting down to enjoy his weekly indulgence of an hour's quiet reading before Saturday supper when the sound of yelling reached his rooms. He put down his book and cocked his ear, listening. No, it wasn't yelling, it was crying. Girls crying. Several girls crying. Something was most definitely amiss.

Ignoring his disappointment, Daniel pushed himself out of his chair and made for the door. The cries were coming from the dining hall, where Mrs. Smiley and the girls ought to be setting out the dishes for supper. Had someone cut themselves? Was one of the girls ill? He started walking in the direction of the noise, half expecting to be ambushed by one of the children or staff coming to get him, but he met no one on his way toward the torrent of girlish tears.

Of all the things Daniel steeled himself to see, a flock of angry girls slamming down tin plates in tearful fits was not on the list. No one seemed to be injured, but each of the five girls on supper table duty that afternoon was crying.

"I want some," the youngest girl moaned as she

slapped a napkin into place. "Why can't we all have them?"

Daniel scanned the room for Mrs. Smiley, hoping for an explanation to the sea of unhappiness swirling before him. He found her, two tables away, having angry words with…with Ida Landway. While Mrs. Smiley was easy to irritate on a good day, Daniel was at a loss for what Miss Landway could have done to not only raise the ire of Mrs. Smiley, but each of these girls, as well.

Dodging past a sniffling nine-year-old brandishing a fistful of forks, Daniel made for the teacher. "Mrs. Smiley, what has gone on?"

Miss Landway's eyes snapped up at the question, and Daniel could see the nurse was upset. It wasn't surprising; despite her cheerful name, Mrs. Smiley's tongue could curdle milk when she got angry—he'd had to have more than one conversation with the woman about keeping her temper under control. When the older woman turned, however, Daniel's jaw slacked.

Baby Meredith Loeman, the youngest occupant of the Parker Home for Orphans at just over a year old, wiggled a pair of bright pink booties at him from Mrs. Smiley's arms.

"I don't suppose I need to explain it to you *now*," Mrs. Smiley snapped.

As if to drive the point home, wails of "I want pink socks" and "Why can't Nurse Landway knit *me* socks?" and "I hate my socks!" surged up behind him.

The only thing stronger than the matron's glare was the look of stunned regret in Miss Landway's eyes.

"She hasn't got a lick of sense, this one." Mrs. Smiley cast a disparaging glance in Miss Landway's direction. "Giving a trinket like that in front of all the girls." She scowled at Miss Landway. "What did you think would happen when you did such a thing?"

"I…I…" The nurse looked at him, her eyes wide and startled. "It's just a pair of *socks*."

Daniel swallowed a weary sigh. This was why gifts were such a tricky business at the orphanage. But before he could explain that to Miss Landway, he needed to calm down the children. "Girls," he began in his best "let's all be sensible" administrative voice, "y'all are already wearing socks. Perfectly fine socks."

"Perfectly *dreadful* socks!" Little Mary Donelley could always be counted on for a dramatic interpretation. "They're plain old white and mine has a hole in the heel."

He walked toward Mrs. Smiley, trying hard not to be charmed by the chubby pink legs wiggling pink booties. Most women he knew would be cooing and tweaking such pink-booted toes. The handmade booties were adorable little things that would have made for a very welcome sight—were they anywhere else but an orphan home. Why? The "I want some!" whine from behind him served as a painful example. No wonder Mrs. Smiley was completely uncharmed by Meredith's clear delight in her present—the poor old woman was likely to have a tiresome evening as a result of Miss Landway's innocent little gift.

Daniel held his hand out. "I wonder if I could take a look at those."

"Gladly." Mrs. Smiley plucked them off Meredith's feet with a huff so loud even Daniel almost winced. Miss Landway certainly looked as if the sound pierced her ribs.

Daniel pocketed the pink socks and nodded in Miss

Landway's direction. "Why don't you and I have a cup of coffee in the other room? Mrs. Smiley and the girls can finish up in here."

Once inside the staff dining room, Miss Landway pulled the door shut behind her with one hand while the other went over her eyes. "I don't know what to say."

She looked as if she might cry, and Daniel was surprised at how deeply her regret touched him. It wasn't right how unfair this place could be to anyone trying to make a difference. Daniel remembered how the need to do something—anything—for these children had nearly drowned him in his first days at the orphanage. He'd given a sweet to one of the girls when she'd banged a finger and found himself amid a similar storm of "Why can't I have one?" howls.

He searched for something soothing to say. "It was a generous and kind impulse, Miss Landway."

She slumped down on one of the dining chairs, distressed. "I had no idea it would cause such a ruckus. I just wanted to put a bit of cheery color…"

"I believe your heart was in the right place." Daniel moved to the sideboard and poured two cups of coffee. "You simply need to learn how to channel such impulses into things that benefit *all* the girls without singling out one." He held up a cube of sugar in a silent inquiry, and she nodded, parking her chin on one hand. "It's one of the most difficult things about working here, and one of the reasons I asked you to clear any ideas with me."

"They're *just socks*." Her moan sounded as if it could have come from one of the girls.

Daniel set the cup and a small pitcher of cream down in front of the nurse. "No, they're not. How can I get you to see that?"

Miss Landway dumped a generous portion of cream into her coffee. The woman did nothing by halves, he was beginning to see that. "So I can't do anything for one of them, I have to only do things that can be done for all of them?" She made it sound dreadful.

"I think what just happened should make that obvious." He collected his own coffee and sat opposite her.

"But they're individuals. Each of them is unique. Their differences ought to be celebrated, not ignored by making sure everything they have is exactly the same."

Daniel remembered that urge, and felt a tinge of regret that practicality had squelched it out of him so effectively. "In a perfect world, I'd agree, but…"

Her eyes sparked. "But nothing. Don't you go telling me we don't live in a perfect world. That's a poor excuse for not letting a baby girl wear pink booties."

She was going to take some breaking in, this one. "I'm not saying Meredith cannot wear booties. But she cannot be the *only one* wearing pink booties." He fished the pink things out of his pocket. "Make them all booties, or socks, or whatever—I've no objections to gifts as long as *every* girl receives them."

"It'll take me months." He noticed her phrasing. She would do it. He could see it in her eyes.

He didn't know where she'd find the time—he didn't know how she'd managed to make the pair he now placed on the table between them. "When did you make these?"

She took a long sip of coffee, which gave him a hint of the answer. "I couldn't sleep last night. Once I got the idea, I couldn't sleep until they were done. This place is starving for color, Dr. Parker. Can't you see that? I just had to do something." She reached out and fingered one of the small pink fluffs. "They made Meredith so happy." Miss Landway looked up at him. "And they made all the other girls so miserable."

He couldn't help but offer her a smile. "In your defense, it doesn't take much in this heat. The smallest thing can set them off. Even Mrs. Smiley can lose her delightful charm." That last remark surprised him—Daniel hadn't joked about Mrs. Smiley's dour personality in months.

"She is quite the heavy hand," Miss Landway replied with a sparkle returning to her eyes.

"She is very good at what she does. Her job is enormous. If you don't realize that now, you will soon. I'm not so sure her firm hand isn't absolutely necessary in order to get things done." He picked up his own cup. "Surely an army nurse can grasp that."

Miss Landway smirked. It wasn't an expression Daniel often attributed to women, but it applied in this case. "Not *this* army nurse." She thought for a moment. "I'll find a way, you know."

"A way to what?"

She nodded toward the door. "To shower those girls in a rainbow of colored socks. You just watch. My mama always said I could teach a mule how to be stubborn."

Daniel believed it. "Really?"

"If I can give each girl socks in as many colors as I can, provided they all get the same number of socks, do I have your permission to do so?"

He didn't see how this would help, but then again he didn't see how he could say no. "Yes. But only if your regular duties do not suffer and only if the gifts are equal for all."

Miss Landway stuck out her hand. "Dr. Parker, you have a deal."

He found himself shaking her hand. The odd feeling in the pit of his stomach forced him to add, "Miss Landway, what will you do if the boys want socks, as well?"

It was a joke, but she didn't take it as such. She gave his hand a comically forceful shake. "I'll just knit faster, Dr. Parker."

Land sakes if he didn't believe her.

Dr. Parker had been right—a weekend started with such discontent quickly dissolved into a marathon of unpleasantness. Ida prayed hard during the Home's simple Sunday church service that her impulsive gift wouldn't do much harm, but the lack of classes seemed to allow the children extra time to acquire cuts and scrapes, sore stomachs and aching heads. This was an altogether different kind of nursing care. While the army had been a flood of dire needs, Ida found her current post to be a wearyingly steady drip of little grievances. It required a particular sort of endurance—and a mountain of grace.

She was just cleaning up after the third queasy tummy of the afternoon—a particular torment in this heat—when Ida heard a rap on her door. Mr. Grimshaw towered over a feisty-looking boy of about eight, clutching him by the elbow so hard the lad looked like a marionette strung up by a puppeteer. It wasn't until Ida let her gaze fall from the dizzying height of Mr. Grimshaw's face that she noticed the boy's bloody knuckles.

"Oh my," she said, reaching for a basin and cloth. "Only one way to get those."

"I imagine you've dealt with a badly thrown punch

or two in the army." Mr. Grimshaw nearly hoisted the boy onto the examining table.

"Usually they come in pairs," Ida replied, peering at the boy's angry scowl. "Where's the other one?"

"Jake Multon is down the hall with Dr. Parker," Grimshaw replied.

"He's hurt worse," crowed the boy, obviously seeing himself as the victor in the scuffle. "I hope he has the shiner for a…ouch!"

Mr. Grimshaw had pinned the boy's good arm with his spindly fingers. "That's enough of that. You'll both be sweating it out in the laundry room for a week if I have my say."

Ida couldn't help but groan right along with the boy. In this weather, she couldn't think of a worse punishment than standing over enormous vats of hot water washing the orphanage's endless stream of dirty linens. "Maybe not."

That raised one of Grimshaw's bushy dark eyebrows. "And why not?"

Ida poured water into the basin and pointed downward, instructing the boy to submerge his bloody knuckles. The resulting yelp answered Grimshaw's inquiry more effectively than any explanation Ida could offer. "Pain aside, young Mr.…."

"Loeman. Tony Loeman." The boy hissed his name through gritted teeth.

"Young Mr. Loeman here will run the risk of infection until the broken skin heals. So unless he can man the laundry vats with one hand, you'll need to find another way for him to pay his debt to society." She handed a cake of soap to the boy. "Scrub when you can stand it. While you're at it, how about you explain what brought this on. Or does Mr. Grimshaw already know?"

To Ida's surprise, both teacher and student gained a look of embarrassed reluctance at the question. Their expressions connected the boy's name in Ida's memory, and she stepped back to park a hand on one hip. "No."

"Jake was making fun of Merrie's socks."

"While I admire your efforts to defend your baby sister's honor," Grimshaw chided, "slugging Jake Multon was a poor way to go about it."

Ida felt as if the world had spun into ridiculous cyclones around one small act of kindness. "It was just a pair of socks!" she declared, more to the whole world than to her present company. She frowned at the boy. "You threw a punch over a pair of *baby booties*?"

"He started it."

Ida looked up at Mr. Grimshaw. "How do y'all survive Christmas?"

"It ain't much fun, but…"

"Scrub!" Ida cut Tony off with the command. She was beginning to see why the Parker Home for Orphans had run through its share of nurses. At this rate, she'd be apologizing clear through to Easter. "Mr. Grimshaw, would you step outside with me for a moment?"

Grimshaw gave Loeman a look that would pin a tiger in its place and then reached clear across the room to open the infirmary door with ease. "Of course, Nurse Landway."

Pulling the door shut, Ida kept one eye on Loeman through the glass as she peered up to the teacher. "I'm dreadfully sorry to have caused such a ruckus, Mr. Grimshaw. Believe me, I had no idea the trouble those booties would cause."

Grimshaw blinked, his face splitting into a smile that looked somehow alarming on his lanky features. "I thought it rather cute, truly. Seems a shame how a spot of kindness gets so poorly repaid."

Ida hadn't expected his reaction. "Why thank you, Mr. Grimshaw. But it seems to me you are doing the paying." She cast a glance at Loeman, now wincing as he gingerly swiped the cake of soap across his knuckles. It stung, no doubt about that, but keeping wounds clean was absolutely essential in this moist heat. "I hadn't thought about there being siblings in here."

Grimshaw's features softened further. "Loeman's one of the sadder cases, actually. His pa's been out of work so long they just couldn't feed them any longer."

Ida's jaw fell open. "Do you mean to say Meredith and Tony's parents are still living? They're not actually orphaned but *abandoned*?" The thought practically knocked her against the hallway wall. "It's a wonder Tony hasn't slugged the whole world."

"He's working on it. This wasn't his first fistfight. That's why I came down so hard on him."

Ida could only sigh and stare in at the poor boy. He looked her way for a fraction of a second—likely imagining she and Grimshaw were out here devising hideous forms of punishment—then returned to his painful task.

"I still think it was a fine thing you did. I know Mrs. Smiley will give you no end of grief for it, but I'm glad to see a kindness paid, no matter what the cost."

After a weekend of awful consequences, the man's encouragement warmed Ida's sore heart. "It's mighty kind of you to say so, Mr. Grimshaw." She glanced up and down the hallway, again aware of how stark the buildings were. "I'm just so aching to put a dash of color into this place. Children should live in cheerful rooms, don't you think? Happy, color-filled places?" It seemed an odd thing to say to a man who seemed a study in black and white every day.

"It's a nice thought, Nurse Landway. Although I could have done with a little less red today." He peered at a bloody smear on his cuff. "Do hope they can get this out in the wash," he muttered to himself before returning his attention to Ida. "I must get back to the library, where the boys are learning chess. Please do send Tony back there when he's done here. While the laundry may not be possible, I'm quite sure Mr. Loeman can play chess with one hand."

Ida put her hand on the infirmary door. These boys needed some place to channel their energy, but she doubted chess was going to fit the bill. What a complicated minefield of a place the Parker Home was turning out to be. *You're going to have to help me find my way, Father*, Ida prayed as she eyed the scowl still filling Tony Loeman's face. *This place makes the army look easy!*

Chapter Six

Ida raised the frame and set it gently on the nail Mr. MacNeil had placed in the wall above her small desk. She looked back at Leanne Gallows before she adjusted the frame so that it hung straight.

"Perfect," Leanne said, smiling. "I like the yellow matting—the room needs it."

"It does." Ida stepped back to admire the brightly framed copy of the "Nightingale Pledge." Ida, Leanne and hundreds of nurses before and since them had recited these words at the pinning ceremony that officially welcomed them into the profession. The piece had been framed in a formal cream matting, but last night Ida had salvaged a few inches off the hem of her yellow curtains and redone the mounting. She'd made a promise to herself to add one bit of color to her world every day, even if it was something as small as a hair ribbon. "And here I thought the army had gotten me used to drab."

"It's not that bad, is it?" Leanne looked around and shrugged. "Well, then again, I suppose it is. Seems sad to ask children to live like this." She clearly caught the look in Ida's eyes, for a smile turned up one corner of her mouth. "Which is why you're plotting something, aren't you?"

"Perhaps."

"Maybe I should remind you about the bit in there about abstaining from mischief," Leanne teased, crossing her arms over her chest. Leanne had given Ida no small amount of grief over the line in the pledge that read "I shall abstain from whatever is deleterious and mischievous," to which Ida had no small amount of trouble adhering.

Ida sat across from her friend. "Socks can hardly be counted as mischief."

"I thought you told me an actual fistfight had broken out over those baby booties."

"Well, yes," Ida admitted, "but we can't blame that one on the socks. In this awful weather, boys are going to be spoiling for a fight no matter what—the booties were only an excuse. I just hadn't thought through the implications."

Leanne laughed. "Imagine that."

"I'll have you know I have Dr. Parker's approval on the idea as long as each girl gets the same number of socks at the same time."

"I've heard of the Parker family, but I don't really know them. What is Daniel Parker like? You've been here a whole eight days. How have you found your new employer?"

Ida didn't have to think much before replying. "Whopping serious."

Leanne laughed. "I imagine half the world strikes you as overly serious. So, then, is the good doctor somber serious, or dedicated serious?"

"A bit of both." Ida looked in the direction of Dr.

Parker's office. The angle of the buildings was such that she could see the windows of his office from her own office windows. She had come down here well past midnight Sunday evening, having forgotten a book she wanted to review, and found his light still on. She knew he left the compound now and then, but other than that he seemed to be continually at his post. "I believe he views his work here as a vocation. He seems to bear the burden of all these youngsters mighty personally. You'd think they'd be fond of him for it."

Leanne cocked her head to one side. "Aren't they?"

Ida fiddled an unruly curl escaping from her pinned-up hair. "They like him, but it doesn't really seem to go much beyond that. It's not as if they are afraid he'll harm them in any way, but they don't look to him for affection—to give it or to receive it. I expect I've gotten more hugs in my week here than that man gets all year. Those little arms can't reach past all that authority to get to the man on the other side, if you ask me."

"Well, I suppose it takes a certain amount of command to keep a place like this from chaos. Soldiers mostly do as they are told. Not so with children."

Ida leaned in. "That's just it—they *do* obey like little soldiers. Take suppers, for instance. The meals here are deathly quiet. Makes me skittish to hear only the sound of so many little mouths chewing. If I could tell Dr. Parker one place to lighten things up, I'd sure start with the meals."

"Will you? Start telling him where to lighten things up?"

Ida blew out a breath and sat back in her chair. "I just won the sock skirmish—or so I think. I might need to ponder when to wage my next battle."

"An army fights on its feet." Leanne recited the saying often quoted by Red Cross knitters as they had stitched up socks for the boys overseas. "So now you're going to start the brightening campaign with a rainbow of little socked feet?"

"Lots of 'em."

"You told me this post doesn't give you a lot of idle time. I admit it's a wonderful idea, but Ida, it could take you a year or more before you get enough socks done."

Ida leaned in just as Leanne's face showed the idea coming to her, as well. "That's why you're going to help me. You did it once before at Camp Jackson. Now we need a much more colorful version of our band of knitters right here."

"Volunteer knitters like we had at the Red Cross. Of course!" Leanne tapped her forehead. "I can't believe I didn't think of that first. It'd be so easy."

"If gals would knit for soldiers, they'd surely knit for children."

Ida watched her friend purse her lips in thought. She knew that look. "I imagine I could have a dozen ladies lined up by tomorrow if I set my mind to it."

"And don't I know what you can do when you set your mind to something." Ida grabbed Leanne's hand. "So you'll help?"

Leanne's eyes sparkled. "Just try to stop me. But we'll need details—how many girls, their shoe sizes, that sort of thing."

Opening her desk, Ida handed her a sheet of paper. "I'm miles ahead of you. We have twenty-six girls. I told them I was inspecting their shoes for mites last night at bedtime, but I really just logged their sizes. I figure if we just divide them up into small, medium and large sizes, we'll have it covered with only three patterns. But the yarn…"

Leanne stood up. "Don't you worry about the yarn. Papa has enough friends in the cotton trade to get that covered. And what Papa can't get, John will." Leanne's new husband, John—a decorated war hero who'd come to South Carolina to stump for war bonds after being wounded in battle—was legendary for his persuasive abilities.

"One rule." Ida held up a finger. "Only bright, cheerful colors. No white. And not one speck of black, navy or army green."

Leanne pulled Ida into a hug. "Not on your life. Pinks and yellows and every cheerful color I can find. I think ruffles on the edges, too?"

Ida imagined Gitch's feet clad in extravagant yellow ruffles and could barely contain the glow in her heart. "Absolutely."

"I can even help from Washington," Leanne said with a sadness overcoming her smile. Leanne and John were moving soon to Washington, DC for John's new post as a diplomatic attaché. Ida knew she'd feel the loss keenly when the couple left. She treasured every face-to-face visit with Leanne, knowing soon they'd be confined to letters and infrequent visits. They'd been partners in escapades—knitting and otherwise—for so long, Ida wasn't sure how she'd keep her spirits up in a place like this without Leanne.

"Of course you can." Ida tightened her grip on her friend. "Socks mail well. But it won't be the same. I shall miss you so very much." They'd been through desperate times together, such as when they'd fought the Spanish influenza outbreak that had almost taken

Leanne's life. Still, Leanne was glowingly happy in her new life and destined for great success in Washington with her dashing husband.

"I won't worry about you having nothing to do here," Leanne said as she pulled away and tucked the list into her bag.

"Do you think we need to supply patterns?"

Leanne thought for a moment. "Not if we gather experienced knitters. Scaling down to small sizes and cheerful colors will be easy for women who knit all those army socks. Honestly, this should be effortless to pull together. I'll stop by the Red Cross on my way home and come back in a day or so with the list of volunteers."

"I was thinking we could assign specific girls to each knitter if we can find enough volunteers. That way there would be a personal connection. I want every chance for these girls to know someone outside those gates cares about them."

Leanne recaptured Ida's hand. "Look at you. I never thought of you as having much of a heart for young ones, but it's so clear you belong here. This place needs my dear Ida's dose of brilliant color."

Ida quoted the pledge behind her. "I shall be loyal to my work and devoted towards the welfare of those committed to my care."

"With only the necessary amount of mischief," Leanne added, giving Ida's hand one last squeeze before turning toward the door. "Oh!" She dodged to the side as a small boy with a very green tint to his face tumbled into the room half held up by one of the older lads.

"Eddie ate dirt," the older boy proclaimed, as though that were all the explanation required.

Ida didn't even bother to ask why but simply reached for a basin with one hand as she waved farewell to Leanne with the other.

Daniel was wrestling with the midmonth invoices and bookkeeping when a knock came at his door.

"Come in."

To have Mrs. Smiley appear at his door with a scowl was a near-daily occurrence at the Home. Her scowl today, however, seemed especially severe. It didn't take a medical degree to diagnose the source of the schoolmistress's current pain.

Daniel removed his glasses. "What has Miss Landway done now, Mrs. Smiley?"

That wasn't entirely fair, but he was indeed weary of Mrs. Smiley's litany of petty complaints. She'd yet to grace any of the nurse candidates with her favor. Indeed, Daniel could never be sure the stout woman had ever found any of the Home staff up to snuff—himself included. Still, she'd been hired by his father, and was practically as much a fixture of the place as the bricks and mortar. As a doctor, he could manage without a nurse, but he could never hope to last a day without a schoolmistress.

"It isn't Nurse Landway exactly, Dr. Parker."

Daniel wasn't sure if that boded well or ill. "Well, then, what is it exactly?"

"That woman just spent the last thirty minutes trying to convince me that knitting involved mathematics. As if I should be tucking yarn and needles inside the girls' textbooks."

Daniel never favored sums and figures as a child,

nor as a man, as his current battle with accounting accurately proved. "Is there math in knitting? I'd no idea."

Mrs. Smiley huffed. "Well, if you want to ask Nurse Landway about it, make sure you've got half an hour to spare. I declare, but that woman can go on."

"She has a certain…" He searched for the right word that would agree with her but yet still defend his new nurse. "…enthusiasm, I'll agree."

"I want your assurance such foolishness will not be entering my classroom." Mrs. Smiley's plump hands planted on her hips. "The last thing I need is those girls thinking about fiddling with stitchery when I've got multiplication to teach."

"Perhaps she was just making conversation." Miss Landway did seem eager to make friends with just about anyone. Perhaps she viewed the dour Mrs. Smiley as an interpersonal challenge.

"Make conversation? That woman has no need to dream up conversation. She has chatter seeping out of her pores, bless her heart." Like generations of Southern women before her, Jane Smiley applied the platitude of "bless her heart" at the end of any negative judgment. Somehow considered the universal absolution of an unkind comment, to Daniel "bless her heart" simply allowed women of good breeding to be delicately mean. The opinion was confirmed by the next sentence out of his schoolmistress's mouth. "If I want my meals in a circus, I'll just head on down to the tavern."

The thought of prim Mrs. Smiley hoisting a mug with the town's multitude of sailors in a tavern was about as ludicrous as it was entertaining. But he couldn't agree with the substance of her complaint. The truth was, Daniel was rather coming to enjoy Miss Landway's way of livening up conversation at the staff dining table. He'd learned things about his staff since her arrival that he'd never known in the years he worked here. Yes, she could be difficult at times, and he was quite sure she'd challenge him on any number of subjects once she settled in properly. His initial reservations, however, were giving way to a reluctant admission that Ida Landway might actually be good for the Parker Home for Orphans. "What is it you'd like me to do, Mrs. Smiley?" He'd learned this to be an effective question—often Mrs. Smiley didn't actually want any action taken, she just wanted her views to be known. Clearly and in considerable detail.

Apparently this was the present case, for she blinked and huffed again, caught up short at the request for a suggestion. While the schoolmistress was never short of opinions, she rarely had suggestions. Miss Landway, on the other hand, seemed to boast an endless supply of both. "Mind she knows her limits, Dr. Parker."

"Indeed I will, Mrs. Smiley." It was, in truth, a valid suggestion. Daniel had already concluded that guiding Miss Landway to see her proper boundaries and not to step on toes would be the key to her fitting in on the staff. He switched the subject. "How is Miss Forley doing in her studies these days? I know she was having some trouble earlier."

Nothing puffed up Jane Smiley like the accomplishments of her charges. "Exemplary. Once Donna put her mind to it, she caught on quickly. I've even asked her to tutor one of the younger ones having trouble with subtraction."

Daniel hoped Donna Forley would be one of the Home's success stories. After losing her mother to illness at an early age, Donna was raised by her father and an aunt until the war, when battle and influenza took them both from the poor child. Life had dealt Donna a terrible hand indeed, and she'd been withdrawn and near starving when she had come to the Home. Now, at sixteen, she was blooming into a confident young woman ready to take her place in the world. She'd managed to establish bonds with the other children, crafting siblings when no blood family existed. Daniel took great satisfaction in the fact that many of the Home's "graduating" classes became makeshift siblings to each other in the outside world. Father had told him, "The Home makes families out of need, not blood," and it was true.

He was almost afraid to ask the next question. "And the business with Matthew Hammond?" Romantic entanglements—even on the most basic teenage levels—were one of the most difficult parts of his job. Young hearts deprived of familial affection often looked for love in inappropriate places. It seemed at least once a week he, Mrs. Smiley and Mr. Grimshaw had to sit down and strategize how to keep Boy A from finding a few minutes alone with Girl B out behind the dormitories. Mr. MacNeil had even once suggested they install a hive of honeybees in that corner to deter "trysts." While Daniel applauded the groundskeeper's creativity, he also knew young hearts would simply seek out another secluded corner. Since then, however, "beehiving" had become the staff code word for teens getting a bit too sweet on each other.

"Settled for now," Mrs. Smiley said wearily. This particular couple had been caught "beehiving" multiple times, making Daniel wish Donna would indeed focus her clever mind on math rather than Math*ew*.

"But it won't be the last, I'm sure." Her eyes squinted in analysis, as if the pair were a mathematical equation. "Properly chaperoned, they might make an appropriate couple."

Daniel sat back in surprise. "Really?" While still eminently clinical, this was the first time he'd ever seen Mrs. Smiley offer anything close to an endorsement of any couple. Just because his curiosity refused to let go, he asked, "How so?"

"When they're not making eyes at each other over supper, their characters do suit each other well." She folded her hands in front of her. "Donna coaxes him out of that shell of his, and Matt calms Donna down. Matt turns seventeen next month, and Donna two months after that. I believe they might actually fare well if they chose to make a go of it after graduation." Again, Daniel couldn't shake the notion that she looked as if she'd just solved an algebra problem, not brokered a match.

Still, Mrs. Smiley claimed to have been happily married for six years before her husband died. As a bachelor himself, Daniel had to at least respect her opinion as the more experienced on the subject of courtship and matrimony. He certainly brought no expertise to the subject; women had mostly bored or baffled him. Not that Mother ever ceased to offer up suitable bridal candidates—that woman's pursuit of a Parker family heir could never be called subtle.

It served him well that most women, while enamored of his social standing, quickly grew tired of the time and devotion he gave to the Home. And for all of Mother's rants about his duty to the Parker legacy to pressure him to find a bride, wasn't *this* the true Parker legacy—this orphanage that his father had built? Daniel knew he didn't measure up to his father in many ways, but he would not cease in striving to give his best to the Home, come what may.

"And what, in your opinion, should we do about that?"

An actual smile broke over Mrs. Smiley's face—a rare sight indeed. "Much as we should do with Nurse Landway—temper their *enthusiasm*." She gave the final word a tone of disdain.

"Perhaps the September picnic could grant them an appropriate social outing."

She considered the suggestion with a hesitant grimace. "Grimshaw and I will discuss the idea and let you know what we decide."

Daniel did indeed feel as if Grimshaw and Smiley outnumbered and overrode him some days. The two of them had been mastering the students longer than he'd been director. Should they ever come to a disagreement, Daniel could never imagine how he would reject either of their suggestions. By God's grace, it had never yet occurred.

There was one subject that might end up testing that theory, however. "Mrs. Smiley?"

"Yes, Dr. Parker?"

"Nurse Landway has asked me for permission to arrange for the girls to receive hand-knit socks from a corps of volunteers." He steepled his hands and chose his words carefully. "I've told her I'm in favor of the project so long as each child receives an equal gift. While I don't much care what color socks the girls wear, I do think the influx of new volunteers could be of use to the Home. I trust you have no objections?"

"Socks? Like Meredith's little ones that caused such

a fuss the other day?" She looked as if she found that a ridiculous idea.

"Yes. Socks. In colors, apparently. I know it seems… unusual…but I can't see the harm in trying, provided no one child is singled out. Any new donations—even if they are time and talents—would be a very good thing for us. And I believe the girls would enjoy it."

"Socks?" Mrs. Smiley repeated, clearly trying to wrap her sensible mind around so ludicrous an idea.

"So it seems. I intend to give my approval, unless you have a reason I shouldn't."

"As long as they mind their lessons, I can't say it matters what's on their feet." Her eyes narrowed. "But I think it's silly."

"I doubt the girls find it so. But I shall keep my eye on things in any case."

"You'll need to do that, Dr. Parker. Mark my words." With that, Mrs. Smiley turned and left the room, muttering something about colors and nonsense and enthusiasm.

Daniel stood and closed his ledgers, glad to now have a task to divert him from midmonth invoices. *Who knows?* he mused to himself as he headed for the hallway. *It might be rather fun to tell Miss Landway she could go ahead with one of her ideas instead of having to constantly rein in her imagination.*

Chapter Seven

Daniel found Miss Landway carrying a load of clean white examination table covers down the hallway toward her office. Her hair, wild as usual, was striving mightily to release itself from the knot she'd wound it in at the back of her neck. Her auburn locks continually struck him as on the verge of escape—which might explain the three different-colored pencils currently sticking out of her bun. Colored pencils. It seems the woman could not even conduct basic correspondence in black and white.

He'd stopped in her office the other day and, finding her gone, allowed himself a moment to take in the scattered collection of sketches and tiny drawings that decorated her papers and notes. He'd also noticed the bright yellow matting with which she'd framed her profession's oath. Daniel couldn't quite decide if he found the bits of color she always left in her wake enjoyable or ridiculous. Perhaps they were both.

He caught up to her and took the laundry load from her hands before she could utter a syllable of protest. "Allow me."

She stopped, sitting back on one hip with—and there was no other way to describe her expression—an annoyed smile. "I'm able to fetch my own linens from the laundry room."

"Oh, I'm sure of that. Still—" he continued walking toward her office "—what kind of example for gentlemanly behavior would I be setting for the boys if I were to be found walking next to you while you carried such a load?"

Nurse Landway darted ahead of him, reaching the infirmary door before he did and standing in front of it. "There are no gentlemen in training to be found here. So I'll be fine and dandy." She reached out her hands for the pile of folded cloths.

"I can at least place them in the cabinet for you." He reached for the doorknob.

She angled in front of him. "I'll be fine, really." With her chin tipped up at him—for he had perhaps half a foot on even her statuesque figure—she looked defiant.

Daniel had the distinct impression she was hiding something. Her eyes darted back and forth and he watched her hand tighten on the office doorknob. He stole a glance over her shoulder to notice faint shapes of color through the thin curtains she had strung over the door's glass window. Rather a lot of color.

"Miss Landway, allow me to enter."

Were she a child, he would call her stance squirming. Given that she was a fully grown woman, Daniel didn't know quite how to describe it. She winced. "You don't want to do that."

Ida Lee Landway was most certainly hiding something. "I'm quite sure I do."

She hesitated again, this time giving a pitiful tug on

the table covers, which Daniel was now sure he would not surrender even at gunpoint.

"Kindly open your office door, Miss Landway." He kept his words polite but his tone firm.

She gave a small whine, ducked her head like a guilty child and pushed the door open.

A riot of color greeted his eyes. Boxes and baskets of yarn in a kaleidoscope of bright hues filled every available surface of the office. It was as if the circus Mrs. Smiley was just bemoaning had arrived and subsequently exploded in the infirmary. *His* infirmary.

Miss Landway cut in front of him. "I can explain."

Knowing he had come to deliver his approval for her little project, he found the entire situation amusing. Still, the sight before him only proved Mrs. Smiley's point: someone needed to mind Miss Landway's limits. And that someone was him. "I expect you shall."

She began rearranging the boxes, as if that would somehow render them invisible. "My dear friend Leanne—Mrs. John Gallows, that is—had the most extraordinary luck when she went looking for donated yarn." She turned to him and laid a hand on her chest in a theatrical gesture. "We had no idea she'd get such enormous and immediate replies when she went asking. It's a blessing, really."

"You sought donations?" He looked around to find someplace to deposit the linens, and couldn't see a single empty surface.

She moved a box to the floor, gesturing for him to put down the stack of cloths, which he did. "Well, not exactly. I was telling Leanne about the whole business with Meredith's booties and the idea I had. I was asking her if she'd help me. There are twenty-six girls after all, and we'd want each of them to have more than one pair of socks, so—"

"We?" he cut in.

Miss Landway planted a hand on one hip. "You did say I could go ahead if I could guarantee each girl received equal gifts." Sparks of defiance lit her eyes—she'd become much more invested in this than he'd realized.

Part of him liked that. Another part of him felt as if he was watching the year's greatest headache form right in front of his eyes. "I did. And I told you I'd think about approving your recruitment of a core of volunteers to assist." He put his hands in his pockets and rocked back on his heels. "I see you didn't find waiting for such approval necessary."

She spun about the room, her hands flung wide. "Well, my stars, I didn't think it'd all happen this fast!"

When he didn't reply, she turned to face him with pleading eyes. It was obvious it would rip her heart out if he told her to send back the yarn. He wasn't going to do that, of course, but in many ways this was the baby booties all over again. Charity may be the heart of the Parker Home for Orphans, but procedure gave it the bones to endure. He had to make her understand that if she was going to last, and Daniel found he wanted this nurse to last.

He pinched his nose and pushed out a breath. "I'm pleased at your initiative, truly I am."

She looked as if she were holding her breath. "And?"

"And I am not going to ask you to send all this back, but—"

"Thank You, Jesus!" She put her hand to her forehead in relief.

"But," he continued firmly, "I would have liked for you to wait until I gave you permission to solicit donations. That was, in fact, why I was coming to see you."

"Well, I would have, but—"

"But?" Daniel crossed his hands over his chest and gave his word all the disciplinary strength he could muster.

Her shoulders fell. "But nothing. You're right. I charged right ahead when I should have waited. I let my excitement run away with my good sense." She folded her hands in front of her. "It's a problem of mine."

"Miss Landway, however did you manage in the army of all places?"

She put one hand up to her hair in a sort of overwhelmed gesture, her eyes popping in surprise when she found a pencil there. She removed it and stared at it as if she had no idea how it had ended up in her chignon. Daniel pointed to her hair and raised two fingers, cueing her to find the two other pencils. Her cheeks flushed pink as she pulled those, as well. "You must think me a ninny," she said with a sigh.

"Actually, I find you rather clever, if a bit…impulsive."

"A bit?" Her eyes lit up at the compliment, and Daniel realized he had yet to tell her he was glad she had come to the Home. He was, mostly. She brought an energy he'd once had, even if it came without all the caution life at the Home had driven into him.

"Perhaps a great deal impulsive. In this case, it has worked out for the best. But I hope Meredith's booties have shown you it doesn't always end that way."

"You're right. You're absolutely right."

Daniel picked up a ball of yarn, one in a light green

that reminded him of spring leaves, and held it up. "So you will come to me with any new ideas and wait for my approval in the future?"

"Absolutely." She took the ball from him as if it represented their agreement. "Oh, in that case I should start right this minute. Do you know Mrs. Smiley's shoe size?"

Daniel couldn't quite follow that train of thought. "I beg your pardon?"

"Mrs. Smiley. I think she ought to get a lovely pair of socks, as well. I'll need her shoe size." Catching herself, she corrected, "Provided, of course, you approve of my making her some. I was chatting with her about all the math in knitting and she didn't seem very taken with the idea, but perhaps some lovely socks could change her mind."

That was an understatement. "Mrs. Smiley is very particular about her methods. She felt your 'chatting' was an attempt to insert knitting into her mathematics curriculum."

Miss Landway's face fell. "She complained to you?"

"She came to me with her concerns." Then, against his better judgment, Daniel leaned in and said, "Mrs. Smiley's life is continually filled with concerns. I wouldn't take it personally."

"Oh, a grouser, hmm?"

While he found the term a bit dramatic, it did fit in this case. "She's an excellent teacher." After a second, he added, "But perhaps even an excellent teacher can use a pair of pretty socks."

"Or slippers." Miss Landway pointed at Daniel, suddenly taken with the brilliance of her improved idea.

"I reckon she'd love a cozy pair of bright blue slippers. Who wouldn't?"

Daniel did not dare to venture a guess as to Jane Smiley's choice in private footwear. He simply smiled, nodded his goodbye and wondered how long it would be before Miss Landway's next outrageous idea.

Ida was carrying a box of medical records down from the attic Thursday morning when she heard it: what sounded like a herd of buffalo stomping at once, and one voice shouting…numbers? It sounded oddly like the military exercises that would wake her up at the crack of dawn back at Camp Jackson, but then there were also grunts and various cracking sounds.

It had to be some sort of calisthenics—she knew the Home had to have some form of physical exercise program, but she couldn't for the life of her guess what would make the sounds she heard. The girls took basic dance and posture, so this ruckus had to be the boys. A crash and a yelp—along with a rumble of laughter— piqued her curiosity and she tiptoed down the hall to take a look.

A dozen or so boys in trousers and white undershirts toed up to a series of lines taped along what was once the big old house's third-floor ballroom. Their foreheads and white undershirts were soaked in sweat—it was broiling up here despite the shutters being thrown wide open—but they looked enthralled as they thrust long sticks at one another. Ida was so shocked by the sight that it took a minute for her to work out that they weren't pummeling each other, they were fencing. Or at least, something like it, as they seemed to be using broomsticks rather than foils.

Their teacher stood at the far end of the room, his face momentarily buried in a towel, for he was as sweat-drenched as the boys. Ida's jaw nearly dropped to discover the man to be Dr. Parker. Shirt open several buttons, glasses off, sleeves rolled up, hair pushed up off his face by the towel and sticking up in all directions, Ida barely recognized him. It was as if someone had taken formal Dr. Parker and dropped him in the center of a wet hurricane for five minutes, then deposited him in the third-floor exercise room.

"No, no, Jerome," he said, walking over to one of the boys. Even his walk was different up here, with longer strides and a freer swing of the shoulders. "Use your knees to advance on your opponent. That way you keep your balance. Like this." And with that, he took a stance and worked his way across the room in a series of very dashing-looking sword-fighting moves. The boys were transfixed, not only because Dr. Parker was very good, but because Dr. Parker used an actual fencing foil. *Boys and swords*, Ida thought. *I'll be seeing the end result of this in the infirmary one of these days.*

Bookish Dr. Parker suddenly didn't seem so bookish. Lengthen out the hair, add boots and a sash, and Ida could very well imagine the doctor alongside the Three Musketeers. Not quite a pirate, but certainly someone with a bit of swashbuckle in his blood. The image before her was so at odds with her notion of Daniel Parker that she had to catch herself before she laughed.

"A lady!"

Evidently she hadn't caught herself at all, for one of the boys—George, if she remembered right—had noticed her and currently pointed his broomstick broadsword at her as if she were an invading enemy.

Dr. Parker's demeanor stiffened up so fast, Ida could have sworn it made an actual sound. "Nurse Landway. You've discovered our Thursday fencing lessons."

"I'm impressed," she said, meaning it. "Looks like fun."

"Girls don't like swords," George proclaimed with all the manly bravado a second-grade swordsman could muster.

"I grew up in West Virginia. I can ride a horse bareback and I can shoot a gun. Why not use a sword?"

George's jaw dropped. "You can shoot a gun?"

"Girls in West Virginia need to learn to hunt, same as boys."

When Dr. Parker raised a "you are not helping the matter" eyebrow, Ida backpedaled to, "Only we confine ourselves to small game like squirrel and possum." She looked squarely at Dr. Parker when she added, "We leave the hungry bears and wild ferocious elephants to the big, strong menfolk."

The doctor checked his pocket watch, conveniently deciding that three-twenty was an excellent time to end fencing lessons for the day. "That's it for today, boys. Rods in the canister in the corner. Use the extra time to wash up before science class—it was hot today."

The older boys, smart enough to realize their lesson had been ended by her intrusion, shot Ida one or two foul looks as they filed out of the room.

"There was no reason to stop early on my account, Dr. Parker. I have four older brothers. I understand the idea of 'no girls allowed.'"

"Quite frankly, I was getting a bit winded in this heat. Some days the boys' enthusiasm outpaces my stamina. They enjoy it so much, though, even if I do hurt the next day. Or day*s*." He made quick work of buttoning up his shirt and cuffs.

"Fencing?" Ida couldn't help but ask.

He put his glasses back on. "Why not fencing?"

"It seems so…" She searched for the kindest word. "…impractical. When are these boys ever likely to use such a skill?"

Dr. Parker picked up the last of the wooden rods and tossed it into a barrel that stood in the corner of the room. "I'll admit, it is a gentleman's sport. But learning to command their bodies, to strategize, to keep a cool head in a fight, to outsmart an opponent rather than outbrawl them? I think those are highly practical skills." For just a moment, a rakish grin filled his face. "But I would be lying if I said it isn't occasionally useful for me to put a few of the older ones in their place. They always think they can best me in a duel." He slid his foil into its case with a defiant air. "And they are always wrong."

Ida crossed her hands over her chest. "I underestimated you, Dr. Parker."

He laughed. "It is, of course, just plain fun, as well. One day I hope to be using more than broomsticks, but from a nurse's standpoint, perhaps that is an advantage."

"Oh," she said with a laugh, "you'd be surprised how much damage a blunt object can do."

"Perhaps to a wild, ferocious West Virginia elephant?"

She narrowed her eyes. "You deserved that."

"I'd prefer the boys not picture you as a gunslinger nurse from a Western novel. Children's imaginations tend to run wild with the tiniest bits of information we give them. I like us to be deliberate in the role models we present here at the Home."

"Oh, and you are nothing if not deliberate. A *deliberate* man hands a dozen boys sticks and sets them loose to whack at each other."

"A deliberate man *trains* a dozen young men how to use those sticks and channels their considerable energies someplace positive so they don't whack *at* each other. Surely the army taught you boys must burn it off somewhere."

Hadn't she had that very thought upon hearing about Mr. Grimshaw's chess lessons? "I heard an officer back at Camp Jackson once say that's why God gave us push-ups." Dr. Parker gestured through the door and she exited the room ahead of him. "Musketeering aside, they do need practical skills, too, don't they? Apprenticeships and such?"

"Yes." Dr. Parker turned, fished a set of keys from his pocket and locked the door behind them. "Most of the older ones take posts at trades around the city, when they can be made to fit around their lessons. I'm careful where I send them, though. Some of the 'apprenticeships' out there aren't much more than indentured servitude. I'm sorry to say the war's left enough orphans that some don't think twice about taking advantage of them. My father had an excellent record for looking out for the children's welfare here, and I aim to keep it that way."

Ida decided it was time to ask the question that had been sitting on her tongue all week. "May I ask you something, Dr. Parker?"

He clasped his hands behind his back. "Well, I've not seen you hesitate yet."

She stopped for a moment, wanting to get the question out before they descended the staircase from the third floor. "Why do *you* think y'all haven't been able to keep someone in the nurse's position here?"

He paused for just a moment, and Ida wanted to stomp on her own toes. *When will I ever learn to keep my mouth shut?*

"Miss Landway, I can't decide if I find your directness refreshing or startling."

"A little of both?" she offered meekly, wondering if her tongue would soon place her at the end of the long line of former Parker Home for Orphans nurses. She'd spent a hundred nights on her knees repenting outbursts of an unguarded tongue—she dearly hoped this post wasn't about to become the casualty of yet another.

Dr. Parker leaned against the banister, which promptly gave a worrisome groan and popped a screw to bounce along the top stair. "I would say," he said wearily as he bent to pick up the wayward hardware, "that it is because it is a big, endless job for which we don't pay nearly as well as we should. We're forever making do and patching up." He rocked the banister back and forth, testing to see if it would hold without the screw. "I spend much of my time beholden to donors, but the money we receive is never enough. Quite frankly, it's my hope the army is better training for what we face here."

The answer satisfied her. Ida was used to uphill battles and making do, and she'd met plenty of nurses who weren't. "Smart thinking."

"I do hope so." He started down the stairs, then stopped. "Oh, but one thing."

"Yes?"

"I must ask you to steer clear of the boys' fencing lessons from now on. We're up here every Thursday from three to four. It really is a 'no girls allowed' thing."

Ida blinked at him. "You're serious."

"Silly, I know, but there are so few things we can give them, and they seem to take to the exclusivity of it. I indulge them."

"So if a female student asked to learn fencing, you'd deny her?"

"Nonsense. It would never come up."

Ida thought of her friend Leanne's husband, Captain John Gallows, and how fiercely he prickled at being forced to learn to knit as a promotional stunt for the Red Cross. Some gender-based "traditions" really begged to be knocked down. "You're sure of that?" Lady Gwendolyn seemed a perfect candidate for Pirate Queen if she wanted to raise a little trouble...

...which she did not. This was neither the time nor the place. *Guard my brain and my tongue, Lord, please!*

"Well, yes, I expect I am," Dr. Parker was saying as he continued down the stairs.

"Of course," she said, following him. *You've got your yarn, why on earth would you go stirring up more trouble?* Ida applied her most congenial tone. "Whatever was I thinking?"

Chapter Eight

Saturday morning passed in relative quiet—three splinters, two sore throats and one very nasty skinned knee. Ida had been at the Home almost two weeks, and was beginning to feel something close to "settled in." As such, Ida took pride in the calm she displayed when Mr. MacNeil pushed into the infirmary with a cluster of irritated-looking boys in his wake. "I've got trouble for ye, Nurse Landway."

Ida's definition of trouble had changed considerably in the past fourteen days. The boys looked in no danger, save a collection of annoyed expressions. "They look rather healthy to me."

"They won't in an hour or so. I found these lads playing with a pile of rocks."

Ida didn't see any blood or bruises, so they hadn't been throwing those rocks at each other at least. "Rocks?"

"A pile of rocks that was sitting under a patch of poison ivy. They'll have gotten it all over the lot of 'em. Should I throw them in the showers?"

She stood up. "Goodness, no. That will only spread

things more quickly." She'd meant to include calamine solution in her list of needed supplies—the tiny bottle she had in her cabinets wouldn't come close to covering the yards of soon-to-be-itching skin standing in front of her. *Time to get creative.* Ida ushered the boys into the office, calculating the number who entered against the amount of baking soda she had in her stores. "Mr. Mac-Neil, would you have time to dash to the kitchen and fetch up all the baking soda they can spare? We'll need more than I have here." The Scotsman nodded. "And some oatmeal!" she called as he ducked out the door. Even the unscientific home remedy could be called into service with this large a case.

Ida stared at the motley lineup, some of whom had already begun to scratch. "All right, gentlemen, off with your shirts. And whatever you do, don't touch your faces." Immediately, as if by command, the one on the end scratched his nose. "I said *not* to touch your face!" She poured water into a bowl and began mixing all the baking soda immediately at hand.

Twenty minutes later, the line of boys more closely resembled a whitewashed fence, patched and smeared as they were with baking soda. She'd commandeered a line of chairs from a nearby classroom and now had them applying the paste to their ankles just in case the offending leaves had wandered into their pant legs. Anything more intimate than that would have to be tended by Dr. Parker.

"Resist the urge to scratch," she warned, "or I'll have to resort to my mama's trick of putting socks over your hands."

"How long 'til it stops itching?" one boy asked, wrinkling his nose repeatedly, trying to sooth the itch without actually scratching. Ida's heart twisted for the boys—it would be a long night. In this heat, it would be a long week—maybe even more.

She couldn't bear to tell them. "Longer than you'd like. But you look to me like a tough lot. You'll get through it."

"They'll have no choice," came Dr. Parker's deep voice from the doorway. He stood holding a pair of serving tongs, a small stack of boys' undergarments and a pillowcase. "Off with your clothes, boys. They'll have to go."

"But there's a girl here!" a boy protested, thrusting a hand so closely to Ida that she had to duck out of the way to avoid contact. Just the thought of being around so much rash had already made her feel itchy. She shot up a prayer of thanksgiving that she had moved all the donated yarn into her rooms in the dormitory.

"There is a *lady present*," Dr. Parker corrected. "One whom we shall thank for her service before we politely request that she leave."

"No need to twist my arm," Ida said, gathering up her paperwork. "I'll come back in an hour to scrub things down and make up some more paste for them to use tonight. Two hours, actually. Lock the infirmary up after yourself, Dr. Parker. I don't want anyone wandering in here until I've washed it all down." Two hours would buy Ida enough time for an oatmeal bath of her own. Poison ivy was nasty stuff—a wily enemy if ever there was one—and a preemptive measure might at least soothe her mind if not protect her skin.

The night was brutally hot, and Ida slept fitfully as she worried about the poor lads and their itchy fate. Finally, just after dawn, she gave up on further rest. After dressing and trying once again to tame her unruly curls in the oppressive humidity, Ida headed down to the staff dining room in the hopes that coffee might be had.

She pushed the French doors open to find a haggard Dr. Parker slumped backward in his usual chair at the head of the table, fast asleep. He'd been up all night from the looks of it. She ought to simply back out of the room and let the poor man doze, but the sight of him glued her feet to the spot. He looked different. Unkempt and unguarded, more human than she'd ever seen him even during the fencing lesson. His dark hair, usually trim and slicked in place, hung mussed over his forehead. The shadow of whiskers peppered his strong jaw in a way that should have made him look rougher than usual, only his face was still somehow gentler than his usual expression. She'd almost forgotten he wasn't much older than her twenty-eight years—he bore himself with such an elder respectability.

He sniffed and shifted in his sleep, and Ida smiled at the uncharacteristic scruffiness of the gesture. She'd thought of him purely as a superior, an administrator, but he was still a man. A very tired, very dedicated man. It struck her, as she smiled at the empty coffee cup and an uneaten plate of toast on the table in front of him, that he didn't smile enough. With his eyes and features, he had a very nice—if rare—smile.

She really ought to leave—he'd be mortified to know she found him this way. The upstanding Dr. Parker mortified—she couldn't imagine such an expression on that face. Then again, looking as he did now, she could. She'd do what she'd do for any friend found in such a state; she'd wake him and send him off to bed.

Turning to the sideboard, Ida placed her hand on the coffeepot, glad to feel it was still warm. No one else was up; evidently the good doctor could make his own coffee. Ida poured a cup, trying to make just enough noise to allow Dr. Parker to wake up with her back turned to him, which seemed the kindest way. Most doctors she knew were light sleepers of necessity.

She heard him shift in his seat again, but when she turned around he still had not woken. Taking a second cup from the sideboard, she poured the doctor a replacement coffee and faced him. "Dr. Parker?" she said as gently as she could.

He grunted, his nose twitched, but still he slept.

"Dr. Parker?" she said a bit louder, then, "Dr. Parker?" again, a bit louder still.

He jerked awake in such a startle of arms and legs that Ida nearly dropped the cup she was holding. "What? What's wrong?"

It was wrong to laugh, but the man looked so wearily disoriented that it was just too hard not to offer him an understanding chuckle as she placed the coffee down in front of him. "Good morning."

He squinted, then ran his hands down his face. "I'm so terribly sorry. I must have dozed off." His jacket was folded over the next chair, his sleeves were rolled up and his shirt was a maze of wrinkles. He blinked and groped for his glasses, which sat on the table in front of him. "What time is it?"

"Not quite six."

He groaned. An entirely human, entirely unadministrative groan. "I'd cut down every hedge on the property if that would keep last night from happening again."

"I suspected the boys would be miserable. I didn't count on them taking you down with them."

"A few of the boys had started to blister. Someone needed to watch them."

There were easily half a dozen people Dr. Parker could have assigned to sit up with the boys. "It didn't have to be you." Still, Ida admired that he'd taken it on himself. For all his procedural nature, the doctor cared deeply about the well-being of his charges. Indeed, he seemed personally invested in every child's welfare, as if he took the burden for all their care solely on his own shoulders—and had something mountainous to prove.

He gulped the coffee down eagerly. "If they had been girls, where would you have spent the night?"

She sighed and sat down. "At their side." How many times had she slept in a chair at the army hospital, keeping watch over a critical patient or even just a frightened one? But that was a nurse's place, was it not? She was no administrator. "How did the hedges get so out of hand?"

"Mrs. Leonard was the one who tended to the plants and flowers. MacNeil does his best, but cobbling this place together on the meager budget we have doesn't leave him much time for gardening. We've become a bit overgrown, I'm afraid." He yawned. "And now we've paid for it dearly." He put his glasses on and started to rise. "I'd best get up there to see just how dearly."

She reached out to stop him, her hand landing on his bare forearm. The touch startled both of them, and Ida drew her hand right back, regretting the impropriety of that gesture toward her employer. She covered the awkward moment by gesturing to the plate of toast and asking, "Is that all you've eaten?"

He began rolling his sleeves back down as if it were

necessary to hide the contact. "They'll be up in the kitchen soon."

"It's Sunday," she corrected. "Not for another hour. I reckon the boys are out cold, so why don't I make you some eggs? I'm not entirely lost in a kitchen you know, even one as large as this." If she could keep him occupied long enough for the rest of the staff to be up, she stood a chance of him letting someone else see to the boys while he managed some real sleep. The army was a fine education in how lack of sleep could muddle a soul's thinking.

"I suppose I could be persuaded."

"You suppose nothing. Nurse's orders." She took the now-empty coffeepot from the sideboard. "And don't think I don't know how doctors make some of the worst patients around," she called as she pushed open the door that led from the staff dining room to the kitchen. "But you make a decent cup of coffee, so you can make more while I scramble up some eggs."

Ida cocked her head toward the kitchen, giving the bleary-eyed doctor her best "do as I say" glare. Her stern look melted into a smile as he followed her obediently into the kitchen.

Daniel was too tired and too hungry to even consider the suitability of being found alone at dawn with the fairer sex in the Home's kitchen. Most of the staff members were women, for goodness' sake, and this was far from the first time a childhood illness or issue had kept him up all night. With fifty-eight children in residence—sometimes more—someone was always sick with something. The pressures of medical as well as administrative oversight that generally came to bear on him were what made an on-site nurse so essential to his ability to keep going.

Last night's itchy, blistering boys, however, had been exceptionally difficult. "I feel as if I've spent the night herding wild boars." He allowed himself a rare complaint while preparing a second pot of coffee. This morning, it felt as if he'd require a third pot before lunch.

"Did the baking-soda paste help at all?" Miss Landway said as she bent into the kitchen pantry. It was too close to their earlier encounter—how had the woman become so adept at holding conversations when her head was stuck in cabinetry?

Daniel spooned grounds into the percolator. "Difficult to say, although if they've slept this late, we have reason to hope. They may owe whatever little comfort they have this morning to your fast action." He added an extra spoonful, wanting the strongest-possible brew this morning.

"You ought to dunk the lot of them into an oatmeal bath when they wake up. It will help with the itch. Yourself, as well. I did so—just to be safe—and told Mr. MacNeil to do the same." Miss Landway lit the fire under a frying pan and set a lump of butter in to sizzle while she broke eggs into a crockery bowl. He watched her out of the corner of his eye. He doubted many of the women in his social circles were such competent cooks. The army had done right by Ida Lee Landway— she seemed ready for anything.

"MacNeil? In an oatmeal bath?" He surprised himself by managing a small chuckle.

That caught her attention. "Why, bless my soul, Dan-

-iel Parker," she exclaimed, an egg still in one hand. "An actual laugh. I wasn't sure you still had one."

Her astonishment stung just a bit. "Am I that serious?"

Sitting back on one hip, her eyes softened as if she'd realized the sharp truth in her teasing. Daniel couldn't remember the last time anyone else had dared a joke at his expense. "I suppose you have to be. But I'd like to think you don't have to be all the time." The pan's sputter pulled her back to the task, and she began beating the eggs with trademark enthusiasm. "What do you do for fun? Other than swordplay, that is."

"Fun?" It bothered him, once spoken aloud, the utter shock he'd given the word.

"Yes, fun. That thing people do when they're not at work."

When they're not at work. When was Daniel ever not at work? When was the last time he'd been anywhere but the Orphan Home and his family home? Men his age often went "out with the boys," but in fact Daniel was *always* with boys—and girls. Perhaps Mother had good reason to declare concern over his social life, or more precisely the lack thereof. Daniel tried to craft an answer that didn't sound pitiful, and when he came up short he simply didn't reply.

Miss Landway banged a spoon against the bowl she was holding. "Mercy, you do have *some* kind of fun, don't you? Is that why this place is so confoundedly gray?"

He squared off to stare straight at her. "What?"

He watched her choose her reply. She had an earful to give him—even half-asleep he could see it boiling behind her eyes—but she was weighing the consequences of such frankness to her employer. Still, the boiling won out, for she launched into a speech, waving the spoon to and fro for emphasis. "There's not a speck of color in this place. Children live here, Daniel Parker, not soldiers. Even Camp Jackson managed more color than these dreary walls. Rooms here should be red and green and blue and yellow with stripes and happy polka dots. Some days I feel choked just walking down the hall." Her volcano sufficiently erupted, she made a *harrumph* sound and began attacking the eggs as they cooked. "Well, that's what I think."

Mrs. Smiley told Daniel what she thought on a regular basis, and that always felt like a weight pressing down daily on his shoulders. Ida Landway's version of the *what I think* speech felt entirely different. Her words poked him, prodded him in ways that didn't feel altogether comfortable, but not altogether unpleasant either. More push than press, if that made any sense. Then again, he'd managed about an hour of sleep in thirty hours—nothing should make any sense at the moment.

"Thank you," he said slowly, "for telling me what you think."

"Well," she huffed, "now *there's* something I don't hear very often. Most times my big mouth gets me into big trouble, which is why I've been trying so hard to mind my tongue here." She cut the fire from under the eggs and turned to him. "But I really do believe it, Dr. Parker. Color changes a heart. There could be so much more happiness in these walls. There could be buckets more joy in these children's hearts, and all it would take is some paint and imagination. God's world is a lovely, color-filled place, and it eats me alive that these little ones can't see it."

Her words were heartfelt; every inch of her body hummed with her belief in what she said. Daniel hired for skill as often as he could, but he always hired for heart above all. It gave him great satisfaction to know that the chance he'd taken on Ida Lee Landway had indeed brought him a woman with heart. Loads of it.

"The Home is that colorless to you?" Practical as he was, he'd never paid much attention to such things. His focus was always the bodies inside the walls, not the walls themselves.

Miss Landway planted her hands on her hips. "Gracious, I just told you the army had more color." She pronounced it like the deepest of faults. "What does that tell you?" She opened cabinets around the kitchen until she found a stack of plates, pulling two out. "Look at these. Plain white. At least they're not tin like in the army, but the children eat off tin plates, don't they?"

They did. With the numbers they served every day, there weren't too many ways around that—but Daniel doubted Miss Landway would see it that way.

She set the plates on the counter beside her then went searching again, producing silverware and—of course—plain beige linen napkins to place down on the counter beside the plates. The children used muslin napkins of much the same color. "No color here, either."

He felt compelled to defend the Home at least a little. "We do have practicalities to contend with, Miss Landway."

She replied by holding up a stack of beige muslin dishcloths. "We're drowning in practicalities, Dr. Parker. I'm not saying we need my granny's china teacups, but honestly, even a blue stripe down the napkins would make a world of difference. The girls could hem

up colored napkins as a sewing project. Embroider flowers on them. Something. *Anything*." She slid the eggs
onto the plates, their sunny yellow color now standing
out to Daniel as he tried to see the Home's bland world
through her eyes. In the few moments of her passion-
ate speech, he'd forgotten how tired he was. She always
managed to impose color onto her nursing uniform, slipping a bright blue ribbon into the rich auburn of her hair,
and he noticed tiny blue flowers embroidered onto the
collar of her blouse. Her whole manner was so vibrant
that he rarely stopped to notice the details, but now that
he did, he had to admit that they were charming. Mean-
while, the comforting, buttery scent of scrambled eggs
and toast filled his senses in a way it hadn't in years.
Had he become that numb to the world and its wonders?

"Perhaps you're right," he admitted, swallowing the
feeling that he'd just cracked open a very large flood-
gate. He rightly feared that this small trickle of his
approval would soon become a tidal wave of Ida Landway's rainbow world.

"I'm absolutely right," she declared. Then, finding
her words a bit presumptuous, she tacked a respectful
"Dr. Parker" onto the end. She picked up the plates and
headed toward the staff dining room as if that settled
the matter. Daniel filled the coffeepot from the percolator and followed her to the table just as MacNeil
pushed through the French doors. The Scotsman was
usually the first up; the rest of the staff would arrive
soon. Daniel found himself unnerved to be discovered
eating breakfast alone with Miss Landway.

MacNeil, on the other hand, looked as if he wouldn't
much mind to find Daniel breakfasting with the Queen
of England. "Saints alive," he said wearily, "I itch like

I've been sleeping with a herd of goats." He pushed up his sleeves to display swaths of tiny red blisters along his forearms. "Have ye got any more of that stuff, Miss Landway?"

She responded by popping off her chair and offering the place setting to MacNeil. "Keep those sleeves rolled down. Here, eat this while I go find some oatmeal in the kitchen. I can wrap those arms up in some napkins while you eat." She headed for the kitchen pass-through, then turned back toward the groundskeeper. "Unless that's not the only place you're breaking out in a rash."

MacNeil's reply was to turn pink and catch Daniel's eye with a mortified expression. It was safe to assume the Scotsman was indeed breaking out in other places.

"Oh," Miss Landway said quietly, her own face coloring. "You just eat up and I'll send you back to your rooms with a bowl of it. Oatmeal and baking soda, that is."

MacNeil lost his embarrassment in a forkful of eggs. "Good cooking and clever. Where'd you find her again?"

Daniel had the strange thought that oatmeal and baking soda were beige and white—Miss Landway's offending colorless shades. Why was he suddenly thinking of everything in terms of hues? "The army," he replied with a smirk as he dug into his own yellow, tasty eggs. "The dull, drab army."

Chapter Nine

Ida sat perched on the edge of her chair Tuesday morning and told the bees in her stomach to hush. She'd faced grisly wounds and battle-hardened generals with less trepidation than she knew now at the prospect of the room of Charleston society ladies currently before her. For all the easy kinship she felt with Leanne, some days the differences in their backgrounds still loomed like an uncrossable gulch.

Ida came from a large, scrambling family up in the mountains of West Virginia. Leanne came from good Southern stock, a comfortable member of Charleston society. When Leanne finally did leave for Washington—which could only be soon—Ida wasn't sure how she was going to get along with the six ladies Leanne had recruited. *Lord, You're gonna have to pave the way here*, Ida prayed. *I'm in over my head.*

Find the good. That's how Mama had taught her to deal with any sticky situation. Ida scanned the room and the refined faces for any trace of positivity. The best thing about the room was the abundance of color and texture. Next to the drab decor of the Parker Home for Orphans, Isabelle Hooper's gaily colored parlor was a breath of fresh air. "You have a lovely home, Mrs. Hooper," Ida ventured to the afternoon's hostess. "Such wonderful colors."

Mrs. Hooper warmed instantly to the compliment. "Why, thank you, dear. You call me Isabelle, now. No need to be so formal."

"I'm Ida," Ida replied, still feeling out of place but glad for the welcome in the woman's kind eyes.

"Pleasure to make your acquaintance, Ida," Isabelle said with a smile as warm as her eyes. "I'm always glad to meet a fellow *I*. And a knitter, too."

"I?"

"Ida, Isabelle. Short of an Imogene down on Broad Street, you're the only other *I* name I know. There aren't many of us."

Ida found herself able to laugh and even manage a deep breath. She reached for the glass of sweet tea Isabelle had set before all the women seated around her parlor. "I suppose that's true. We ought to look out for each other." Feeling braver, she managed a wink. "All the other vowels are likely to be jealous, us being so exclusive and all."

Isabelle fanned herself. "Gracious, but you are a clever one. I do believe we'll get along just fine."

She was like Mama, Ida thought to herself, just with fancier trimmings. Welcoming, quick to make a friend and fond of a good laugh. A lump of shame settled in Ida's stomach where the bees had been. Why had she made assumptions just because Isabelle seemed to be exceedingly well off? Rich folks could be as kind as poor ones, just as poor folks could be as mean as those with wealth. Dr. Parker had allowed her to seek these volunteers and donations of yarn, and that meant rubbing elbows with Charleston's upper tiers. She was going to have to learn to look at these people by their character, not their ledgers. Still, coming from someone whose entire childhood home could fit inside the living room where she currently sat, it was hard not to feel small and fretful.

"Have you been knitting a long time?" Ida made herself ask, picking up one of the myriad balls of colored yarn that sat in baskets at the center of the circle of women.

"My mother and grandmother were talented knitters. Mother with all kinds of needlework." Isabelle pointed to a set of exquisitely worked pillows lined up on a settee in the corner. "Those are hers."

"They're wonderful." And they were. It was clear from the designs where Isabelle got her love of color. "Mercy, but I think I'd never let anyone sit on those— they're worth framing."

Now it was Isabelle's turn to laugh, leaning in as if to share a secret. "You're half-right—no one but Chester is allowed to sit over there."

Ida was just taking a breath to ask what earned this Chester fellow such special privileges when a dainty white poodle the size of a bread box trotted into the room and hopped onto the couch to settle himself in a space she only now realized was left between the groupings of pillows.

"Yes." Isabelle chuckled as she answered Ida's unasked question, "That would be Chester. He doesn't take up much space, so I indulge him."

Given the twinkle of affection in Isabelle's eyes, Ida guessed that Chester must live a very indulgent life indeed. "I had a dog once, growing up," she offered. "They are grand company." She pictured Spud, the loud and wiry mutt she and her brothers chased growing up. It was hard to categorize Spud and Chester as members of the same species. Still, dogs were indeed great company, which made Ida wonder if the good Dr. Parker would ever consent to something so unpredictable as pets on the Home grounds. She couldn't see it—the man had been forced to stretch his mind to embrace colored socks, never mind something that ate and barked and required cleaning up after. Still, she could almost picture the delight in the children's eyes were they to get a visit from well-behaved Chester. How much trouble could an occasional visit from such a small dog be? "If you ever deliver your socks in person to the Home, would you bring Chester?"

The idea raised Isabelle's gray eyebrows. "Chester?"

"The children have no pets, and I think the chance to play with and pet a dog would be such a treat for them. The girls at least. Some of the boys might be a tad rough for a…" She scrambled for the right word to speak of Chester's rather dandy nature. "…gentlemen like Chester."

The older woman pondered the idea, one eye squinted in consideration. "I shall have to consider that. I've never been to the Home, you know. Of course we give—everyone does—but I've never been active in the cause before now. And visit? Well, I don't mind saying I fear it would be such a dreary place."

Everyone does not give, Ida corrected silently, remembering a surprisingly frank lament Daniel had recently given her over dwindling contributions. *But I aim to change that, one sock at a time.*

At that moment, Leanne stood and gathered her notes to begin the formal portion of the gathering.

"Well," whispered Ida to Isabelle, "it certainly can be dreary, but I like to think we're about to change that."

"Thank you, first of all, to the gracious Isabelle Hooper for opening her home to us this morning. I know so many people have fled the heat to The Islands or farther north, but I am delighted to find y'all here and willing. Ida, I wonder if you would tell the story of baby Meredith's booties. It would help the ladies understand what we're up against."

Ida told the story of poor Meredith's booties and the confrontation those innocent pink feet had launched. She was a good storyteller, and it pleased her to see compassion or humor or sadness reflected in the eyes of her audience. At the right moment, Ida reached into her pocket and produced a lone, sad white sock. Plain, graying and with a lamentable hole in the heel, it seemed to tell the whole story of the Parker Home for Orphans in a single object.

Then, timing it carefully for full dramatic effect, Ida produced Meredith's booties. Her heart leaped at the oohs and ahhs that erupted from the women, some of whom even clapped. "It breaks my heart to think of all those girls without a single bright, cheerful thing that someone made with love for them. It's just socks, I know, but didn't the war teach us that it's so much more than just socks? I want each of these girls to know someone cares enough to give them something pretty. The scriptures tell us 'Happy are the feet of those who bring good news.' I dearly hope you'll join me in bringing good news and happy feet to these children."

"Of course we will," declared Isabelle in such a voice

of enthusiasm that it dared any woman in the room to consider otherwise. "If my own feet were any smaller, I'd march you right up to my armoire and dump out my stocking drawer for you to take back this afternoon."

The room erupted in laughter, and Ida caught Leanne's eye. It had begun. Leanne handed out single sheets of paper with the instructions written out. "There are three sizes of patterns, but if you have a pattern you know well and can adapt to a size close to one of these, that will work just fine. It's variety we're looking for here, so be as creative as you like. At the bottom of each of your sheets is a list of girls. There are six of you here, so we've assigned four girls to each of you. Since there are twenty-six girls total, Ida and I will take the final two girls."

"Look," said Ida, pointing to the list that had been given to Isabelle, "another *I*." How could she have forgotten there was an Ingrid at the Home? Ida was also pleased to see both Gitch's and Donna Forley's names on Isabelle's list. She was growing especially fond of both girls.

"Another *I* indeed. Perhaps I will need to pay you all a visit. And bring Chester."

Of course, Dr. Parker would be aghast at the thought of Chester's appearance at the Home. Ida knew, however, that it would take only one visit for the children to capture Isabelle Hooper's heart. And if that required the chaos of a little white dog, well then, it was a tiny price to pay.

"Socks?" Mother looked as if she found the idea preposterous.

"I suppose I ought to be thankful we don't live in a

climate that requires sweaters." Daniel's spine stiffened at the look Mother was giving him. They were sitting on the porch again, discussing the Home. Lately his weekly visits to his mother had become a chore. He loved his mother, and was grateful for all the support she'd given him in taking over the Home when his father died, but lately her staunch support had begun to wane as he began to implement his own views. Consciously or unconsciously, it was becoming clear to Daniel that Amelia Parker had expected him to simply replicate his father's administration. Any divergence from "the way things have always been done"—such as the one he'd just described in Miss Landway's little project— was met with a scowl.

It had begun to be "Miss Landway's Little Project" in his head, although every day it seemed less and less "little." His industrious new nurse did not deserve the look Mother was giving down her nose at the moment. Daniel surprised himself by stooping to name-dropping to gain her approval. "Leanne Sample Gallows—who happens to be a dear friend of Miss Landway's, by the way—has gathered some very prominent names to lend a hand."

"However did she manage that?" Mother inquired as though it were an impossible feat, blotting her forehead. Again Daniel was struck by how sour she appeared of late. "Most families of prominence are out of town this time of year."

Daniel swallowed the "Well, *we* are not out of town" that was simmering on his tongue. Mother seemed to try his patience so easily lately. His days of fleeing Charleston's heat for The Islands farther along the coast or up into the cooler mountains for weeks at a time were long gone, surrendered to the weight of his responsibilities. If he was going to live up to his father's memory, he couldn't give the Home less than his full time and attention. Besides, he had little reason to wish himself anywhere other than town. The midsummer temperature was decidedly uncomfortable, but Daniel did not fear malaria and other summer-borne diseases the way other Charlestonians did. As for comfort, Daniel welcomed the idea of migrating the full population of the Home to some cooler summer locale one day. Present circumstances, however, gave no indication that such luxuries could come his way anytime soon. The best he could do these days were the pair of treasured concrete bathhouses the Home had off one of the dormitories. The cool, sheltered swimming "holes" made summers bearable at the Home, and while it had been one of his father's only amenities to the compound, it was certainly the most appreciated.

He took a sip of his coffee, trying again to ignore his mother's customary glare of bafflement at his beverage preference. He pressed on in the conversation. "Did you know Isabelle Hooper hosted the lady knitting volunteers for their first meeting yesterday?"

"Well, of course I knew that!" Mother snapped, as if the mere hint that she was not aware of all Charleston's social events would not be tolerated. "She invited me."

This was news to Daniel. Miss Landway had been dutifully providing him with project updates, asking his opinion on some issues and even waiting for approval before acting on others. She seemed so energized by the progress that he'd come to enjoy and even anticipate her reports. Just a few days ago, Miss Landway had shown him her current work on Mrs. Smiley's surprise blue slippers, holding them up with a pride of crafts-manship that made him grin. As a matter of fact, Daniel now found himself hiding an amused smile every time Mrs. Smiley complained about her aching feet. Mrs. Smiley's grousing producing a smile? That alone served as evidence that Ida Landway was proving to be a great asset to the Home.

"You declined Mrs. Hooper's invitation?" Daniel felt a pinch of annoyance. Normally, Mother had her hand in everything to do with the Home. He didn't think she could knit, but according to Miss Landway at least one of the recent volunteers was new to the skill and had received many eager offers from potential teachers, so that proved no impediment. No, he suspected his moth-er's decline had little to do with yarn and needles, and that bothered him. Whatever bee she had in her bonnet these days, she shouldn't be taking it out on a project to benefit the orphans.

Mother puffed herself up at his question. "I had a previous engagement."

Daniel's annoyance pinched harder. "I'm sure you could still participate. As a matter of fact, I'm positive that a prior engagement needn't stop you. Mrs. Gallows will be moving to Washington, DC soon and plans to knit her socks there and ship them to the Home."

"How very dedicated of Mrs. Gallows, bless her heart." When he grunted his disapproval at the snide tone, Mother squared her shoulders. "I fail to see how such an odd form of support is at all useful. Whyever do the children need colored socks?"

He'd had the same initial reaction, of course, but Miss Landway's persistent arguments had turned his opinion. He had the uneasy feeling that the nurse would be shifting his opinion on many topics in days to come. Looking at his mother, currently mired in her mental monuments of "how it is done," Daniel reminded himself that new ideas were worth exploring. The day he couldn't entertain a new idea that acted for the children's benefit should be the day he handed over administration of the Home to someone else.

"I don't think this is about necessity, Mother," Daniel countered, keeping his voice more pleasant than his current mood. "I've come to agree with Miss Landway's fresh assessment that while the children's garments are plain and practical, they are without any cheer whatsoever." He poured himself more coffee, noticing the many colors in his mother's good china. Was it in fact more pleasant to drink coffee from this cup and saucer than from their more utilitarian Home counterparts? Perhaps. "No one is saying that we don't meet the children's physical and educational needs," he went on, "but Miss Landway believes the Home ought to be a visually joyful place. Happy to look at. Cheerful to be inside. She contends that the environment can sway the children's mood and outlook. I must say, I'm coming to see her point. We are serving the children in many important ways, but I am open to the idea that we could be more creative in boosting their spirits."

"Boosting their spirits?" Mother found this as inappropriate as colored socks, evidently.

Daniel leaned in, a little shocked at his own urge to defend a scheme he'd found absurd a mere week ago. "I'm surprised at your reaction, Mother. Do not orphans deserve to be happy? I wouldn't divert funds from their food or education for this, yes, but if pretty socks give them some pleasure and their creation brings new friends to the Home, I don't see how I could possibly object."

When Mother looked as if she might be formulating a list of how he could object, Daniel pressed on. "It serves no useful purpose for you to buy a new hat, but it makes you happy. It is human nature to want beautiful things around us."

"I am not an orphan." Her mouth drew into a sour little bow. "I am not surviving on·the kindness of others."

She'd just inadvertently made his point. Daniel did not want the children to merely survive. He wanted them to thrive, to grow into full and healthy adults who contributed great things to the world despite the poor hand war and poverty had dealt them. How had Mother come to lose sight of that goal he knew she once shared with his father?

Daniel put down his coffee. "Mother, you are among the most charitable women I know. I admit, this is unconventional, but we are living in a new age and perhaps new methods are called for. I find I can't understand your objection." It was the closest he'd come to an outright challenge of his powerful mother's position in many months, and he didn't regret it. Yes, Amelia Parker had once moved philanthropic mountains in Charleston. Still, Daniel couldn't dispute that in her short time at the Home, Ida Landway had done more for it than his mother had all year. Hadn't his father once told him, "When God shows you the path, start walking"? It was time Daniel Parker stepped out onto his path.

"I don't object," Mother balked, startled by his challenging tone. "I just find it…frivolous."

"Come to the Home the day the socks are delivered,"

Daniel challenged. "I think you will find the children do not agree with you."

Mother waved him away. "Goodness." It was her stock reply for when she did not have a reply, and Daniel's cue that he had won this particular battle. For now.

Walking back from his visit an hour later, Daniel passed by the hardware store to pick up a few things MacNeil had requested. He stopped in front of the window, taken aback by the display. "Montgomery Ward's Coverall House Paint—the Best Paint for Your Money" the arrangement boasted, showcasing a pyramid of paint cans in two dozen or so colors. The style of painting homes in an array of colors had indeed caught on in recent years, a fashion completely ignored by the Parker Home for Orphans. With amusement, Daniel noted that the paint came in fifty-gallon drums at a considerable discount. With a piercing shame, he noted that the color closest to the Home's current walls was named #36: Deep Drab. *When God shows you the path, start walking.*

Daniel walked inside the store.

Chapter Ten

Ida smiled at the face Gitch made while she applied a bandage to the girl's finger. "Better today?" The cut was tiny, but Ida knew that sometimes "care" went beyond a small strip of well-tied gauze. In fact, Gitch had been in to have her bandage changed every day since the small mishap on Monday with some scissors, and it was clear her repeated visits had nothing to do with medical necessity.

"Not much," Gitch proclaimed, inspecting her new bandage with a carefully displayed doubt. Ida found the girl's face so sweet, her smile so charming with its half gaps of just-budding teeth, that she couldn't find it within herself to shoo the child from her office.

"Oh, I imagine it will be better in no time. You've taken excellent care of that finger. I wouldn't wonder if you became a nurse yourself one day. You've got the knack, I can tell."

That pronouncement lit the girl's face up like a lantern. "Really?"

Ida returned her gauze and scissors to their drawer under the examining table. "Absolutely. I've got a sense for it, being a nurse myself and all. You've got caring eyes, and that's important."

"So do you, Nurse Landway. I'm glad you're here." She pointed to the watercolor of some flowers Ida had tacked to the wall yesterday. "That one's new."

"It is. Do you like it?"

Gitch studied the painting with narrow eyes worthy of an art critic. "Not as much as the blue one. But it's nice."

"Well," replied Ida, "it's nice to know I'll never have to worry about false praise from you." The child was as honest as the day was long—often with mixed results. Ida could see much of herself in Gitch. Perhaps that's why she had grown so fond of the child. She'd grown fond of all the children beyond any of her expectations. It was becoming easier to see why Dr. Parker worked the long hours he did. To leave something undone for any of them poked at her conscience like a physical pain. Just Tuesday she'd woken twice in the night to check on a child who had developed a worrisome cough.

Despite having been duly treated, Gitch seemed in no hurry to return to class. She stubbed her shoes against the exam table, fiddling with the dingy pinafore tied over her dark blue dress. "Can you make me one of those?" She pointed shyly to the band of yellow daisies Ida had embroidered on the collar of her white blouse. "You could put it on my pinafore."

Ida heard Dr. Parker's voice cautioning her from the back of her brain. To decorate one child's pinafore would likely start an avalanche of requests, or complaints of preferential treatment, as the baby booties had done. Still, while the socks would soon be ready for twenty-six girls at their current production rate, the child's clothing seemed to cry out to Ida in its colorless sadness, twisting her heart. It was so hard to have to do everything in batches of twenty-six when she saw each child so clearly as an individual. Still, she wanted to show Dr. Parker she had learned her lesson.

A solution hit her just as Gitch's lower lip began to pucker out. "You know, you're smart enough to learn how to do this yourself."

"No I'm not." Gitch's self-doubt grew a lump in Ida's throat.

"You are. Besides, how will you ever know if you don't try?"

"I suppose."

"Have you ever sewn? Mrs. Smiley has taught you basic mending, hasn't she?" Mrs. Smiley was all about practical skills. Surely she would have taught the girls how to mend their own clothes.

"The older girls."

"Well, this is like sewing, only with colors—so it makes a picture. It only looks hard. I've done it since I was not much older than you—and you, Lady Gwendolyn, are loads smarter than I was back then." Ida took every opportunity to praise anything she could in the children, for they seemed to be so thirsty for affection and affirmation. Mrs. Smiley was effective and efficient, but Ida could see the girls needed to feel loved in even the smallest of ways.

"What about Donna? She's smart."

Donna Forley was indeed very clever. Ida had taken an immediate liking to the older girl who'd been her first guide around the Home. Ida wasn't alone in her affections, for Donna had caught the eye of Matty Hammond, and everyone at the Home knew the young couple had eyes for each other. "Do you think Donna might want to learn, too? Or any of the other girls?"

"Learn what?" Dr. Parker's voice came from the doorway, where he stood with a large parcel in his hands and the most extraordinary expression on his face.

"That." Gitch pointed with excitement at the collar of Ida's blouse, proving that the injured finger worked just fine indeed.

"Pardon?" Dr. Parker looked understandably baffled.

"Gitch asked me if I couldn't embroider the hem of her pinafore with flowers like my collar."

Dr. Parker's face took on a "haven't we been over this?" expression.

"And I was just asking Gitch if she'd like to learn how to do it herself, and perhaps all the girls if they wanted."

The doctor's expression softened. Ida raised her eyebrows at him as if to say, "See? I have learned my lesson."

"Nurse Landway says it's like sewing, only with colors. She says I'm smart enough to learn, but I'm not so sure."

Dr. Parker smiled. Ida took no small pleasure in the fact that she saw a great deal more of the doctor's striking smiles lately. "I expect there's only one way to find out."

"That's what she said." Gitch sighed. The child's eyes fixed on the parcel. "Whatcha got?"

Ida was glad the child asked—she'd been wondering the same thing, given the doctor's unusually cheerful expression.

"What do I *have*, Miss Martin?" When she nodded, he continued, "I have a surprise for Nurse Landway."

Ida couldn't have been more stunned. "A surprise? For me?" She didn't know what to make of it.

Dr. Parker set the parcel on the counter, and the package made an odd metal *thunk* as it landed. Whatever it was, it was heavy. He nodded toward it as he stepped out of the way. "Go ahead, open it."

"You got a present!" Gitch was practically jumping up and down.

Ida gave the doctor a tentative grin. It surely wasn't yarn, so she had no idea what he could have brought her as a surprise—especially with that look in his eyes. "I won't know for sure until I open it, will I?" She stepped forward, slipping her finger under the twine and pulling until it released the brown paper wrapping.

Ida gasped.

Eight magnificent tins of what could only be paint stood in a perfect stack. Paint! And in the most glorious colors! She read the names aloud, running her hands along the square of color on each label in euphoria. "Canary, Sky Blue, Cherry Red, Lettuce Green." Each one as vivid as the next, eight splendid tins of bright, beautiful color. Daniel Parker had brought her paints—Ida couldn't think of a single gesture that would bring her more joy. The affirmation in his "surprise" raised a lump of deep gratitude in her throat. "Oh, Dr. Parker, they're wonderful." She read the next row. "Moss Green, Deep Blue, Wine Color and Pink Tint. They're all just beautiful. Beautiful," she repeated, at a loss to describe what the arrival of these tins meant to her. Ida surely hoped her face showed the thankfulness filling her chest, for no words could even come close.

"There's a whole rainbow in there," Gitch said. "You could paint anything you wanted with all those colors."

"Maybe just start with the window trim in the girls' common room." Ida could see it in Dr. Parker's eyes— he understood exactly what this gift would mean to her.

"How? Why?" Her breath tingled in her chest as she ran a hand across the set of tins again. So much color. Such an extravagance of hues. Had he brought her even just one tin, she'd have been pleased. But eight? Had he presented her with a box of jewels or a trip around the world, Ida could not have been more pleased.

"Let's simply say—"

"I'm gonna go tell the other girls we're getting pretty colors in our rooms!" With one last look at the brilliant stack of cans, Gitch ducked around Dr. Parker to speed out the door.

"*Going* to go," Dr. Parker called after her, then turned to face Ida again. The room suddenly felt too small for so grand a gesture. She'd been standing closer to him at breakfast the other day and not felt as intimate as she did just now with yards between them.

"Why?" she repeated softly.

"Because you are right. It is too drab in here. We've lost sight of the wonderful views around us. I can't make flowers bloom like Mrs. Leonard did, but you have a gift for bringing color into the world. I'd be foolhardy not to let you use the talents God gave you to make the children's lives brighter."

He could not have said anything more perfect in all the world. "I don't know what to say."

He smiled. "Miss Landway at a loss for words? Grimshaw would never believe it."

Mr. Grimshaw and the boys—they deserved color, too. "If the girls' common room meets with your approval, may I have your permission to do the trim in the boys' room, as well?"

He crossed his arms over his chest, teasing in his eyes. "Am I to understand you are both asking permission and waiting for approval? Are you quite sure you're Ida Landway?"

Something fell away between them. The carefully tended wall of employer and employee slipped down to reveal a timid, fresh partnership that went beyond children, medicine or education. When she heard him say her name, her view of him shifted from Dr. Parker the institution, and took a small step toward Daniel Parker the man. The man who had just brought her paint to bring beauty into this tiny world they shared.

"Quite sure," she said, wishing the words did not sound so breathless. "Thank you. Thank you more than you can ever know."

"The Sky Blue is my favorite," he said in the tone of a secret. "What's yours?"

"All of them. Every single one of them."

There was a moment of powerful silence, as if the air itself had changed between them. Ida wanted to look anywhere but into his eyes, but at the same time couldn't pull her gaze away from their intensity. He seemed both bothered and more comfortable, which made no sense at all.

"Yes, well," he said, taking his glasses off and then putting them right back on again, "I'm glad you like your surprise."

"Oh, I do—I really do." Her words came out in a tumble to match the one in her stomach, and Ida fought the urge to put her hands up to the heat she felt rising in her cheeks.

"Yes. Good. Well then, it's almost time for fencing."
He stuffed his hands in his pockets.

"Oh, you wouldn't want to be late for that. And
thank you again. Really."

Dr. Parker coughed, nodded once at her, nodded
again at the tins of paint, and then fumbled from the
room.

Ida stared after him. *Well, I never!* She couldn't remember a time she'd been more shocked—and for an
army nurse, that was saying something.

Daniel stared at the ceiling and tried to get the sparkle in Ida Landway's eyes out of his mind. It wasn't
working.

He'd been especially vigorous in fencing this afternoon, unnerved as he was by how his simple gift
seemed to change things between them. He hadn't intended for the gesture to become so important...had
he? No, surely not. It was an impulse, a "wouldn't it
surprise her if I..." ambush of a thought that came over
him as he passed the hardware store window.

An impulse would have been one can of paint, Daniel
argued with himself. *You bought her eight.* How was it
that this woman could annoy him to pieces and intrigue
him to distraction at the same time? He found her vitality energizing, even if it was the kind of electricity just
as likely to shock as it was to provide power.

Folding his hands behind his head as he lay on the
couch in his parlor, Daniel allowed himself the luxury
of dissecting his thoughts on Ida Landway. She was
unlike any other woman he'd known—socially or pro-
fessionally. She wasn't a socialite by any stretch of the
word, but neither was she as coarse as her backcountry

upbringing would dictate. Down-to-earth, perhaps, but Daniel found the lack of pretense refreshing. He never had to guess what Ida was thinking—she spoke her mind, with force and clarity. After all, thanks to her nursing scholarship from Columbia, she was an educated woman.

He'd known plenty of well-educated women, but many of them had struck him as dull while Ida had such a wit about her. He recalled the verbal sparring they'd had when she discovered the boys' fencing. Ferocious West Virginia elephants? The boys still talked about her appearance, even at today's class. He liked matching wits with her, just as much as he enjoyed dueling with the older boys. Only with the boys, Daniel could be assured of a victory. Lately, it was difficult to know who came out on top in any conversation with Ida Landway.

Why have You brought her here, Lord? It was a valid question—even though Daniel had sought out an army nurse and reviewed her file, he couldn't escape the same notion Ida had: that God Himself had brought her to the Parker Home. The children adored her, but it was more than that.

Daniel rolled on his side, frustrated. Out of the corner of his eye he spied Meredith's pink booties, still sitting on the windowsill waiting to be returned to the toddler's feet once Miss Landway's sock project came to fruition. She'd turned so many things in his world upside down in the space of three weeks—he ought to be firmly put out by it.

Only he wasn't. It was as if he hadn't even recognized the rut he was in until she came and startled him out of it. Routines were comfortable, predictable and efficient. He'd liked, even depended upon, his routines. Ida's disruptions—and there seemed to be a new one every day—were irritating, uncomfortable…and filled with all the vitality he and the Home lacked.

Maybe, just maybe, time would settle them into a smoother working relationship. So far she'd done more good than harm, and Daniel found he didn't like the thought of the Parker Home without her in the infirmary.

It's only been three weeks, he told himself as he rose to get ready for bed. *Give her time. She may surprise you.*

He laughed at himself as he doused the light in his parlor. *May surprise you?* She'd done nothing but surprise him from the moment she set foot on the property.

Chapter Eleven

Friday just after lunch, Daniel was going over plans for an upcoming outing with Mr. Grimshaw while the boys were out in the yard when the calamity broke out. The shouting, yelling and—what was that yappy noise?—came through the window in such a burst that both he and Grimshaw sprang to their feet and made for the window that looked out onto the grass.

There, with her back to him in a circle of noisy boys, stood an impeccably dressed woman. A small white creature ran in crazed circles at her feet. When the woman turned toward the animal, Daniel was shocked to recognize the visitor as none other than Isabelle Hooper. MacNeil, who had evidently just let her in through the visitors' gate, stood beside her with a baffled expression on his face. Mrs. Hooper, it seemed, was here with her dog—if that indeed was what that thing was. Mother had told him stories of Chester the ridiculously coddled poodle, but he'd never met the animal—until now.

"A dog?" Grimshaw balked, scratching his forehead. "Someone's brought a dog?"

Without attempting to hide his displeasure, Daniel sighed. "I expect this is Nurse Landway's doing."

"A dog?" Grimshaw repeated, clearly at a loss for other words as the noise level kept going up in the yard.

Daniel had been hoping for a quiet Friday afternoon. A series of academic tests taken this week had left the boys boisterous and argumentative under the strain. Yesterday's fencing had been a lesson in chaos—and now this. This was a poor time for any visitor, much less Isabelle Hooper and her dog. He'd been trying to gain Mrs. Hooper's attentions for any number of months now, but this? A surprise visit—and one with Chester to boot—hardly seemed destined to end well. *Lord, deliver me!*

No one was going to deliver him from this but himself, it seemed. With a grumbling sigh, Daniel lifted his coat from the back of his chair and began to roll his sleeves down to button the cuffs. "I'll go greet our guest. Guest*s*. Grimshaw, would you be kind enough to run by Miss Landway's office and ask her to join me in the front room?" Daniel hated the thought of admitting the jumping, running beast into his parlor, but he could think of no other way to keep the boys away from the yapping dog long enough for a conversation to take place.

By the time he made it to the front gate and Mrs. Hooper, word of the dog's presence—or just the high-pitched bark—had evidently reached the girls, for he found Mrs. Smiley vainly trying to herd the girls back inside away from the dog. For a panicked second, Daniel could not tell if the sounds emanating from Isabelle Hooper were cries of fear or laughter. Thankfully, a closer view showed that the woman seemed to be as amused as the dog as it leaped from lap to lap and hand to hand, barking and jumping.

"Good afternoon, Mrs. Hooper," Daniel shouted as he made his way into the circle of excited children surrounding the woman.

Mrs. Hooper produced a rubber ball from her handbag—an act that made Daniel's eyes pop in surprise—and handed it to the nearest boy. "Here. Chester simply loves to chase this."

"Here, Chester, here, boy!" cried the boy, followed by a chorus of "Here, Chester!" seemingly from every child in the yard. Chester, good sport that he was, proceeded to chase the ball and plant happy licks on everyone he could reach.

"My goodness, Ida was right," Mrs. Hooper said, adjusting her hat, which had slipped off to one side. "They really do enjoy each other."

Daniel motioned two boys apart so that Mrs. Hooper had an exit from the circle. "Miss Landway asked you to bring…" He found himself hesitating just a bit before addressing the dog by name. "…Chester with you for a visit today?"

"Well, actually I do think we talked about a time next week, but Chester and I were on this end of town and it is such a lovely day. Besides, I found I couldn't wait to meet my girls."

Daniel looked toward the door behind Mrs. Hooper, willing Ida Landway to appear on the scene and explain. When she did not yet appear, he ventured, "Your girls?"

"Oh, that's right, we're to keep this a secret, aren't we?" She pulled Daniel to the side, completely unalarmed that her four-legged associate was mired in a mass of cooing, petting, giggling children. Daniel feared the small dog might be crushed, but Mrs. Hooper seemed to harbor no such concerns. "The girls I'm knitting socks for," she explained in a whisper. "We've each been assigned four, and I found I wanted to meet them before I put on the final touches."

Daniel had no idea how to respond. The whole thing baffled him on multiple levels. Visits? Assignments? A dog?

"Mrs. Hooper!" came Miss Landway's voice from behind him, a very satisfying panic pitching her greeting high. "I thought you and Chester were coming next week."

"And we are, dear, but…" The woman's eyes darted back and forth between Daniel and Miss Landway, picking up on the tension now strung between them. "Perhaps it wasn't the smartest idea to just show up."

"No, truly—"

"It's quite fine—" Daniel and Miss Landway both gushed refutes at the same time, moments before a red ball sailed through the air, just missing Daniel's forehead and causing him to duck.

Daniel straightened, determined to take control of the situation. "We always welcome visitors, Mrs. Hooper, but we'd have been so much better prepared to receive you if you had let us know you were coming."

"Pshaw, Dr. Parker. I require no reception. You have other concerns than receiving old ladies."

Concerns that involve a crazed dog, Daniel thought as he applied a casual smile. "Why don't you come into the front room and we can have a chat there. Chester will welcome a bit of rest from his many…admirers, too, I expect."

"Delighted." She turned to the children and gave a

small whistling sound, which brought Chester to her side immediately, much to the dismay of the children. "Give me some time to talk with Dr. Parker and Nurse Landway, children, and I promise Chester and I will come back outside for another visit."

In response to that promise, Mr. Grimshaw displayed an amused resignation while Mrs. Smiley's face was pinched tight with irritation. Clearly, the pair of teachers had come to the same conclusion Daniel had: hope of any further classroom accomplishments for the afternoon had just disappeared.

"I was going to tell you—" Nurse Landway started in a whispered voice just behind him.

"Next week?" Daniel threw back over his shoulder as softly as he could manage, only barely able to keep the irritation from his voice. It was going to take every ounce of control he had to make Mrs. Hooper feel as if her visit was the high point of his day. Here he'd just been thinking how nicely Miss Landway was finally fitting in—he'd gone and bought her paints, for goodness' sake—and she went and did something like this. An animal visit! An *invited* animal visit!

A whining chorus of "Why can't Chester stay out here with us?" and "We never get to play with dogs!" sounded in his ears as he held the door open for Mrs. Hooper and Miss Landway. Mrs. Hooper looked as if the whole thing had been great fun. Miss Landway had the good sense to look guilty.

"Isabelle," said the nurse, "why don't I go arrange for some iced tea and coffee to be brought while you talk to the doctor. And perhaps a dish of water for Chester?"

"A fine idea, dear. And darling of you to think of

Chester. He's had quite the exercise with those youngsters. But coffee?"

Miss Landway managed an "I'm so sorry about this"
smile as she nodded toward Daniel. "Dr. Parker pre-
fers coffee."

"In this weather? Goodness, I don't know how you
stand it."

"Thank you, Miss Landway," Daniel said, motioning
toward the small setting of tables and chairs. He didn't
know whether to admire Miss Landway's cunning exit,
or be annoyed at having been left alone to entertain Mrs.
Hooper and Chester. The latter was eyeing him with
large pleading eyes and a panting pink tongue, oblivious to all the chaos he'd just caused.

"I'm glad for the chance to speak with you, Daniel.
I know your mother well, you know."

Everyone does, Daniel thought. "It's too bad she
wasn't able to join your project."

She waved the comment off. "Oh, come now, we both
know she wasn't ever interested. I asked her to be polite, really. She's done more than enough for the Home
over her life already." She began petting the little dog,
who had settled himself delicately into her lap. "I find
this a most creative project. You've quite the talented
nurse there. I'd never have thought to look to the army
base for a nurse for your Home, but I dare say it's been
a great success."

Daniel wasn't sure *success* was the word he had in
mind at this particular moment. Still, the woman's kind
words bore out a surprising truth: he had assumed the
volunteer ladies' enthusiasm had been won by Leanne
Gallows, but perhaps Ida had a greater hand in it than
he'd realized. "Miss Landway is a very creative person."

"I've become rather invested, knitting these little socks. I hadn't expected that to happen. I want to meet the girls I'm knitting for. Actually, I'd like to continue meeting them, and I know some of the other ladies feel the same way. I'm hoping Miss Landway and I can devise a way to maintain a personal connection with the girls over the year. Do you think that can be arranged? A sponsorship of sorts. You know, cards on birthdays, gifts at Christmas, that sort of thing?"

Daniel removed his glasses. "It's a lovely sentiment, Mrs. Hooper, and I do appreciate all you're doing. It just might be a bit more difficult in practice."

"Miss Landway seems to think you are capable of anything. Surely arranging for small kindnesses for some of the girls shouldn't pose a challenge."

Here it was again: the never-ending battle of "some" versus "all."

"I'm not against kindnesses. I welcome anything we can do for the children. But please understand, it creates new problems if *some* children get things and others don't. I'm sure Miss Landway told you the story of the pink booties that launched the whole project of socks for her."

"Oh, she most certainly did." From the look on Mrs. Hooper's face, the story did little to dissuade her. He was going to rue the day those little pink booties came into his life. Was? He already did.

Ida walked into the room just as Dr. Parker was talking Mrs. Hooper out of getting further involved. Her heart sank to hear the doctor's practical, discouraging tone. She'd begun to have such high hopes for him when he'd purchased the paint, only to have them dashed again today. "So I can't do things for the four children I've knit socks for?" Mrs. Hooper's voice was actually sad.

"I'm not saying that exactly. I'm saying that we must ensure that the children are treated equally."

"I know it's hard to realize," Ida offered at the disappointment in Mrs. Hooper's tone, "but comparison is our worst enemy here. We want each child to feel special, but it is so hard when close quarters make it impossible to hide if one child has a treat that the others do not. Please don't let that discourage you. We really do want your help."

"Well, I suppose there's only one thing to do, then." Ida held her breath, fearful Mrs. Hooper would give up when she was sure the older woman had so much love to give. If she gave the children on her list even one-quarter of the devotion she showed to Chester, it would be an abundance to the girls. "We'll have to ensure that all the women get involved."

Ida sank into a chair as someone from the kitchen set a tray on the table between her, Mrs. Hooper and Dr. Parker. Suddenly this small impulse to knit socks for one girl was ballooning into something much larger than she could ever have imagined. Ida put a hand to her chest, astonished. "You'd do that?"

"It's a sizable commitment, Mrs. Hooper," Dr. Parker advised.

"Well, of course it is," Mrs. Hooper dismissed. "But really, what in life worth doing isn't?" Chester perked up at the bowl of water the server set at Mrs. Hooper's feet, hopping from her lap to tuck his white nose noisily into the bowl. "Now, there you are, Chester. Look how kind they are to you here." She turned her gaze to

Dr. Parker. "I rather like the idea of making a personal connection. I serve as a patron for several fine artists. Why not become a patron to orphans, as well?"

"You'd have to get all the women equally involved," Ida admitted. "We simply can't single one group of girls out for special treatment." She felt compelled to add, "Even though they all are so very special, don't you think?"

"I've been thinking I needed a new project. Why not this?" Mrs. Hooper accepted the glass of iced tea Dr. Parker offered. "Now, just to be clear, 'equal' doesn't have to mean 'identical,' am I right? As long as each child receives the same amount of attention, am I free to treat each child individually? If one child likes licorice, and another likes peppermint, I don't have to buy them both licorice, do I? I hardly think that's a true kindness."

Dr. Parker picked up his coffee cup. "Are you telling me you want a one-on-one relationship with each child?"

"Well, not all of them. Just my four. And each of the other five ladies will foster relationships with their four. Think of us as…well, a little band of surrogate aunties."

Or fairy godmothers, Ida thought. "That's so much more than we'd hoped for, Mrs. Hooper. I don't know what to say."

"That's easy." Mrs. Hooper laughed. "Say yes."

"It's not really my yes to say." Ida looked at Dr. Parker. He couldn't possibly disapprove of such generosity, could he? Not when Isabelle Hooper was offering such an abundance of attention to the girls. "Please, Dr. Parker, I do think this could be wonderful."

Daniel Parker had the good sense to know when he was outnumbered. Quite frankly, the way Mrs. Hooper was grinning, Ida thought she would sit here until sundown making arguments if Dr. Parker declined. She'd have to thank Leanne ten times over for getting this wonderful older woman involved—dog and all.

"I'll agree," Dr. Parker said after entirely too long a pause. "As long as treatment feels equitable to each girl. Which reminds me, the setup you've suggested leaves two girls unassigned."

"Oh, that's right. Leanne and I are making socks for two of the girls. We'll have to do something about that."

"I'll take them on," Isabelle said. "I've raised six children—I'm used to doing things by the half dozen." Chester chose this moment to walk over to Dr. Parker and plant his wet snout on the doctor's knee. Ida tried not to laugh as the little dog looked up at the man with pleading eyes. Daniel set down his coffee cup and gave the dog an obligatory pat, receiving a bevy of licks for his kindness.

"My stars. Chester is always fond of children but he's very choosy with his friends when it comes to adults. You should be honored he's taken such a shine to you."

Dr. Parker looked many things, but honored wasn't one of them. Ida hoped Chester knew enough not to hop on Dr. Parker's lap—she didn't know what the good doctor would do with that.

"I'll have all their agreements lined up by the time we come with the socks next week. Ida tells me there's an afternoon later this month when the boys are on an outing. I wouldn't want them to feel left out—not that I imagine any of them pine for pink socks."

"Mr. Grimshaw is arranging for them to tour the navy shipyards," Dr. Parker confirmed, trying to politely extract his hand from Chester's continual licks.

"Miss Landway will coordinate your visit with me." He caught Ida's eye with an expression of command. "Although today was a…delightful surprise."

"Oh, yes, a delightful one," Ida added.

"A bit chaotic at first," Mrs. Hooper said, "but I think even Chester enjoyed himself. I promise I won't raise quite such a ruckus when we come back. Still, I think Chester would enjoy becoming a regular visitor here, if that's all right with you, Dr. Parker."

Ida hid her smile in a glass of iced tea. Dr. Parker really was outnumbered at the moment. "How could I refuse?" he said, his voice tight but cordial. Ida expected to hear a great deal about this once Mrs. Hooper was out of earshot.

"Another thing. Could you prepare a list of the girls' birthdays for me? I'd like to ensure the girls get birthday and holiday cards, among other things. And Bibles. Do the children have Bibles of their own? Because if they don't, I should like to make sure that they do— boys included."

"We have many Bibles in the library, but the children do not own individual books."

"Surely you'll make an exception in the case of the Good Book, won't you?"

Ida began to wonder just how much Isabelle Hooper was going to get away with in a single visit. "It sounds like a fine idea—if you approve, of course, Dr. Parker." She felt a tad guilty about adding her endorsement, given how little chance Dr. Parker had of refusing Mrs. Hooper, but if God had sent Isabelle Hooper as such a blessing of generosity for the Home, who was she to object?

"It's a lovely gesture," Dr. Parker said, his voice still tight and Chester still lavishing his hand with licks.

"That's enough, Chester, leave the good doctor be." She made a small snap with her fingers, which halted Chester's licks immediately and sent him scurrying to sit obediently at Mrs. Hooper's feet. Ida had never seen a dog so impeccably trained.

Daniel was trying to discreetly mop his wet hand with a napkin from the serving tray when Mrs. Hooper put down her iced tea and patted her lap once, which was Chester's clue to hop into her arms. "Well now, I think I've taken up quite enough of your time. I see the children are still outside, and I expect they'll want another round of fetch with Chester before I go." She turned to Ida. "Thank you, dear, for coming to us for help. I look forward to our little project more than you know."

"I do too, Mrs. Hooper." Ida took the hand Mrs. Hooper offered.

"You must remember to call me Isabelle. Not in front of the children, of course, but I think we'll be seeing a great deal of each other." She rose, dog in hand as if he were as much an accessory as the beaded handbag at her wrist. "Would you take me back out into the yard, Dr. Parker? You may throw Chester's ball first, if you'd like."

Ida watched the doctor lead Isabelle out into the yard, hiding a smile behind one hand. *Oh, Father, have I done a good thing or a bad thing? I can't tell if You've sent us Isabelle to bring blessings or if I've sent Dr. Parker a whopping aggravation. Surely only You know.*

Chapter Twelve

Dr. Parker had in fact given Ida a wide berth for the rest of the afternoon, keeping to his offices rather than hunting her down to complain about Chester's surprise visit. Ida surely wasn't going to go seeking him out. Instead, she spent a luxurious evening rearranging the paint tins, reveling in the task of dreaming up color combinations. Moss Green and Wine for the trim in the boys' areas, Pink Tint and Sky Blue—or maybe the yellow—for the girls. Could she dare talk Dr. Parker into something so extravagant as a mural? How lovely that would be in the dining room, if she could ever find the time for such a task. Find the time? Today Ida felt as if she could give up sleep for a week and paint all night if not for the lack of light that made such an idea impossible.

Yes, the blue and yellow together, she decided as a knock came on her sitting room door. She'd told the girls they had permission to visit her anytime, but this was the first occasion a child had taken her up on the offer.

Ida opened the door to see a red-eyed Donna Forley

standing there twisting her skirts with anxious fingers. "Goodness, Donna, you look a fright. Come in."

Donna dashed into the room and vaulted herself onto Ida's small couch, dissolving into sobs. This was no medical emergency, but a crisis of another kind, surely. Most likely one with the name Matty Hammond. "Oh, Nurse Landway, it's just awful."

"I'm sure it feels that way," Ida said, wondering what spat Donna and Matt had gotten into this time—the usually love-struck couple had often been arguing of late. "Why don't you tell me all about it and we'll see what can be done."

"Nothing," moaned Donna in true teenage despair. "Not a thing."

"Well," said Ida, pulling a handkerchief from her side table drawer, "tell me all about it anyway."

Donna heaved out a handful of further sobs, then sat upright and pulled in a dramatic deep breath. "He's been just beastly."

Ida found the adjective a bit novel worthy, but kept silent and only offered a hand on Donna's arm and a soft "How so?"

"He says he doesn't want to marry me."

They were nearly of an age; it shouldn't have surprised Ida that orphans met and married in homes like this one. If she had to pick any two from the Parker Home who stood the best chance as a pair, it was surely Donna and Matthew. "Have you two been talking of marriage?"

"We *were*." Donna made sure Ida understood the past tense of that word.

"Do you know what changed Matty's mind?"

"Sense," Donna spat out like a curse. "Matty says it doesn't make sense to get married soon."

Oh. So this was perhaps not about rejection, but impatience? "Are you saying Matty still wants to marry you but not just right now?"

"A year after we graduate. A *whole year*. Honestly, Nurse Landway, I'll die of waiting."

Ida felt a little humor might serve the situation. She made a grand show of taking Donna's pulse. "Hmm. I'm quite sure you're not in any danger of imminent death. Mr. Hammond might break your heart, but he won't stop it from beating, I guarantee that."

Donna made a face, but at least she stopped crying.

"I take it you don't want to wait."

"Why?" It never ceased to amaze Ida how children could string that word out to be such a long, agony-filled syllable. "Why should we wait when we're in love?"

"Well, did you ask him why *he* thinks it makes sense to wait? Matty seems like a clever fellow to me."

"He wants to have a job. He's choosing a job over me. He could find a job after we get married, couldn't he? Why does it have to come first?"

Having a secure income before marrying seemed like a sensible course of action to Ida, but Donna didn't seem ready to hear that right now. "You want to be together now, don't you? Hearts never want to be sensible, do they?" After so many years on her own, could she really blame Donna's young heart for wanting to know it would never be alone again?

"I think it makes all the sense in the world to get married as soon as we can. I don't want to be out there without him."

"Out there" was a term Ida had heard the orphans

use for the world beyond their years at the Home. "Out there" was by turns wonderful and scary, depending on the child and any number of circumstances.

"It doesn't sound to me like you'll be without him at all." She took Donna's hand. "I reckon he wants to get himself settled in a job and be able to provide for you, and that's a fine thing for a man to want to do. Shows mighty good character."

"I won't care what kind of job Matty gets. I'll love him no matter what."

"He's blessed you love him so much, Donna, but men are funny about such things. God's crafted most of them—not all of them, mind you, but most—to be providers. They need to know they can take care of the people they love. It's why Dr. Parker works so hard to see that all of you have food and clothing and books and such." She soothed Donna's hand. "If you ask Matty if the heart part of him wants to marry you tomorrow, I'm sure he'd say yes. He loves you. Anyone can see that."

Donna sniffed. "He says he does."

"He's just trying to do right by you the best way he knows how. The head part of him is trying to be sensible and have things all lined up before he takes you as his bride. That's an admirable thing. What you have to do is convince the head part of *you*—" she tapped Donna's forehead affectionately with her other hand, her own heart cinching in sympathy for the love-struck young woman "—to be patient enough to let him."

The girl seemed to be wrestling with the idea. Finally, reluctantly, she admitted, "I didn't think of it that way. I told him he must not love me enough if he doesn't want to marry me right away."

Oh, dear. Ida could see how that remark turned a

conversation into an argument. "If you're asking me, I think it means he loves you very much. You're blessed he does, too, even if it means having to wait a whole year 'out there.'"

Donna fell back against the sofa cushions. "Whatever will I do out there?"

Ida sat back to meet the girl's eyes. "There are wonderful things to do at your age. I went to nursing school. My cousin worked in a shop, my friend became a baker. Ever since the war, there have been all kinds of things women can do. You know the US Congress passed an amendment giving women the right to vote last month, don't you? That just goes to show it's a fine time to be a woman your age, Donna, really. I hate to say 'wait and see' but it's true."

"He hurt my feelings so much, I stomped out of the yard. Matty must hate me right now." She looked at Ida. "Why is this so hard?"

Ida laughed. "Honey, I wish I knew. Seems to me the battle between heads and hearts has been going on as long as time itself. Just seems harder when you're young, I think."

"You're smart," Donna said, drying her eyes again. "Is love hard for you?"

That was an enormous question. "Some parts come easy to me. Others I mess up the same as you."

"When were you in love, Nurse Landway?"

It had been a very long time. "Oh, there were one or two soldiers who caught my eye back at Camp Jackson, but the timing never did seem right." It was half of the truth. Watching her friend Leanne and the deep, life-changing relationship she had with Captain John Gallows had redefined love for Ida. She'd known infatuation, and some mighty strong attractions, but the kind of soul-mate love John and Leanne had? That hadn't come her way yet. "I never did mind being on my own. Oh, I like company and such, but I'm fine with waiting until God sends the right man along. And that's just it." She straightened, wanting to make the point to Donna. "God's got it all worked out. You need to trust that. If the Good Lord means for you and Matty to marry, nothing on this earth can stop that from happening. Even if it takes longer than you'd like."

Donna leaned in. "You ever kiss a fellow?"

Ida laughed at the combination of awe and secrecy in Donna's tone. "I've had some mighty fine kisses in my day. But a man who loves you for who's on the inside, one who wants what's best for you for the rest of your life and not just what his urges are telling him at the moment? A man like your Matty? Well, that's a whole other kettle of fish. Love like that is more powerful than any kiss, I tell you. Don't you let any of that nonsense out by the beehive tell you any different."

Donna's eyes popped wide, making Ida laugh harder. "You know about the beehive?" The staff thought "beehiving" was their secret word, and the teenagers thought the code was theirs. Each side thought the other didn't know what "beehiving" was. Ida saw the whole thing as complicated nonsense—why on earth didn't folks just come out and say what they meant?

"'Beehiving' has been going on as long as time itself, too, you know. It just goes by different names." Ida felt another point needed to be driven home. "But you be careful about such things. Love is a powerful notion, and it can run away with your judgment." When Donna nodded, Ida went on, taking both of Donna's hands in hers. "I want you and Matty to have a bright, clear future. Dr. Parker, Mrs. Smiley and Mr. Grimshaw do, too. Only it's up to you and Matty to make it happen." She wiped a stray strand of hair from the young girl's face, glad to see the tears gone and a smile in their place. "You come to me anytime you need advice or have questions, okay?"

"Thanks, Nurse Landway."

"Now, you get on to bed. It's late and you have classes in the morning."

Donna yawned at the mere suggestion of the hour. "I do."

Ida rose and gave the girl a hug. "Your *I do*s will come in good time, I promise."

Daniel stared at the line of books on the Home's library shelf, waiting for something to catch his eye. Sleep eluded him despite the late hour, and nothing in his personal library seemed to suffice. He pulled out a volume of Greek dramas only to shut it again. *What I really am*, he decided, *is hungry*. There had been some very good ham at supper tonight, and he was sure there would be some left in the kitchen.

He met Mrs. Smiley in the hallway, startling her as she came from that direction. He was in shirtsleeves and open collar given the lateness of the hour, and almost apologized for his appearance when the matron stared at him sharply. She, on the other hand, was still fully dressed. The woman never ventured out of her quarters in anything but full proper dress—even in emergencies, even in the middle of the night. If Miss Landway ever succeeded in making her wear blue slippers, he'd never know, for she would never stoop to don such things in public.

"I'm hungry," he said in unnecessary explanation.

"Are you, now?" For some reason her arched eyebrow bothered him even more than usual.

"Is there any of tonight's ham left?" He really did try to make his question sound congenial.

"Why should I know a thing like that?"

Daniel found himself too weary to dodge the woman's piercing glares. He simply offered a "Good night, Mrs. Smiley," and continued on his way in search of a ham sandwich with a glass of milk.

Chapter Thirteen

Daniel made his way toward the kitchen, pleased to see light peek from under the door. Grimshaw was often known to fix himself a sandwich at this hour, and Daniel smiled as he pushed open the swinging door, ready to have a conversation with the teacher.

What he found instead was Miss Landway hauling the aforementioned ham from the icebox. A loaf of bread and a pitcher of lemonade already sat out on the counter. She startled so at his appearance that he had to dash to her side to keep her from dropping the large hunk of meat.

"Mercy! I just about sent that tumbling," she yelped as together they maneuvered the ham to the counter. "You scared me out of my skin."

"My apologies, Miss Landway. Seems we had the same fond memory of tonight's ham."

She shook her head. "I mostly needed something to take my mind off the conversation I just had with Donna Forley." She put her hand dramatically to her heart. "The tribulations of young love."

"Another spat?" Daniel reached for a carving knife.

"Not really. More like a misunderstanding." She opened a cabinet and pulled out two plates.

"Aren't all lovers' quarrels rooted in misunderstandings?"

"Now that," Miss Landway declared as she put the plates down, "sounds like something a man would say."

"I take offense…I think," Daniel teased. Somehow, in the confines of this kitchen at odd hours, he found Ida Landway delightfully easy to talk to. Under more official circumstances, she could be vexing, annoying even, but here, talking of everyday things, he found her effervescent.

She laughed, proving his point. "Matt told Donna he wanted to wait until they were a year out from graduation before they married, so he could secure a job first. Donna took it the wrong way and stomped off thinking he didn't want to marry her at all. It would be sweet, actually, if it weren't so taxing."

"She's impulsive," Daniel agreed as he piled a slice of bread with savory ham. "Matt is good for her."

"Impulsive's not all bad," Miss Landway countered, looking as though she knew every bit how impulsive she herself was. "Donna is very good for Matty. Some things in life require a leap of faith, and it'll be Donna pulling Matty over that leap."

Daniel gave her a doubtful glare. "Now that, Miss Landway, sounds like something a woman would say."

"What do you say we leave off the titles after midnight? I'm just Ida. Ida who needs a sandwich. And maybe one or two of the cookies I saw in the pantry."

Daniel wasn't quite sure he was ready to peel off another layer of formality between them. Then again, perhaps she was an impulsive Donna to his sensible

Matthew and this didn't need his gift for overthinking things. After a moment's pondering, he consented. "Well, then that makes me hungry Daniel, who wouldn't decline one of those cookies, either." He topped both sandwiches with a second slice of bread and slid one plate over to her.

"Oh, no," she said, unscrewing the jar next to her, "it needs mustard."

That was Ida—forever embellishing the world around her. Which reminded him: "Have you decided how to use the paint?"

"Oh," she said, slathering a frightful amount of mustard on her sandwich, "I've buckets of ideas."

That didn't surprise him. He was half-stunned the Home hadn't drowned in colors already. She really was trying to be deliberate about the process, wasn't she? "Such as?"

Her eyes lit up at the encouragement. "Well, I've mostly decided on wine and moss in the boys' common room and Sky Blue and yellow in the girls'."

"No pink?" He'd made sure pink was in among the tins, knowing her fondness for the color.

Ida licked a glob of mustard off one finger. "Too obvious."

"Well, one mustn't be obvious." He was making jokes and sandwiches with Ida Landway at midnight in the Home kitchen. The Dr. Parker part of him was startled at the concept. Daniel, however, was enjoying himself. This friendly, spontaneous meal felt the direct opposite of his endless porch luncheons with Mother.

"I have an idea," Ida said carefully as she cut her sandwich into four triangular quarters and arranged them on her plate.

"Yes?" Daniel recalled Chester's vexing visit earlier today and fought the knot growing in his stomach.

"What do you think of a mural on the dining room wall?"

A mural? He'd been thinking only in terms of using the colors for trim. As a matter of fact, he distinctly recalled agreeing only to the girls' common room trim, and noticed Ida had already started talking about the boys' common room.

"You want to paint a mural on the dining room wall?" A mural sounded, well, radical. Then again, could he expect any less considering he had as much as handed her a palate in his gift of paints?

She frowned. "You hate the idea. I knew it was too much."

"I do not…hate…the idea. I don't love it, either, to be honest. It is a big jump from our current…" He hunted for a word, seeing the Deep Drab paint tin label in his mind's eye. "…decor."

Ida cocked her head to one side. He'd learned she did that when biting back a strong opinion. "This house has paint on walls. It does not have a decor. I don't see any reason why we can't change that."

"I appreciate your enthusiasm, but—"

"Oh, please," she cut in, "please don't use that phrase. You've no idea how many times I've been 'appreciated for my enthusiasm.'" She looked straight at him, eyes afire. "I know what that really means, Daniel. I've heard every polite form of 'no' there is, I assure you."

Daniel shook his head. "You are by far the most direct woman I have ever met."

She didn't seem to be one bit fazed by his pronouncement. "Well, then, I don't think I'd like whatever female company you have been keeping." She picked up one neat triangle of her sandwich. "I find directness to be a fine thing, and too rare in some parts. Seems to me men are direct all the time. Why not women? What's the point in being all coy and elusive? If it's worth saying, it's worth saying outright, that's what I think."

"I don't believe I'm ever at a loss for what you think." It was true. He had friends who took great satisfaction in navigating Charleston's social maze, but Daniel was neither good at it, nor enjoyed such complexities. Ida Landway was no coy Southern rose—she was a full-blossomed sunflower, impossible to ignore or misunderstand. She offered no hidden agendas to uncover, no subtleties to misinterpret. It was refreshing. And, if he were honest with himself, it was becoming rather appealing.

"Well, I find myself at a loss for what *you* think."

Daniel chose the most direct words he could. "I think I would rather wait until we see how the colored trim in the girls' common room goes before I even think about a mural."

She smiled. Ida had the most engaging smile—it seemed to light up her whole body, not just her face. "I can live with that. But we should do the boys' common room as well—equal treatment and all, just like you said."

She had him there. In for a penny, in for a pound. "Well, yes."

"Thank you. I appreciate your approval."

He picked up one half of his own sandwich. "I appreciate you actually asking this time." When her resulting smile converted the knot in his stomach to an unsettling ripple, Daniel changed the subject. "Do you think Donna can live with waiting a year? I told Matt that while I've always been in favor of them as a pair, I thought it would be sensible to wait until their finances were more secure."

"You put that idea in Matty's head?"

"Of course I did."

Ida leaned in. "I suppose lacking a father, you're the closest thing Matty has. Donna, too. Why, I wouldn't be surprised if Matt came to you asking for Donna's hand—where else would he go?"

"He has." Daniel hadn't told anyone—not even Mr. Grimshaw—that Matt had come to him with just that request two weeks ago. It had warmed his heart and startled him at the same time.

"Matty came to you asking to marry Donna? And you told him to wait?" The way her eyes narrowed, Daniel couldn't tell if Ida thought that was good or bad.

"Not directly. We spoke of providing for her, and for the family they might someday want. Given his history, it's understandable that Matt is very concerned about giving Donna a good home. I simply suggested that it might be easier once he had a secure post. They are still very young, even if they are quite good for each other."

"Here I was wondering how Matty got so sensible at his age. I don't know if I'm more impressed that he came to you with questions, or that he was willing to listen to the answers." She leaned on one elbow. "Seems a shame to make them wait, even if it is sensible. They're so darling together. I don't think anything could stop me if I were Donna and I had my heart set on running off with a fine young man like Matthew Hammond." Then, as if it were a perfectly reasonable question, Ida looked at him and said, "Why haven't you married? You're of more than sufficient age."

Ida watched Daniel practically choke on his sandwich. Why had such a rude question popped out of her mouth like that? Mercy, but she needed to learn how to guard her tongue! "I'm sorry. I had no business asking such a thing."

"It is a very…direct…question, I'll give you that." Daniel took a drink of milk, recovering from the apparent shock of her ill-mannered curiosity. "I wish I had a direct answer. I suppose," he ventured, putting down the glass, "it is the unusual nature of my role here. This isn't the kind of post where I lock up the office and come home for dinner promptly at six."

She was just beginning to grasp how much of a burden running the Home could be—physically and emotionally, but socially, as well. Daniel had always shown such singular passion for the place that, until meeting with Isabelle, she hadn't thought about his outside life. The truth was that Daniel *had* no outside life—or very little that she could see. Did he choose to make it that way? Or merely accept the isolation as a consequence of the time he saw fit to devote to his vocation? Either way, it was unsettling—in any number of ways—to think of the man in front of her as "Daniel," with interests and tastes of his own that had nothing to do with the Home, rather than merely as her employer, "Dr. Parker."

"Surely there's someone…" She began the sentence, but found herself unable to finish it. Why on earth had she let Donna's drama pull their conversation into such unsuitable waters?

"There was a young woman once," Daniel began to

her surprise, "when I was not much older than Matthew. I'm afraid I lacked Matt's charisma with females, and it felt like years before she even recognized my existence."

Daniel wasn't handsome in the traditional sense—he would never command a room the way Captain John Gallows did—but he had deep, intelligent eyes, a strong jaw and a wonderful, if rare, smile. Ida remembered how he'd looked when she had found him sleeping in the staff dining room and felt her heart skip a little. He kept himself under tight rein, but there was far more to him than the carefully controlled exterior he usually presented. His laugh, for example, was delightful. And he had certainly looked dashing enough in the fencing class. Had he been more like that as a young man? Would she have noticed him were she Donna's age?

"But she did notice you? Eventually?"

"We had a very brief, very carefully orchestrated courtship." His face did not show this to be a happy memory.

"And then?"

Daniel sighed, lifting his sandwich with such an air of "life goes on" resignation that Ida felt it push against her chest. "And then Sarah Jane met another, far more exciting man who swept her away from me."

"He stole your girl?" Ida balked.

That brought a dark laugh from Daniel. "Well, now, that's a direct way to put it, yes. It certainly felt that way at the time. But I soon realized Sarah Jane was never really mine to start with. The whole thing was more contrivance of her parents than any real affection on her part. But I was sure I loved her. As sure as one can be at that age."

"I think you can be. Donna and Matty are sure. But since then?"

"Oh, my pedigree ensures that I'm invited to all the proper events, where I find I have a respectable line of women seeking attention. But as I said, once they get to know me better, the demands of the Home don't sit well with them. They quickly learn there are better prospects elsewhere." He said it with such an astounding lack of bitterness that Ida's heart twisted. He was a fine man. Everyone deserved to know love, especially someone who gave himself so completely to others the way Daniel Parker did.

She looked up to find Daniel staring at her. "And you?"

Ida hadn't expected him to turn the conversational tables on her, but fair was fair. "Oh, there were the usual infatuations growing up. And I will say there were soldiers at Camp Jackson who showed a very flattering level of interest, but mostly I've just wanted adventure more than romance. I was never sure I could trust my impulsive nature, anyways. Today's perfect man always seemed poised to end up as tomorrow's silly regret."

"A very independent view." He was still staring, and the attention was making her stomach wiggle under the scrutiny. "Will you remain independent, then?"

"Oh, no, I'd like a fine match whenever God gets around to it. I figure His timing is bound to be better than whatever I might ask for, anyways." She looked down at the remaining quarters of her sandwich, surprised at how his eyes could fluster her. "For now, I'm just glad to be here," she said, just because she wanted him to know how fond she'd grown of the Home. "I think God's put me right where I belong."

"I was just thinking the same thing," Daniel said. There was a warmth to his voice she'd never heard before. "I'm very glad you came to the Home."

Ida started to say a polite "Thank you, Dr. Parker," but found she couldn't. The unnerving possibility that it was the *man* rather than the doctor saying such words caught her up short. Ida sputtered out a soft "Thank you," sounding entirely too much like teenage Donna rather than independent Nurse Landway.

There was a still, quiet moment where they sat looking at each other, seeing each other, Ida thought, in a different and unexpected light. In the bright sunshine of day, the moment would have vanished, but here in the soft glow of the kitchen lamp so late at night, it remained. A dangerous man-and-woman *what-if* that had very little business existing between the Parker Home for Orphans nurse and its doctor administrator. From the look in Daniel's eyes, it caught him as much by surprise as it had Ida.

She could see him take the thought and pack it away behind the shell of duty he so often wore. Truly, it showed that clearly on his face. Ida felt a small chill, as if he'd pulled the warmth out of the air between them with his decision. "You make a fine addition to the staff, and the children adore you." Despite the warm words, his tone was businesslike once more.

"I think they are wonderful," she said, still reeling inside from the way his unguarded stare had caught her breath. "All of them." A part of her—a much larger part than she had realized until just now—wanted to halt the door she was watching him close. There was something between them, something that had come uncovered when he brought her the paints and had shown itself even more tonight. Only another part of Ida agreed that whatever it was should be put aside for the sake of the Home and its precious charges. That was the wisest course of action, wasn't it?

"It's late," he said finally, his eyes pronouncing closure on the moment far more than his words. Without finishing his sandwich, Daniel rose and headed for the door. "Good night, Nurse Landway." The use of her title was no accident.

Ida smoothed one hand against her skirts. Yes, that was the wisest course of action. "Good night, Dr. Parker."

She stared at the door long after it had swung shut, trying to make sense of the swarm of thoughts in her head. No sense came, and she collected the uneaten portions of both sandwiches and tucked them in the icebox. She'd only thought herself hungry—yet another silly regret—for now she had no appetite at all.

Chapter Fourteen

Mr. Grimshaw burst into the infirmary with an alarmed look on his face. "You'd better come. And bring supplies—I don't think Dr. Parker ought to be walking just now."

Ida dropped the box of gauze padding she was holding. "Dr. Parker?"

"The boys were getting rough with each other. He stepped in, and got caught in some of the shoving. He hit his head on the fence. Hard."

Ida grabbed the portable first-aid kit she'd created for when injuries could not come to her. She started to ask the teacher if Daniel was bleeding, but a smear of blood on Grimshaw's arm gave her the bad news. She added two extra packs of bandaging to the kit—head wounds could bleed frightfully even if they weren't serious. "Let's go. You can tell me more details on the way."

"I don't think he blacked out, but he was talking funny when I left." Mr. Grimshaw, usually hard to ruffle, seemed disturbingly grave.

"Where is he bleeding?"

The teacher touched his left eyebrow and ran his finger down along close to the side of his eye, making Ida suck her breath in through her teeth. This could be a serious injury. "Who do you call when the doctor is sick?"

Grimshaw blinked. "Dr. Parker's never been sick. Never been hurt before, either."

Ida mentally calculated the distance between the Home and the nearest hospital. Unless the doctor's life or sight were at stake—which she dearly hoped wasn't the case—they'd have time to get him to whatever medical attention she wasn't qualified to give.

They dashed through the Home hallways until Ida could have found her way by the sound. Children yelling, Mrs. Smiley shouting, younger children crying; the commotion gave Dr. Parker's position away clearly as she headed out into the yard behind the kitchen.

Slumped like a rag doll against a rusty portion of the Home's massive wrought iron fence, Daniel sat motionless. Well, not entirely motionless—he clenched and unclenched one fist and the part of his face she could see worked in bloody grimaces. Donna and Matthew were attempting to herd the children away from the gruesome scene while Mrs. Smiley was holding a wad of dish towels—now more red than white—against one side of Daniel's face.

"Coming through," Ida said, her voice cutting the commotion to silence as the children parted between her and Daniel. She flipped open the kit and knelt in front of Daniel next to Mrs. Smiley. "Dan—" She stopped herself, grateful to catch the error before she made it in front of the matron. "Dr. Parker?"

His eyes worked to focus on her. He squinted—his glasses were off and lying bent on the ground somewhere to her left—which sent him into a hissing wince of pain. "Fence." Grimshaw was right; his words were slightly slurred.

"Here, let me," Ida said to Mrs. Smiley, gently taking the soaked cloths from the teacher's hand. She took the smallest of peeks at the wound, careful to hide her reaction from the present audience. Daniel had a deep, angry gash running dangerously close to his left eye, which was already boasting bright red splotches where the white of his eye ought to be. Feeling the battle calm the army hospital had bred into her, she returned the cloth as she caught Mrs. Smiley's gaze. "The children need to be elsewhere. We don't want them seeing us carry Dr. Parker like a bloody corpse out of here."

Mrs. Smiley's command snapped into place, and she rose with authority. "The children will follow Mr. Grimshaw and me back to the classrooms. Dr. Parker is injured, but he will be fine and Nurse Landway will see to his treatment. Off with you now, make room. Those who need water may stop in the kitchen."

Daniel brought a wavering hand up in the air to catch Ida's. "Blurry," he said, spitting blood out of his mouth from where he'd split his lip open. She hoped Daniel was describing his thoughts and not his eyesight.

"I'll bet that smarts," she said, forcing a false amusement into her tone. "Forget the fencing—you'll look like you lost a boxing match by tomorrow morning."

He grunted. That meant he'd heard her and could understand her words. She took comfort in that. Taking a quick glance behind her to ensure the children were retreating, Ida peeled the dishcloths off Daniel's forehead, willing herself not to show any reaction. She'd seen enough drastic wounds to know how to keep her composure, but tending to someone she knew well was different from treating scores of anonymous soldiers. His wound was deep and jagged, and it had indeed caught the edge of his eyelid. He'd need a hospital, and most likely a surgeon.

"He hit right there, I'd say." Mr. MacNeil squatted beside her, pointing up to a spot where it looked as if the fence jutted in from a falling tree or some other blow. Ida's spine ran cold as she saw the blood streak on the rusted black metal. Daniel had chosen a particularly dangerous place to catch his fall.

"Run to the telephone in Dr. Parker's office and call Roper Hospital," Ida whispered to Mr. MacNeil as she began pulling gauze and antiseptic from her kit. "Tell them we need an ambulance. Ask them to use the side gate. Meet them there and try and keep this out of the eyes of the children as much as you can."

"Don't let the children see this." Daniel began to rise until Ida put a hand on his chest.

"They've gone, but don't you move. You're hurt. More than I can treat, I'm afraid. We'll get you to Roper as soon as we can." When MacNeil had gone, Ida moved in closer. "Here, see if you can hold this up." She guided his hand to the red-soaked pad of toweling. She didn't like how flimsy his usually strong hand felt and how wobbly it moved through the air. She pressed her hand on top of his, cueing him to hold the cloths tight against the wound. Leaning in, she tried to capture his attention. "Daniel, can you see me clearly?"

He licked his swollen lip. "Somewhat," he muttered. "One side…blurry."

Ida dearly hoped it was simply the blood seeping into his eye that blurred his vision and not something more. She soaked a gauze pad with antiseptic and began dabbing around the edges of the wound, eventually easing his hand up to begin working near the deeper gash. "You've cut yourself close to that eye. I'm sorry, but this is going to hurt."

He winced as she applied the medicine to the narrow end of the laceration. He let out a groan through gritted teeth as she swapped out the drenched cloths and replaced them with a wad of gauze soaked in antiseptic, pressing as hard as she dared. For a moment, she thought he was mumbling nonsense words, but she soon realized what he was saying.

"Genesis, Exodus…Exodus…I can't remember what comes next."

She couldn't help but smile, frightened and worried as she was. "Leviticus," she cued. "Almost done. My part at least. I can't vouch for what they'll do to you at the hospital."

The bleeding was slowing somewhat, but she could only imagine how much the strong antiseptic stung in so large a facial wound. *I saw rust on that dirty fencepost, Father*, she prayed. *Spare him from tetanus or anything else. We depend on him.*

Looking back at Daniel, she watched the focus in his good eye wander and fade for a moment. "Daniel," she urged, grabbing his free hand. "Daniel, stay with me. You've taken a hard hit to your head and there is a serious wound near your eye. You're going to the hospital because I think you need to see a surgeon. Do you understand?"

She could see him try to pull his thoughts together, his jaw working and his fingers tightening around her hand. "That bad?"

It was difficult to keep a wounded soldier calm,

but in those cases she could always hedge the information she gave a patient in order to keep him from unnecessary worry. How could she do that with an informed doctor? Perhaps it was a blessing Daniel seemed confused—she would surely not stay calm if she knew she was facing extensive stitches, surgery or the chance at any of the handful of nasty complications a rusty, dirty cut could give.

She decided on the gentlest version of the truth. "Bad enough. We've slowed the bleeding, though, so that's good."

His breathing shallowed, and he started to shake. "Ida…"

Daniel was going into shock. Ida looked up and around, willing the ambulance orderlies to appear through the side gate.

"The children…all the blood." He began looking around as if he could rise and begin to clean up after the accident.

"Shh," she said, pushing him back down against the wall. She was glad he was too hurt to put up much resistance. "Keep still. The children are all fine and back in their classrooms."

That seemed to soothe him a little. How very like Daniel to be more worried about how the children might be affected by seeing him hurt than by his own pain or injury. She was struck again by this extraordinary man's tireless devotion to his work. *He needs to continue, Father. Spare him from harm.*

"What comes after?" he asked vaguely as his eyes fell shut.

"After what?"

"After Leviti...Leviti..." He was having trouble forming the word, and that frightened her.

"After Leviticus?" she finished for him, hating how his brow furrowed and winced with both pain and effort. "Why, it's Numbers, of course."

"Numbers," he repeated, his focus returning just a bit.

"Daniel, open your eyes and look at me."

He obeyed, making an enormous effort to stare directly into her eyes. They were inches apart, her heart surging toward him in pity and concern. She squeezed his hand.

"Good, good, much better. Stay with me. After Numbers comes Deuteronomy."

"Deuteromony," he mispronounced. He ran his tongue across his split lip again, fumbling with something in his mouth that he eventually spit into his hand. "I broke a tooth."

Ida stared down at the chip, gleaming white against the blood smears on his hand. "Your flawless charm is doomed."

"Ha," he moaned, followed by a decidedly inelegant, "Ow."

A commotion behind her alerted Ida that the orderlies had arrived with their canvas gurney. "Over here, gentlemen. Head wound. Four-inch laceration, rather deep, adjacent to the left eye." She pointed up to the offending bent fencing. "From that."

"Thank you, Nurse," said the orderly, grimacing at the bloody scene before him. "We'll take it from here."

There was a line of searing pain from Daniel's hairline down past his eye, ending in a throbbing ball somewhere along his cheekbone. He hadn't blacked out when they stitched him up, although he'd almost wished for it. He wasn't fond of anesthetic—most especially on himself—even though he knew the doctor working on him. Somewhere in the midst of the treatment he'd had the ridiculous thought that he'd rather stitch himself up than let someone else do it.

That was a silly thought, since he could barely see between the loss of his glasses and the bandage over his eye. Touch and feel told him he was in a bed at Roper Hospital, but his world boiled down to the two feet he could see in front of his face.

"How do you like my needlework?" A voice came from his left. Dr. Michael Hartwick appeared in Daniel's field of vision.

"I hope it looks better than it feels," Daniel said with a grimace.

"I'd imagine it looks *much* better than it feels," Hartwick agreed, "and it looks rather awful."

"Thanks for the encouragement." Daniel reached up to touch the bandages over his eye. They felt a mile wide, and his head felt as if it had swollen to twice its size. "The eye?"

"You were very fortunate, Parker. Another half an inch, and it would have been a very tricky business indeed. As it is you'll just keep us company for a few days and sport a very dashing scar. Here." He handed Daniel his bent glasses, now boasting a crack in one lens. "I had the office contact your mother about seeing to another pair, but you won't be needing the lens you broke for at least another week. Can you get them on over the bandages?"

It was awkward—and no doubt comical looking—

but Daniel managed to get the glasses on only a bit off-kilter. He sighed in relief as the world came into focus again. It had bothered him immensely not to be able to see well in circumstances that already stole much of his control.

"Who is your new nurse?" Hartwick asked. "Most unusual woman."

Now, there was a description with which Daniel could heartily agree. "She is indeed." He ran his tongue along his swollen lip again, feeling as if his personality had been stuffed into some giant's face. It seemed as if he tasted blood every time he swallowed, and while he could have used some supper, he found the prospect of eating daunting enough to go hungry.

Hartwick began moving his finger back and forth in front of Daniel's face, cuing him to follow with his good eye. "You've run through your share of nurses over there. Think this one will stick?" Hartwick was just making conversation as he checked Daniel's vision; the man had no idea how vital a question he was asking.

"She's an army nurse," Daniel replied. "I don't think we can scare this one off."

"Clever thinking."

"Where is she?"

"Oh, she was here for about an hour when we brought you in, keeping close tabs on you. She left when you dozed off after the procedure. Bossy little thing, isn't she?"

"She's not shy about sharing opinions, I'll grant you that."

"Well, she did a fine job hauling you in here." Hartwick sat back, satisfied with his examination. "I'd keep her if I were you."

Daniel thought about how he'd focused on her eyes when the world spun in confused circles around him. As his thoughts had tangled there on the ground, she'd held him in place. She'd been calm and efficient. He remembered the soft warmth of her hands and how it felt different from the hard coolness of the metal fence. Yes, keeping Ida Landway would be a very good thing indeed.

Chapter Fifteen

Daniel was in the hospital four days, although to Ida it felt like four weeks. After that first day, she'd stayed away despite how much she wanted to go every hour and check on him. She was not Daniel's family. He had his mother tending to him, and quite frankly she was needed here at the Home with the doctor out of commission.

Ida kept herself busy tending to nursing tasks, helping out the other staff as much as she could and working with Isabelle to coordinate the delivery of the socks. Despite regular reports of Daniel's recovery, everyone had seemed on edge and in an especially sour mood with him away from the Home.

Now—Friday and the first of August—the whole Home had brightened this morning with the good news that Daniel was coming home today. In fact, the doctor was due here any minute, and Ida was tacking a series of floral watercolors up in his room so he'd have something pleasant to look at while he recovered. According to Mr. Grimshaw, Daniel had staunchly refused his mother's demands that he convalesce with her at the Parker house, which didn't surprise her. She'd meet the formidable Amelia Parker minutes from now, but she'd heard enough stories to hint that Daniel's mother would be a suffocating nursemaid. Provided he weren't too gruesome a sight—and that was certainly a danger given his injuries—Ida knew the company of the children would be Daniel's best medicine.

The door opened behind her and an elegant woman with Daniel's dark eyes and piles of graying curls bustled into the room. She looked startled to find Ida in Daniel's private quarters, casting her eyes up and down Ida before pronouncing, "You must be the army nurse."

"Ida Landway, ma'am. I was just ensuring everything was ready for Dr. Parker's return."

"I'm sure everything is more than ready," came Daniel's weary voice from behind the woman.

Mrs. Parker stepped aside, letting Daniel into the room. He was upright, but battered looking. The paleness of his complexion made his dark eye stand out even more. Eye, not eyes, because the left side of his head was covered in a thick bandage. An artist would have a field day with the spectrum of blue and purple bruises along the left side of his jaw. Her prediction that he would look as if he'd been in a boxing match was not so far off. His expression, what she could see of it, told Ida he knew on some level the sight he was. It was a sentiment she'd seen so often among soldiers—craving company but worried they were too unsightly to have it.

"You're sure about this, Daniel?" Mrs. Parker was clearly not happy with her son's choice to recuperate at the Home. Mothers were the same everywhere—no matter their son's age, they wanted to tend to them under their wing when hurt.

"Quite certain, Mother. There's no need to make this more than it is. Besides, why go to the expense and trouble of bringing in a nurse when I've access to a fine one here?" He moved gingerly over to the chair in his study alcove, settling himself in it as if to underscore his decision. "The children have been upset I've been gone and they'll be happier knowing I'm here. Even if I do look a bit of a monster."

"Oh, I wouldn't say that," Ida argued. The children of the Home were made of stronger stuff than to let such details keep them from the Dr. Parker they needed. "I suspect most of the boys will be rather impressed, and the girls will coddle you." She offered Daniel an understanding smile. "You may wish for a bit less attention before the week is out."

She was sorry for the last comment, for Mrs. Parker jumped on it. "My point exactly. You need rest and quiet, Daniel."

"What I need, Mother—" Daniel put just enough edge in the respectful tone of his voice to let his mother know the point was not open for debate "—is to get back to work. I'm simply injured. I'm not an invalid. I'm grateful for your concern, but I'm endlessly tired of just sitting and having people fuss over me."

Mrs. Parker huffed, fiddled with her handbag, but offered no reply. Ida thought that wise; Daniel looked at the very edge of his temper. Time for a diversionary tactic. "Mrs. Parker, I'm sure it's been a difficult day for you. Would you like me to see to some tea for you in the dining room while Dr. Parker settles in?"

Mrs. Parker looked surprised, but pleased at the opportunity for a graceful exit from the room's mounting tension. "Thank you, Miss Landway, I'd like that."

"Right this way. I'll make sure you have time to return to your son before you leave. I'd like you to see all the cards I had the children make for Dr. Parker while he was away."

As quickly as she could, Ida guided Mrs. Parker to the dining room, where a flurry of colorful cards were tacked to the staff dining room French doors waiting for Daniel's first meal back at the Home. The woman seemed to find the display rather baffling. She peered at one drawing after another, inspecting the hearts, flowers and other sweet images that filled the wall. "You had the children do this?"

"They wanted to—I only gave them the supplies and paper."

"How charming." Mrs. Parker's tone was that distinctly Southern mix of sweet and sharp that made Ida wonder if she really did think so. Ida didn't know what to make of her reaction—what woman would not be charmed by such a show of affection for her son?

"Your son does marvelous work here, Mrs. Parker," Ida offered. "He's a very fine and honorable man. You must be so proud of him. Take a moment to look at all of these and I'll be back with tea in a jiffy."

She quickly ducked into the kitchen and had the servers there put together a small service of iced tea and sandwiches. She also asked them to dish up some of the cold soup she'd recommended, along with anything else that would require little chewing, and send it to Daniel's quarters. When she brought out the tray to the staff dining table, she found Mrs. Parker staring at Gitch's card. It was an adorable drawing of a duck with bandages on his little yellow head.

"You show a great admiration for my son," Mrs. Parker said.

"He is a mighty fine doctor and does quite a job running this place. I've never seen a man so devoted to his work. As sorry as I was to see him hurt, I am glad the children have a chance to let him know how special he is to them." Ida set the tray down.

"My husband ran the Home for years during the war, you know, back when it was smaller. It's a terrible price of war that the Home has grown so much in the past few years." She looked at Ida with a softer expression than she'd shown in Daniel's quarters. "I do know what a thankless, endless task running this place can be." She sighed. "I sometimes wonder if the strain of it all sent Harold home to Heaven earlier than was necessary."

Ida hadn't thought about that—this woman, of all people, knew how much it took from a man to run the Home. A pang of sympathy shot through Ida's heart. Given what Mrs. Parker had lost, was it so hard to understand why she hovered over her son so? "Dr. Parker Senior must have been an extraordinary man." That wasn't false flattery. Often Ida had looked at the portrait that hung on the Home's library wall and wondered at the man who'd set out to meet such an enormous need. Daniel had made a great many changes and improvements, but it was Dr. Harold Parker who had the initial vision. He was the man whose example Daniel strived to match.

"He was." Mrs. Parker took a long drink of tea, then reached into her bag to produce a hanky and blot her brow. "My, but the day has been hot and tiresome." In truth, Mrs. Parker didn't look all that well herself, but it had been a difficult day for everyone.

Ida ventured a friendly smile. "I somehow suspect Dr. Parker is not the most cooperative of patients. Physicians rarely are."

"He will try to do too much too soon."

"If it helps," Ida confided, "I share your worry. You should visit every day, and I promise that all the staff and I will keep a close watch on him. Personally, I plan to march him back to his quarters to rest at least twice a day no matter how he protests."

The older woman picked up a sandwich from her plate. "I admit I was not in favor of Daniel bringing a military nurse here to the Home. Daniel speaks very highly of you, however."

Ida didn't know what to make of her words. They had more a tone of resignation than of approval. Ida chose to extend the tired woman the benefit of the doubt and offered a smile. "I'm very happy to be here, really I am. I think your son is doing marvelous, important work."

Mrs. Parker's lips pursed just a bit. "To hear Isabelle Hooper speak—and my but she does go on and on about it, bless her heart—you're the best thing that's happened to the Parker Home since my son."

It was hard to think of joyful, generous Isabelle having anything in common with the formal, proper Amelia Parker. Ida didn't know what to say except, "That's very kind of you, Mrs. Parker. And kind of Mrs. Hooper, as well. Leanne—Mrs. Gallows, that is—and I are just thrilled with all she's done for the children."

"Ah, yes, the knitting." Again, such a carefully neutral comment that Ida couldn't hope to guess what Mrs. Parker truly thought of the sock project. After a disturbingly lengthy pause, she added, "I suppose I really ought to help with that. I do know how to knit, you know."

Ida thought about how Isabelle had scowled over Mrs. Parker's refusal to join the other knitting ladies. While her laconic statement wasn't a ringing endorsement, was Amelia Parker coming around to the idea? Perhaps God was going out of His way to show Ida how much good she could do in Charleston. "I've some yarn and the pattern in my office. I'd be delighted to fetch them for you before you go."

"Have you any pink? With only one son, I've never had the chance to work with pink yarn."

She was indeed coming around. Suddenly Ida wanted nothing more than to give Mrs. Parker something pink and fluffy to knit, and she felt a smile shine all the way to the bottom of her heart. "I've got loads of pink, Mrs. Parker, loads of it."

Daniel had agreed to spend his first full day back at the Home within the confines of his rooms. He didn't much like the prospect of not being out in the classrooms and yards, but he was desperately tired from not sleeping well, and he quite frankly thought his current appearance might give some of the younger children nightmares. His brow seemed to stab him with pain every time he blinked, and the stitches had started to pull, making him feel as if his face were an overfilled balloon about to burst. The broken edge of his tooth bothered him immensely, both because his tongue seemed to find it every ten seconds and because Daniel thought it made him look like a hoodlum.

At lunchtime today, Donna and Matthew had both brought him their card from the staff dining room doors. "Glory, but you're a sight!" Matthew had proclaimed, sucking air in through his teeth with a grimace. "It's

like the whole side of your face is one giant shiner."
Donna had swatted him for that one, but Daniel would
have laughed if it didn't hurt so much.

"You look like a brave warrior come home from a
terrible battle," Donna had proclaimed.

"A terrible battle with a fearsome fence post," Daniel had joked, wanting to put the worried look on the
young woman's face to rest. "I'm fine, I assure you."

Ida knocked on his door shortly after Donna and
Matthew left. "Are you ready for your excursion?"

"More than ready. I'm going mad in here."

She chuckled and shook her head. "I doubt that. But
I do have a special surprise for you."

The short walk to the staff dining room tired him
more than he'd expected, yet the sight that awaited him
was more than enough to reinvigorate him. Ida had
told him about the display of cards, but even her vivid
description didn't prepare him for the bright, splendid
splash of colors and shapes that filled both French doors
and spilled over onto the door frame, as well. And the
endearing messages! It was all he could do to keep the
lump in his throat from swallowing him whole right
there in front of her. He was glad she'd arranged it so
that he was alone in the room when he saw it; he was
rendered weak and speechless.

"Wonderful, isn't it?" she said quietly after giving
him a long time of silence to take in the display. He
was grateful not to have an audience for the emotions
welling in his chest.

"It's extraordinary," he choked out, staring at the
drawing Gwendolyn had done of a duck all bandaged
up as he was. She had signed it "G," and he recognized
Ida's handwriting underneath: "Because that stands for

Gitch *and* Gwendolyn."" His soft laugh very nearly dissolved into tears.

"They love you. You know that, don't you?"

Did he? They respected him—that was clear—and
many of the older ones admired him, but had he allowed
himself to think of their feelings toward him or his toward them in terms of genuine love? Professional devotion, charity, certainly—but love? Then again, what
did these precious children need more than to love and
be loved? It seemed dangerous and absolutely essential
at the same time. Ida's question struck so close to home
that Daniel found he couldn't hope to form words, just
a hard swallow and a slight nod. He was grateful she
simply stood beside him in silence, not pressing him
for further admissions. As it was, he felt exposed and
brittle, as if she'd seen way too far inside him.

When he could speak again, he chose a lighter subject as they walked back to his quarters. "What have
you done to my mother?" he asked.

"Your mother?" The innocence in her words didn't
match the secretive smile.

"The woman was knitting in my presence this morning. Pink socks. With white lace ruffles, evidently."

"Ruffles?" Ida asked, mock surprise on her face.
"Goodness, Isabelle must have really gotten to her."

"It's unheard of, I assure you, and I want to know
how you did it."

Ida folded her hands in front of her as if the task were
simple. It was not, by any means. As a matter of fact, before today Daniel would have classified it as impossible.
"I simply showed her how irreplaceable her son was."

That made Daniel laugh. "Mother already considers
me essential." *Entirely too important*, he added silently,

wishing he had a little less of his mother's attention and oversight. "That can't be it. I saw the way she looked at you when we arrived. Now she's knitting pink socks. What have you done?"

She kept walking, the amused look still lighting up her face. "I took her to see what you just saw. I thought she should see how much the children love and need you. I talked about how important you are…to them."

The fact that she felt compelled to add "…to them" said everything her words did not say. Daniel's mind brought back the vision of her staring into his eyes, touching his cheek, imploring him to stay awake and alert as they waited for the ambulance. Lots of things were foggy about that day, but the care in Ida Landway's eyes and words was not one of them.

"Those cards are an astounding thing. I expect I'll keep them the rest of my life." He couldn't find words for what was going on inside him regarding Ida. He wasn't sure it was safe to even speak about, fearing that voicing any of the strong sentiments he currently had might give them even more strength. A huge part of him was drawn to the color and energy that poured from her. Everything looked drab without her. The bland Home he'd once considered practical now seemed thirsty for the wash of vibrancy she added wherever she went. She'd pried something open in his spirit that refused to go back to its proper place.

"They look lovely, all brilliant and bold like a loud, cheerful rainbow. All waiting to be delivered at whatever pace you're ready to receive them." She'd contrived some plan whereby each day, starting with the older ones, one or two children were allowed to take their cards from the door and bring them to him. Donna and Matthew had been the first, and Daniel was amazed again at her ability to create something so suited to his condition. He really was worried how the children would take his ghastly appearance.

As if she could hear his thoughts, Ida smiled softly and added, "You look much better today."

Daniel cringed. "No, I don't. I rather think I look even worse. I know you're a fan of color, but I'd prefer less of these horrid hues on my face and the use of both my eyes."

She laughed as he opened the door to his parlor. "Well, you are colorful, I'll grant you that. But don't you let that stop you from seeing the children. I'll talk to the younger ones first, if you think that will help, but I tell you, their imaginations are coming up with far worse than how you really look." She stopped and put a hand on his elbow as they entered the room. "They need to see you, Daniel. They need to know you are healing and coming back to them."

She was right, of course. Some part of him knew that. It was only that the accident had thrown him, made him realize how much of the Home rested solely on his shoulders. He'd never been incapacitated in the way he had been over the past four days, and it had shaken him. God was waking him up to the lonely nature of his position and his life, and Daniel knew much of that awakening was coming from the woman in front of him.

"You are wonderful with the children, Ida. You're wonderful with people, period. You turn everything inside out, but somehow it's better that way." It was the closest he could come to saying how she'd changed his life—the words he spoke were daring enough as it was.

She held his gaze, making Daniel feel exposed and

wondering if his own eyes had said what he'd held back from revealing with words. He needed so much more time to think about what was happening between him and Ida Landway. So many things were at stake, so many things could be hurt by him simply giving in to this rush of strange new emotions. A romantic entanglement would complicate things, to say the least. There could be little hope of escaping their difference in social status. Too many conclusions would be drawn about him as an employer taking up with one of his employees. The Home thrived on its integrity—even with the best of intentions, any perception of impropriety could cost the Home much-needed donors.

"Mama always said I love to upset the applecart."

The air hung too warm between them, his guard too close to falling after sleepless nights and painful days. Daniel struggled to push the conversation back to safer subjects. "When will the socks be ready?"

He watched her pull back, watched the space between them fold itself back up into professional boundaries. "Next week. I think we should wait until you're feeling better anyway."

"And the common room trim?"

That brought a smile to her face. "I finished the girls' room while you were gone. It was a good place to channel all my fretting."

She'd worried about him. He'd known she would, of course, but to hear her speak it out loud sent a little glow of affection into his chest. He'd actually worried about her, as well, wondering how the children would react to his gruesome exit. "Do they like it?"

"Oh, they love it." Her eyes sparkled. "It only took two days and it was like Christmas when it was all done.

Gitch just stood there with her mouth open and said she'd never seen anything so pretty in all her days. I let each of them help with one of the baseboards. It took a lot of cleaning up, but they were so proud. Gitch wants to show it to you personally when you're up for a tour."

Daniel settled himself in a chair. "After today, I've been thinking you should go ahead and do a mural in the dining room."

Ida's eyes went wide. "You do?"

"If that gallery of cards doesn't show how much a burst of color will do for a room, I don't know what does." The thought had come to him the moment he saw the wall, saw how the colors changed the room— and changed his heart.

"Oh, Daniel, really?" Her face was downright radiant.

"I know better than to give you any false encouragement. Although," he added, "I will ask to see sketches first for approval."

Her smile broadened with such warmth that Daniel felt it in his fingertips. "And you shall have them." She paused for a long, potent moment, and he noticed the white blouse she wore today had little blue flowers embroidered on the collar and cuffs. She simply could not bear her nursing uniform to be completely without color. "I am so very glad you are back and well."

He was glad, too. Daniel was beginning to think he simply could not bear for his life to be completely without Ida Landway.

The question was, what to do about that?

Chapter Sixteen

"It's already August," Leanne said to Ida when they met in Leanne's house on Ida's next free afternoon. "I can't believe we will be moving in less than a month," she exclaimed, followed by an enormous hug. "Oh, Ida, how I will miss you so! I know Washington isn't clear across the country, but it feels as if there will be too many miles between us."

The separation loomed before Ida in the same way, but she wanted to encourage her friend. "Good things are waiting for you in Washington, Leanne. I wish you were staying, too—but John has such a bright future ahead of him in Washington. It takes the sting out of your being gone."

"And what about your future here? You've already weathered your first crisis with Dr. Parker's injury. Are you happy at the Home? Is it the right place for you?"

"I do think so. I feel like I've made a real difference, and that's mighty satisfying."

"So you think you'll want to stay?"

"Yes." Ida looked again at her friend, caught by her

particular expression. "Why so many questions about if I'm happy here?"

Leanne looked at her hands. "Well, it's selfish of me to bring it up, but John has heard about a position in Washington. It seems a perfect fit, and goodness knows I would love to have you near, especially since..." Leanne's face flushed.

"Since what?"

Leanne leaned in. "Since John and I are thinking we might be ready to start a family."

"A family!" Ida grabbed Leanne's hand. "That's wonderful news. You'll be a splendid mother, Leanne, I just know it." Broad smiles filled both their faces. "And think of all the knitting—booties, caps, sweaters, even itty-bitty socks in dozens of colors!" The two friends fell into joyous laughter. "Oh, who wouldn't want to be there for that?"

"I'd hoped you would. The post is a nursing position at Walter Reed Hospital. And Ida, their rehabilitation programs include both art and knitting. I'd never ask you to leave the Home if you are happy, but this seemed so perfect I just had to let you know." Leanne leaned in. "They hinted they might take John's recommendation into high account."

Ida sat back in her chair. "Well now, that is something to consider. I'm happy here, but a nursing position in a major hospital with an art and knitting program as part of the accepted treatments...well, that does sound as if it was tailor-made for me."

"John talked to one of his doctors here and learned that Walter Reed Hospital has a fine reputation, especially for its art programs."

Ida thought about all the effort she had to make to

get any kind of art into the Home. Sure, she was making progress, but it seemed an uphill battle at best. To serve in a place where art and color were welcomed as vital instead of dismissed as a luxury? The idea drew her instantly. "Washington." Ida tried out the idea on her tongue, feeling surprisingly torn. A big city? The nation's capital? Wouldn't all the folks back on the hillside in West Virginia be surprised at scrawny little Ida growing up to consider a post in Washington, DC?

"Will you think about it? John says they will give him a copy of the posting with all the information. The job opens up in October, just a month after we settle in. You could even stay with us until you get settled yourself."

Ida put a hand to her forehead in astonishment. "I was barely sure I would win the position at the Home. To have a post come looking for me like this? The world sure is changing."

"I think the twenties are going to be an amazing time, don't you? And not just for you and me, but for the whole country. The whole world." Leanne sighed. "When I think back to how things were in the war, it feels like a lifetime ago."

"Doesn't it? Some days I look around me, at my apartment with three rooms—*three* rooms!—and the army feels a century away instead of just a year."

"I don't want to lure you away from the Home if you're happy there, Ida. That place is so dreary that I'm sure they need you. Only when John told me about this just after I was telling God how much I'll miss having your nearby, well, I couldn't help but think maybe it was His gift."

"It does feel like something only the Lord could or-

chestrate," Ida admitted. "But moving again so soon
after coming to Charleston feels like I haven't given
the Home a real chance. And I'd never want to leave
Dr. Parker shorthanded without a nurse."

"If you gave your notice soon, he'd have time to
find one. You could even see if Camp Jackson could
send another."

Another army nurse dealing with all those dear little
children? Ida was surprised how the thought disturbed
her. She may have been at the Home for only a short
time, but she'd come to think of many of the children
as "hers." She wanted to see Gitch's teeth come fully
in. She wanted to see Donna and Matty settled together.
But she could always come back and visit, couldn't she?
She could even be one of Isabelle's "Aunties," as she'd
come to call them, sending cards and gifts and knitted
socks to some of the girls.

And then there was Daniel.

He was coming around to her way of thinking—
the tin of paints, the common room decor and even the
soon-to-be-approved dining room mural proved that
he was. She liked working with him very much—perhaps a bit too much—even if they did find themselves
at odds over a dozen tiny issues. There was no denying
that she'd found herself thinking of Daniel frequently—
and often in the wrong ways—since his accident. The
last thing she needed on her first professional post out
of the army was to become emotionally involved with
her employer. Could this new post be an ideal solution?
Besides, she'd be foolish not to at least explore a post so
perfectly suited to her skills, wouldn't she?

"Okay, then, let's see how this plays out. Have John

let them know I might be interested and they can send me the details and…"

Leanne took both of Ida's hands. "I was hoping you would say that. I know it could all fall through, but it could be so perfect. I'm sure I could face whatever Washington brought us if I had you near. And who knows? A city like Washington has to be filled with handsome bachelors—maybe God has the perfect man up there waiting for you alongside that perfect job."

Ida laughed. "Now you're getting ahead of yourself. I hardly think a slick city man would take to the likes of me." She thought of how easily Leanne navigated the parlors and teas of Charleston whereas she found them nerve-racking and foreign. "I can barely wade my way through Charleston's social muck, much less someplace like Washington."

"Nonsense. Nothing scares the Ida Lee Landway I know. Now, are you all ready for Friday's big delivery?"

Friday was the day Isabelle, Leanne and all the other Aunties were delivering the socks. "When I think of all those happy little toes wiggling in all those color-ful socks, I think it'll take weeks for the smile to leave my face. It's gonna feel like Christmas—I can hardly wait." Ida was about to burst from anticipation, and so were most of the girls. Of course, the girls thought they were just getting socks, but Ida knew they were getting a year's worth of attention and their own "Auntie." She was having trouble keeping such wonderful news to herself.

"I'm glad the good doctor is up and about to see it, too. It would have been such a shame for him to miss it. Of course, I expect he'll be seeing these socks every day for months to come now, won't he?" She held up one hand. "Which reminds me!" Leanne bustled to a sideboard and pulled out a small bag, which she held out to Ida. "I got to thinking it shouldn't be the female students who have all the goodies on their feet. I know you told me you were working on slippers for Mrs. Smiley, so I simply followed your lead. Open it."

Ida opened the small tissue parcel to see the softest slippers, knitted in a sunny yellow yarn with great big yellow-and-white daisies gracing the toes. They were the most cheerful thing she'd seen, like wearing a sunrise on each foot. "Oh, Leanne!" Ida slid her hands into one of the luxurious slippers, the soft mohair a fuzzy cloud against her fingers. "They're positively decadent. I love them."

"There's more…well, more thanks to Isabelle. She sent these over when I told her you were coming today." Leanne held up another package Ida hadn't noticed she was holding. "She said to give it to Dr. Parker."

Leanne opened the wrapping to show a pair of beautifully crafted argyle socks made from a fine lightweight merino wool. They were appropriately dark in blue and gray, but a single run of yellow stitches crossed over the traditional diamonds to give the socks a bit of color. They were an extraordinary bit of craftsmanship. Ida looked at Isabelle. "Isabelle made these?"

"She told me a friend of her sister's did the work. But we were talking about how to do something for the boys in the fall, and Isabelle decided this might help Dr. Parker come around to the idea."

Ida felt her cheeks heat at the thought of giving Dr. Parker such a gift. "Why doesn't Isabelle give these to Dr. Parker herself on Friday?"

"I asked her the same thing." Leanne nodded. "Do you know what she said?"

"What?"

Leanne's eyes went wide. "She said she didn't want Amelia Parker to be scandalized by the sight. I think our Isabelle has a bit of the rebel in her."

Ida held up the socks. "Could you imagine what Mrs. Parker would do if she found Daniel wearing these?" It was ill-mannered of her to be sure, but the bit of the rebel in Ida was curious to find out.

The girls' common room was a festival of color and noise. Today was Sock Delivery Day, and Daniel found himself dead center of a sock delivery party he could never have imagined. Christmas, it seemed, had nothing on Sock Delivery Day. Just when he thought he'd seen the limits of Ida's impact on the Home, she turned around and instituted a holiday—right down to the Happy Sock Delivery Day banner strung across the now color-trimmed windows.

Daniel was grateful his wounds had healed a bit, for the sound and commotion held the likely makings of a spectacular headache. He'd been avoiding loud noises and bright lights since the accident, but knew better than to try to bow out of this event. Part of him truly had wished to leave such frivolities to the ladies, even before his injury. As it was, the sounds of excited girls and the smell of tea and sugar cookies commandeered his tender senses. *It's not so bad*, he told himself. *It's rather fun. Or at least it could be, if you tried.*

"This one is called Canary and that one is Sky Blue." Gwendolyn had him by the hand, leading him around to the windows, baseboards and bookshelves as she pointed out the different colors Ida had painted.

He knew this, of course, being the one to purchase those paints, but he wouldn't stop the girl's animated explanations for all the world. She looked enthralled, beaming with pride and excitement, as were all the girls. He hardly had to ask, "Do you like the room's new colors?"

"Oh, yes, Dr. Parker. I love 'em. Makes me think of blue skies and sunshine, and those are happy thoughts." She crunched up her face to examine Daniel's, which still boasted a bandage over his eye. "Can you see all of this with only one eye?"

"Yes," Daniel replied, reaching down to scratch Chester behind the ears. The dog had spent the past half hour running from one child to another collecting pets and treats. Thankfully, he hadn't barked—Daniel was sure the yapping would've been the one thing to drive him from the room. "My one eye is working extra hard so that the other one can rest and get better."

Gwendolyn peered closer, making Daniel wonder if she wouldn't up and lift the bandage to see the wounds for herself. "Joshua says you'll have a great big scar." She drew the last three words out for grotesque emphasis, much as Daniel expected Joshua had. "Will you?"

Daniel was surprised he could laugh at her drama, and glad it no longer hurt to do so. "Well, I don't know about a great big scar. Maybe a small one. Nurse Landway says I should be able to take the bandage off the day after tomorrow, and then you can look and tell me what you think."

He thought maybe she might flinch at the invitation,

but instead she leaned in, narrowing one eye in pint-size analysis. "I think medium-sized," she declared.

"I'm glad to have your opinion, Dr. Martin."

"Maybe just 'Dr. Gitch.'" She giggled, reaching down to pet Chester herself. The dog licked her generously, then darted over to check in with his owner. Mrs. Hooper was chatting excitedly in the circle of ladies who were busy arranging packages and cookies on the far side of the room. Gwendolyn tugged on Daniel's sleeve. "Will you look at all the Aunties Nurse Ida brought us?"

The term *Aunties* fit, in a dangerously familial way, for each woman had taken to heart her responsibilities toward a specific set of girls. It was starting today with socks, but according to Isabelle, the relationship would continue on throughout the year. He'd often thought of implementing a sponsorship program such as this, but had never gotten around to doing so. Anytime one matched a child with a sponsor like this, it was precariously easy for the child to begin to fantasize that the sponsor would adopt them. Yes, it happened, but the sad times it did *not* far outweighed the splendid times it occurred. Daniel hated to risk anything that might bring the children even the smallest sense of rejection.

Today, however, everyone seemed bursting with happiness. Daniel looked around the packed room, stunned again that the plans of a single nurse with a desperate pair of knitting needles had bloomed into the large-scale joyful chaos in front of him today. It was a hot afternoon—hardly the weather for lots of socks—but no one seemed to notice the temperature for all the bright colors and noise.

"Well now," Isabelle announced, clasping her hands

together, "who'd like to get started?" Daniel winced as
Chester gave in to his yappy nature and sounded his approval as the girls shouted theirs. The rush toward the
table of packages and sweets was thunderous.

Even his mother was smiling. She was certainly surprising him these days.

For that matter, he was surprising himself. Ten minutes ago, as he was walking over to the common room
with Ida, he'd hoisted up one trouser leg to show the
outlandish argyle socks she had given him earlier from
Isabelle. Her eyes had popped as wide as her smile. If
Mother had noticed his unconventional choice in ho-
siery, she'd not admitted it.

"Your names are on each of the packages," Leanne
Gallows said, her voice near laughter as she tried with
Ida and Isabelle to bring some sense of order to the glee-
ful, colorful pandemonium that had ensued. The girls
were ecstatic about the rainbow of socks they received,
cooing and shouting and holding their gifts up for others to see. For all his worries, Ida had managed it perfectly. Every girl received the same gift of four pairs
of socks in just her size, and yet each set was unique to
the recipient. No girl seemed jealous of any other girl's
gift, and Daniel knew each girl well enough to see how
the socks suited their personalities. He couldn't possibly have hoped for a better outcome.

"Look at them!" Donna was turning her foot to and
fro as if she were on a magazine cover. Shoes were
strewn about the room as each girl tried on the quartet
of socks she had been given. *Socks.* He'd never have
guessed socks to be so important. To Daniel, they were
just the layer between foot and shoe, one of a dozen

identical dark pairs to be plucked from a drawer each morning as he dressed.

Except, of course, for today. Recalling the burst of amusement he'd felt as he donned the pair Isabelle had made him—stately gray and navy diamonds with a rebellious yellow streak running through them—Daniel supposed socks could indeed "make the man." Or at least make the man smile.

"You're smiling." Ida came to stand beside him, beaming herself.

"Not as broadly as you," he replied, tucking his hands in his pockets.

Ida hugged herself, clearly delighted with the level of joy and color in the room. "Look at them. Happy as puppies, every one. I reckon this is the happiest place in Charleston right now."

Daniel laughed, as well. "You may be right." He looked at her, as seriously as he could while one-eyed and surrounded by mayhem. "I owe you an apology."

"Why?"

"I doubted you could do this." He glanced down, ashamed of his judgment. "I assumed you could not do something both equal and individual, and I was wrong."

A warm glow touched her eyes. "You were watching out for the children. I can hardly fault you for that." She looked out over the room. "Besides, even I didn't think it'd turn out this wonderful. Isabelle Hooper is an answer to a prayer, isn't she?"

Chester, after multiple attempts, finally jumped up high enough to snatch one of the cookies a child had left on the edge of the table. "She's something, all right." He returned his gaze to Ida. "I am grateful. To her and to you. I was worried the Aunties wouldn't work, that the children would get their hopes up, but I shouldn't have been so concerned."

She touched his sleeve. "Yes, you should. It's who you are to worry over them, to want to protect them. That's not a bad thing, as long as you spend some time on the sunny side." She folded her hands in front of her, something Daniel had come to realize she did when solving a problem.

"You're thinking."

She blinked and shrugged her shoulders. "Shows, hmm?"

"All over your face."

"I'm just wondering," Ida said, hands crossed over her chest and eyes narrowed in thought, "about the boys. Mr. Grimshaw has them today, but…"

Daniel had seen this long coming. Ida would be hatching an idea for them on the heels of this success, as sure as he breathed. "Ah, the boys."

Her fingers drummed against her elbows. "They'll feel left out if we don't do something for them, but socks won't cut the mustard with that lot. We'll just have to start with what we have."

Daniel looked at her. "And what do we have?"

Ida's face filled with mischief. "Paint. We'll start with painting their room, and pray the Good Lord sends the right idea while we paint."

Daniel swallowed hard. "We?"

Ida's hands went to her hips. "Well, near as I can tell, you'll have to help me. I can't very well plant myself in the middle of the boys' common room all by myself, and you need something to do."

"I'm happily occupied. I'm busy, in point of fact."

Her lips pursed into a supervisory scowl. "You are not supposed to be doing paperwork."

He felt like a chastised student. "Light reading."

"Why then, light painting should prove a perfect distraction." He could practically watch Ida set her determination upon him. He knew what that meant: she'd press her point continually until he relented. Really, was it such a burden to spend time with the boys helping Ida paint the room? If it gave the lads half the joy today was giving the girls, could he really refuse? And, when he was honest with himself, the prospect of having to spend considerable time in Ida's company, watching her do what pleased her most in the world, ignited a warm expectation under his ribs. These days there were few places that gave him as much pleasure as Ida Landway's company.

"I've only one eye," he refuted. Daniel spoke negative words but was unable to keep his tone anything short of amused. "My aim will be off."

"Your *depth perception* will be off," she corrected, equally playfully, "and you won't be needing that to paint window trim. My two-year-old nephew could paint window trim. We'll have it done in an afternoon if the boys stick to the task."

"*If* they stick to the task." There was that. Here, at least, the odds were in their favor—every girl had her own Auntie. Some days those boys felt as if they needed two adults to every rambunctious student. Putting paint into those hands might prove dangerous indeed, and Daniel did not think he could roust up a herd of "Uncles" to improve the ratio.

Ida shrugged. "What's the worst that could happen?"

Daniel concocted a list of half a dozen potential disasters in the space of a few seconds. "I could lose the good eye I have left."

Chapter Seventeen

"I declare, you look as if you've been in a brawl,"
Mother said with a sigh, tilting Daniel's chin this way
and that as he stood unbandaged before her in her living room for his usual weekly luncheon.

It was his first outing with both eyes, and he was
rather proud of himself. Perhaps that was why her examination annoyed him, as if he were a boy sent home
from school for fighting. "I did strike a wrought iron
fence, Mother. There were a lot of stitches. I think I'm
rather entitled to look pummeled."

"Well, you do." Her expression changed from one
of judgment to one of concern. "Does it hurt? Can you
see well out of that eye?"

He thought of Robby's declaration the other day that
he looked like a pirate and managed a small smile.
"Yes, it hurts. And yes, I can see well enough. Still,
I'm glad to be out and about."

Mother shook her head. "You never were one to sit
around." She sat down in her favorite wing-back chair.
"When you twisted your ankle at the boathouse that

one summer, I feared your father would have to sit on you to get you to rest it."

He remembered that summer when he was fourteen. He was old enough to have a good deal of independence, yet young enough to have no responsibilities. He probably had dreamed of being a pirate that summer, or any number of world adventurers. The century had barely turned, and it seemed as if the new era spread out wide and wonderful before him.

Of course, then had come serious schooling and wars, epidemics and poverty. And then Father died at the end of the war—one of countless victims the Spanish influenza had taken—and the Home became Daniel's cause to take up. He had stepped dutifully and purposefully into the role of Home director. The family would never seek an outside candidate to replace Harold Parker. No one, however, could have foreseen the coming demand. The war left so many children alone and destitute, and the Home became Daniel's all-consuming life's work.

Mother seemed to sense his faraway thoughts. "He'd be proud of you, you know," she said softly. "Although I don't know what he would have thought of all this sock business."

Daniel tried to imagine his father sporting argyle socks, and tossed the thought away as improbable if not impossible. He was wearing dark socks today, and for an impetuous moment wondered if he should ask Mother if she'd noticed his choice of foot covering that chaotic day. He chose another risky question instead. "What do you think of Miss Landway?"

Mother snapped her fan open now that the afternoon's small breeze had dissipated. "Well, I must say, she isn't at all what I was expecting from an army nurse."

That was certainly true. "Indeed."

"The children seem to like her well enough."

Daniel nodded. "She gets along very well with the children. The girls adore her, and the boys will at least listen to her."

"All that colloquial charm, I suppose." Mother said it with just enough edge to let Daniel know where she placed Ida on the social ladder. "She certainly likes her knitting."

The comment made Daniel realize his omission. "Thank you, Mother, for making a pair of socks. I realize you found it rather silly at first, but I do hope you've seen what a grand project the whole thing turned out to be."

"You know Isabelle—it's nearly impossible to say no to that woman once she gets an idea in her head."

Daniel felt the same way about Ida. "Perhaps that is why she gets along so well with Miss Landway. I've found it just as pointless to say no to her."

Mother turned to look at him. "Have you?"

"The woman is relentless," Daniel said, laughing. "But I have found her to be a wonderful addition to the Home."

Her fan stilled. "Really?"

"I think I'd become a bit…stodgy…before Miss Landway came along. She brings a fresh energy I hadn't realized we needed. And you saw what she did with the girls' common room—they haven't stopped talking about it yet."

Mother laid her fan in her lap. "Daniel…"

Daniel stilled, realizing how much he'd just said

and how he'd said it. He wasn't sure he was ready to have this conversation—even with himself, much less his mother.

She shifted in her seat to face him square on. "Son, you haven't allowed yourself to become...emotional... about this woman, have you?"

He didn't answer. He didn't really know *how* to answer that question in light of her tone.

"She's a likable girl, I'll grant you that, but Daniel, she is your employee. She's of no family of consequence that I can see. Surely you recognize what an unsuitable idea such a thing would be." Mother leaned in. "Don't think I haven't noticed that she is sweet on you. Goodness, all those cards, all that attention...it's obvious. You're going to need to be careful."

Daniel blinked, caught up short. "What?"

"She idolizes you. And why shouldn't she? I'm sure this is a great step up from her army duties, and you seem to spend so much time together lately."

"We work together, Mother." Daniel was still trying to grapple with his mother's revelation of Ida's feelings for him. He barely had energy to battle with her opinion of it. "There is nothing between us."

"Well, I should hope so. She's enamored of you, son, and that's a problem. You're going to need to deal with that."

He'd known it on some level. He'd felt the attraction between them from that evening in the kitchen. Or rather, he'd felt it coming from *him*. The sensation was so different from the polite diversion he had felt in the presence of other women that it was impossible to ignore. Ida Landway invaded his thoughts. He found himself wanting to know her opinion on far too many matters.

All of that was manageable when it remained his problem. When the attraction confined itself to his side of things. To know—well, Daniel supposed he had always known but to now have it confirmed by his mother of all people—that Ida felt the same way threw everything out of proportion. It made it all seem too real, rather than just his misguided illusions.

Should he deny it? Tell his mother she was seeing things that weren't there? But could he say those words when he didn't believe them to be true? Where Daniel's social life was concerned, Mother often saw things she wanted to see. If Ida's feelings were evident enough that Mother saw them even when she *didn't* want them to exist, that could only mean that Ida's emotions might be as strong as his.

He chose to downplay the truth, convinced that outright denial would never work in this case. "I do enjoy her company."

He knew the minute he said it that his tactic had not succeeded. "I enjoy the company of cats, Daniel, but that does not make them suitable social companions."

Daniel walked to the window, needing both air and a moment to gather his thoughts.

Mother rose and followed him. "Daniel. For years you have dodged the subject of a suitable wife. I've tried to be understanding. It's a new era, and you young people have modern ideas about such things. I know you are devoted to the Home, but perhaps, child—" she put her hand on his shoulder in a rare display of maternal warmth "—you have let it make you lonely. This infatuation—and that is what it is, if you ask me—simply tells me it is time for you to find a wife. And a man in your position needs to be smart about such things."

Mother wasn't entirely wrong. He was feeling—for the first time—the hole in his life left by his bachelor status. But to call what he felt for Ida "an infatuation" couldn't have been more wrong. Daniel held a higher respect for Ida than he did for all of the "respectable" potential brides Mother had paraded before him in the past years. To him the whole process had been like sorting through a rack of coats tailored for other men; all serviceable but none of them truly fitting him.

The idea crystallized almost before his eyes, his thoughts coming into startling focus: Ida fit him. Everyone agreed she fit into his professional life. The issue was that he knew she fit into his personal life, as well. Clearly, society wouldn't see it that way, and he couldn't escape that he was a man whose respectability had high consequences. And an employer who shouldn't become emotionally entangled with those under his command. Either one of those could produce scandal, and that could mean a loss of charitable support for the Home when funds were already stretched to their limit.

Mother, her hand still on his shoulder, turned him toward her. "Sit down. I want to tell you something." Her face had such a stoic set to it that he returned to the chairs without another word.

"Do you remember Mr. Shepler?"

Daniel had been quite fond of the man who had held Mr. Grimshaw's post before Fritz had come on staff. "Of course I do."

"Do you remember when he took the position up in Maryland?"

"The boys' academy in Baltimore. I remember it. It was an excellent opportunity for him."

Mother folded her hands in her lap. "It was a move your father arranged for him in order to save the Home from a delicate matter."

"I beg your pardon?"

"Michael Shepler had grown fond of the house cook at the time. And she of him. Michael was an educated man of good family, a man with prospects. This cook was just that—a good cook from somewhere here in the city."

Daniel saw where this was heading and didn't care for it. He rose and returned to the window.

"It was an unsuitable match by all accounts. Michael was too young to recognize the cost to the Home if he and that girl had kept on. The Sheplers were large donors to the Home. They kept on as donors, Daniel, because of what Harold did in the best interests of both the Home and their son. Your father did what was right for a man in his position. He'd have removed the cook if that had been the easier solution, but when he learned of the post up in Baltimore, it became best to arrange for Michael to go."

Daniel turned. He'd always attributed such social manipulations to his mother, but his father? This was a side to the man he'd revered that he didn't care to see, especially not in this instance. "You're suggesting I find someplace else for Miss Landway to go?" The notion shot a hollow hole in his stomach.

"If it's necessary, yes. It would be in everyone's best interests. Surely you are mature enough to see that. Be reasonable, Daniel. A nurse, however fine, is expendable. You are not. She's a simple girl—we can't depend on her to understand the consequences. If you can't get this…distraction of yours under control, then you must take action."

His mother had always been a demanding woman, but she'd never stooped to ultimatums. "Action?"

She put her hand to her forehead. "For goodness' sake, Daniel, either find a wife or remove Miss Landway."

"I don't think either of those actions is necessary," he said with a glower, swallowing the urge to shout.

"Of course you don't." She dismissed his reply as if he were an impetuous young man run amok by his passions.

"I think it's best we never have this conversation again."

She glared at him. "If the situation continues, then that will not be possible and you know it. Face facts, son. Something must be done."

"I think what must be done," Daniel said as civilly as he could manage, "is that I should go now." He could hear her indignant huffing as he turned and left the room.

It had been a stroke of genius to suggest the boys help paint their common room. With Daniel not yet up to leading fencing lessons, they were getting squirrelly and needed something to do. Ida sent up another silent burst of thanksgiving heavenward as she stood with Daniel in the room now readied with drop cloths, brushes and paints. "Honestly," Ida chided as Daniel gave the supplies a dubious look, "you could have done this with only one eye. Now you've got two—it ought to be a cinch."

When the boys were finally let into the room, Ida found herself wondering if this was such a good idea after all. The boys were nearly uncontrollable in their eagerness and paint was rather, well, permanent. Yes, they'd covered the furniture that hadn't already been removed from the room, but Ida did wonder if the floor and walls—and possibly even the ceiling—would survive the process. Still, in order for things to be truly equal, she had to include the boys. Word of the "Sock Circus"—as Mrs. Smiley had dubbed it over the weekend even after receiving her lovely blue slippers—had spread, and the Home's male population was feeling left out.

"I don't think anything with you is ever a 'cinch,'" Daniel mused. "My life has become considerably more complicated since your arrival." It was amusing to watch him attempt a good-humored scowl with one eye still red and swollen.

Ida pushed up the sleeves on the artist's smock she'd donned for the occasion. "I prefer the term 'lively.'"

"Can we start now?" Little George Masters looked as if he couldn't stand to wait another minute. He was poised over the baseboards with a tin of dark green paint as if at the starting line of a footrace. She'd assigned the baseboards and doors to the boys, while keeping the windowsills and higher trims for her and Daniel.

"Matty, would you make sure George gets off to a good start?" Ida said with an encouraging air, hoping her eyes said "and keeps most of the paint on the baseboards?"

"Yes, ma'am," Matty said, swapping the large brush George had picked up with a much smaller one. *Smart young man*, Ida thought, even more convinced that

Matty and Donna made a fine pair and would do well in life.

They worked for a whole ten minutes before the first mishap. A whack and a quiet "oops" made Ida and Daniel both turn their heads to see a small puddle of green spread along the drop cloth by the west door. Ida heard Daniel's "I told you so" sigh.

Nonsense. She'd expected this, and was ready for it. "Don't fret, Robby. Just scoop up the cloth and put it in that bucket over there. Use a rag from that pile by the wall to clean up whatever has seeped through, then lay down a fresh cloth."

She watched in a combination of amusement and concern as Robby followed her directions, oblivious to the dribble of green he left in his wake as he walked to the bucket and dumped the cloth in. No one had better require nursing services today—the three hours she'd allotted for this one wall weren't going to be enough at this rate.

Evidently fearing for his institution's floor—and perhaps rightly so—Daniel walked over to Robby and his green dribbles with a long-suffering look on his face. For a moment, Ida held her breath, praying Daniel would not scold the child for his carelessness. Even Robby looked as though he feared the worst. The old Daniel most certainly would have scolded, but she had sensed a fundamental change in the doctor lately.

"Robby," Daniel began, bending down to the boy's height, "let's fix this together, shall we?"

The relief in Robby's face matched the swelling in Ida's heart. Daniel had always cared deeply about the children, but a distinct tenderness had sprung up between Dr. Parker and his charges recently. She hated to see him injured, yes, but she couldn't ignore the fact that his wounds had given the children a chance to show how much they cared about him, and it had loosened the stiff bindings he kept around his heart. Even the way he looked at her had changed.

And oh, what an unsettling change that had been.

Ida stood back, watching Daniel interact with Robby while she pretended to be stirring some paint. He looked so different now. He couldn't wear his glasses easily with the injured eye, so he went without more often than he normally did. His hair, usually neat, had been so continually mussed by bandages that it now stuck up in odd directions. The effect shaved years off his serious features, making him look a bit of the ruffian. The artist in her longed to capture this moment and sketch it a dozen different ways. Daniel looked different, stood differently, spoke differently. Was it wrong that she found the differences so appealing?

Her heart turned over inside her chest, humming with the knowledge that she was losing her heart to the doctor. That was a riskier proposition than all the boys and all the dripping paintbrushes combined. *This could be wonderful or awful*, Ida cried out to God in the silence of her flip-flopping heart. *Father, what are You up to here?*

Daniel was crouched on the floor beside Robby— something she'd never seen him do before—taking the rags Robby offered one by one to sop up the trail of green spots. "Look at that," Daniel said.. "All gone, as if they were never there." Daniel pointed over the baseboard. "You're doing fine work, Robby. Let's go finish all the way down to the corner, you and I together."

Ida felt her throat tighten. "Sure, Doc!" Robby said.

Doc? It was hardly a term Daniel had allowed before. She watched to see how he would respond.

Daniel tilted his head to one side, his good eye narrowing above a furrowed eyebrow. "Doc, hmm?"

Robby stilled. "Well, I don't know your real name, Dr. Parker."

A small smile began at one corner of Daniel's mouth. "Dr. Parker is my real name."

"I mean the *other* one. You know, like I'm Robby."

"Oh." Daniel folded up the last rag. "I see. Well, in that case, my real name is Daniel." She could see the gears in Daniel's head spinning, trying to figure out how to explain social protocol to an eight-year-old. "Only…"

"But Mr. Grimshaw told us we aren't s'posed to call grown-ups by their real name. I mostly just wanted to know. Only 'Doc' is kind of fun, isn't it?"

Ida swallowed a laugh. Daniel was no more a "Doc" than she was "Lady Ida." She sat back on her heels, entertained to watch how Daniel would navigate this social mire.

"It's not my favorite," Daniel said kindly. "Let's find something else. We can think while we paint."

Robby, who had never objected to "Dr. Parker" before as near as Ida could tell—nor had any of the other children, for that matter—looked pointedly dissatisfied. He wanted to call Daniel by something friendlier than Dr. Parker. Many of the girls had begun to refer to her as Nurse Ida, so that's where he must have gotten the idea. Good Southern civility dictated the use of *sir* or *ma'am* outside of family—but this *was* a family. It was the only family Robby had ever known. It was part of why Isabelle's idea of the Aunties was such a powerful one.

They kept on painting, but Robby was coming as close to a pout as any eight-year-old boy would allow. Ida longed to step in and distract him, but something told her to let Daniel sort this one out on his own.

To Ida's surprise, it was Robby who made the next move. "What about 'Dr. Dan'?"

Ida winced. She'd known dozens of Dans or Dannys in her day, and Daniel Parker struck her as neither. Again, she held back—her bedside manner told her this was a pivotal moment for this particular patient. Daniel's face was kind, but didn't hide his dislike for the nickname. Ida clutched the tin of paint she was holding, waiting for something even if she didn't know what.

Daniel held up his paintbrush. "How about Dr. Daniel?"

Robby looked up from his painting, squinting as he tried the thought on for size. "It fits." He proclaimed his approval with a wave of his paintbrush—one that sent a spattering of green onto Daniel's chin.

Ida sucked in a breath. To her delight, Daniel began to laugh. Robby raced over to the bucket of rags and grabbed one off the top, mortified.

"Thank you, Robby. And don't worry—I'll clean up just like the floor."

"I'm...sorry...Dr. Parker." Robby clearly thought his carelessness was going to earn him a stint at the laundry basins.

"I'm sorry, Dr. *Daniel*," Daniel corrected, chuckling as he wiped the paint from his chin. He made a face at Robby. "Does the green go with my black eye?"

Ida let her breath out as Robby began to giggle. "Not

at all," the boy replied. "And your eye is really more of a purple, if you ask me."

"Well, good then. I'll match the windows. They're a sort of purple, I suppose."

The two went back to painting, but Ida could barely move. She'd always suspected Daniel could be less rigid, less cautious, but she hadn't expected to see this tender, endearing side of him. She wanted to run for her sketchbook, to capture the curve of Daniel's smile and the gleam in his dark eyes, but she didn't want to move for fear of breaking the wonder of the moment. *Thank You, Lord, for that. What a gift.*

She'd known her prayer was silent, but Daniel looked up as if he'd heard her gratitude. He held her gaze over Robby's head, the hint of a smile on his lips and just the faintest smudge of green still on his cheek. He'd recognized the step he'd just taken as much as she did, and the astonishment of it showed on his face. He was, at that moment, the handsomest man Ida had ever known.

She pressed her hand to her chest and gave him a smile of her own, eyes stinging with the threat of tears. All the while, boys busily painted baseboards, oblivious to the huge shift two hearts in the room had taken.

It was a wonder what a little color could do to the world.

Chapter Eighteen

Something had been wrong with Daniel the rest of the week. He'd been glowing the day of the painting, but much of the stiffness had returned to his demeanor. Ida felt she was watching all the new joy she'd seen in Daniel evaporate in front of her eyes. She'd been so fond of the "new" Daniel, so overjoyed to see the new connections he seemed to have with the children. This slip back toward the "old" Daniel now seemed twice as regrettable. It was as if his new openness had made something worse—only she couldn't understand why.

With no classes on Sunday, it was usually the easiest day to talk to Daniel. She'd tried to seek him out all day—worried that, at the very least, his eye had taken a turn for the worse—but he seemed to be avoiding her. Now it was nearly nightfall, and the day seemed to be stretched tight as a drum between them. Was she imagining the change in the way he looked at her? Before today, when they could catch each other's eye over a task or across the room, she would feel a burst of warmth between them. Today, despite the oppressive heat, Ida could almost shiver at the change she saw in his glance.

Confused and tired by the time night fell, Ida decided to take the direct course. As soon as the children were settled for the evening, she went looking for him. He didn't answer a knock to his parlor door, nor was he in the library or any of his usual places. Finally, after searching every other place she could think of, Ida found him sitting on one of the bathhouse benches. He looked deep in thought, staring at the patches of moonlight reflecting on the water as if he were gazing out to sea.

"It's pretty," she offered, not knowing what else to say. It *was* pretty, in an unusual way. Boxy as the bathhouse was, it took on the quality of a reflecting pool in the breezeless darkness, and it was certainly one of the coolest places on the compound.

Daniel didn't look up. "I do some of my best thinking here, strange as that sounds."

Ida chose a bench next to his rather than sit on the same one beside him as she might have done earlier in the week. He seemed to need space. "Everybody needs a thinking spot, I suppose."

"Where is yours?" When he looked up at her, the only word she could think of to describe his expression was *lost*.

Tucking her hands under her knees, she replied, "I haven't picked one out for here yet. Back at Camp Jackson, there was a particular bench up on the hillside. You could look at the whole camp and even some of the countryside. I always thought the wide view helped me keep things in perspective. Getting up above my problems, you know?"

Daniel shrugged. "We've got no high spot here."

"I'll find a spot. Or, I suppose I should say, I'm sure the spot will find me."

He looked at her for a long moment before saying softly, "You have such faith that things will work out. It seems so much easier for you."

Ida wanted to laugh—if he only knew how much she worried about things lately—but it seemed wrong to make light of his comment. "God's been kind to me."

Daniel didn't reply to that, only stood up and walked to the far corner of the pool. The structure wasn't especially large, but she felt the distance between them sharply and wondered if he'd moved away from her intentionally. He seemed to be drawing back into himself, retreating, and she wasn't going to let that happen. She stood up herself and walked to the side of the pool where he stood.

"Daniel, what's wrong? What's happened?"

"Nothing."

"That is so far from true, I could be a mile away and know something's happened. You seemed to change so much while we were painting, but yet you've been quiet and sour the rest of the week. Don't try to deny it. I'm a stubborn lot, if you haven't yet figured that out."

Daniel leaned back against one of the columns that framed the structure. "You're wonderful."

Well, that wasn't what she was expecting. The way he said it, Ida couldn't shake the notion that her "wonderfulness"—whatever he meant by it—was a problem. "Thank you—I think. Whatever do you mean?"

"You've changed this place. You've brought things I didn't even know were missing. Things aren't running nearly as smoothly as before, and for some insane reason I'm glad for the disorder. It's better. The children are better." He let his head fall back against the column, his shoulders sagging a bit. "I'm better."

The two words pressed against her heart. "It's what nurses do. We make things better."

Daniel smiled a bit and shook his head. "You are a fine nurse, Ida, but all of it is so much more than ointment and bandages."

Ida's heart stilled. So he had felt the strength of the connection between them. It was silly to think he hadn't—it was so strong Ida often wondered if the whole Home felt it. The night, already quiet, seemed to hush to a stillness that was nearly church-like. Somewhere off behind her, Ida could hear the sounds of the Home settling down for the night, and it struck her how much those sounds had become a part of her life. In a way she never expected, she fit in, felt at home, felt as if she had purpose and belonged here. Daniel was such a huge part of that—did he know? "I'm very happy here. In a way I never expected to be." Ida dared a step toward him. "What is it, Daniel?"

"It's you." He put his hand to his forehead, squinting and looking up as if he'd find the right words in the rafters. "I...it's all...I don't know if..."

His look was such a combination of confusion and pain and wonder that whatever piece of her heart Ida had been holding back slipped right through her fingers. It was here, between them, and powerful. "I know," she said, brave enough to finish the thought he could not. "Me, too."

Her directness seemed to startle him out of the cloud he'd been carrying around him. "Ida." He was trying so hard not to feel it, to fight what was growing between them. She wasn't quite sure how, but his resistance seemed to dissolve hers. This was real and precious, no matter how puzzling. This was worth the risk.

He stood motionless up against the column, looking at her with fear and wonder in his eyes. She walked toward him, confidence coming with every step. Once there were only inches between them, he shook his head and nearly whispered, "It's not sensible." His tone was so transparent and yet so intimate that even she knew he didn't believe that to be a true obstacle.

"I don't think it's supposed to make sense. If it helps, I'm scared, too. You're right that there's a load of reasons why this isn't sensible." She looked up into the spectacular intensity of his dark eyes. "Right now they don't seem so important."

Daniel's hand left his side and turned palm up, open and asking for hers. He was reaching for her. The gesture was physically small, but Ida knew how enormous it truly was to Daniel. She slipped her hand into his, feeling something deep and vital settle into place between them. She tightened her grip around his hand, and when he returned the grasp, she knew they'd stepped over the imaginary line they both had been drawing for days if not weeks. A fragile joy spread around her heart, as still and quiet as the night around them.

"You are so…extraordinary. In so many ways I never expected." His free hand went to her cheek. "You're an absolute gift, Ida."

Ida had been called a great many things. Unusual. Spirited. Spunky. Odd. Some had called her special or unusual, and she tried to be happy for her unique character the way Mama had taught her. Her strong nature had been an asset sometimes at Camp Jackson, but just as often it got her into trouble. Right here, right now, Daniel's eyes told her that those very qualities were what touched him most, what made her special. To be a gift to someone like that? To each of these children and this exceptional man? Ida felt as if the "gift" was from Daniel and the Home to her, not the other way around.

Color and shape were how Ida saw the world, not words. Words weren't her language—and at this moment they failed her. Except she knew she would remember the particular shade of Daniel's eyes right now, reflecting the pearly glow of the moonlight off the pool, every day forever. She would always know the shape of his brow and the arc of his smile when he laughed—and oh, what a joy it was to release his laughter. Having no words, nor wanting any if they weren't absolutely perfect, Ida touched the place where his wound began down by his cheekbone, and stood on tiptoe to plant a feather-light kiss there.

His hand gripped hers and she heard Daniel suck in his breath. "Ida." He said her name with such a close, cherishing tone that Ida felt her heart break wide open. She kept her face close to his, her eyes still closed, afraid to move for fear of shattering the fragile moment.

Ida felt Daniel's one hand leave her grasp, and she opened her eyes when both his hands cupped her face. When he stared down at her, eyes wide and suddenly fiery, Ida could barely breathe. She would follow those eyes anywhere, would pay any cost to stay in the brilliance of their gaze. The moment hung between them for what felt like forever, awash in discovery and defiance. And then Daniel dipped his head and kissed her. Gently at first, like the gentleman he was, and then more like the warrior he had become in her eyes, battling against all the elements set out to drag these precious children down. He was so strong. Ida felt that the power of his focus and drive could buoy her against any foe. With his kiss humming through her body, bursting brilliant light into corners of her spirit she hadn't realized had gone dark, Ida felt as if together they could accomplish anything.

She belonged with him, and he with her. It was an irrefutable fact, an unopposable force no matter what sensibility said. Decorum might frown on her station beside his, tongues might wag at a well-born doctor taking up with a nobody nurse, but none of that mattered. God brought her to the Home to complete Daniel, while Daniel and the Home completed her. It was a harmony only God could orchestrate, a harmony she felt in Daniel's touch and the exquisite brush of his lips against hers. *Bliss* wasn't too strong of a word for the burst of light and color Ida felt pulsing through her.

"I ran out of ways to fight it," he said, pulling her fully into his arms so that her head rested against his chest. The moon and quiet seemed to fold around them, holding time still and the world at bay while they discovered each other's heart.

"Hearts are powerful things," she said with a sigh, marveling at how perfect it felt to be in his arms. There could be no argument against such perfection, she thought, certainly not any that mattered. She looked up at him, feeling ready to defy anyone who thought this wasn't exactly how God had it planned. "Do you really think anyone will disapprove so much?"

"Yes," he said, the word almost a sigh. He pulled her closer still, as if to protect her from the objections he saw coming. "But right now I can't bring myself to care." The statement was so unlike the Dr. Parker she had first met at the Home gates that she smiled. He must have felt her smile, for he looked down at her. "You've brought out the radical in me, Ida."

"I'm too happy to regret it," she admitted. "I feel like I'm ready to burst." She reached her hands around his neck and kissed him again, wanting to show him how happy his affections made her.

Ida's happiness swallowed him whole, and Daniel gladly drowned in the glow of her boundless affection. When she threw her hands around his neck as if he were the whole world to her, Daniel's heart shifted in a way he knew would change him forever. Her enthusiasm, however delightful, pulled Daniel's forehead down to bump soundly against hers, right at the most tender spot of his still-healing brow.

"Ouch," he said and then winced, seeing stars even as he couldn't wipe the smile from his face.

Ida cringed and laughed. "Oh my goodness, look what I've done." She planted another of her most tender kisses on his brow, and Daniel could have sworn the pain disappeared instantly.

He took her lovely, glowing face in his hands again. "Look what you've done? I look everywhere around this place and I see what you've done. You've touched everything, and all of the Home is the better for it. I know I am."

She sighed and leaned against him. He wrapped his arms around her, astounded at how right she felt in his embrace. This simply could not be wrong—everyone else had to be in error, for nothing about this struck him as anything but perfect.

Ida angled her face up to look at him. "How are we going to do this?"

Daniel looked down at her, then up at the moon. "I have no idea." She settled more tightly into Daniel's arms and he felt his happiness grow stronger the closer she was. She was light and warmth, drawing him in like a moth…

…to a flame. Yes, this was going to be a very tricky business indeed. "I wish it weren't so complicated." Then again, was it really that complicated? Could a man in his position simply decide to do what made him happy? Could he have the kind of trusting faith Ida did that it would all work out in the end as the Lord intended?

She returned her head to his shoulder. "God had better finish what He started."

"What?"

"I've always felt like God worked it so I'd be here. At first I didn't know why, but I do now. So He's simply going to have to work all the other complications out."

Help me keep her, Daniel prayed as he held Ida in his arms and looked out at the Home he loved. *She belongs here, and I want her to belong with me. I just don't know how.*

Chapter Nineteen

Mrs. Parker poured tea into two lovely china cups Tuesday morning, setting one in front of Ida. "Thank you for coming."

"I'm delighted you'd like to make another pair of socks," Ida said, feeling something off in the woman's expression. She didn't really think today's visit was about wanting to knit more socks.

She'd been nervous about meeting with Daniel's mother this morning, not having a chance to ask Daniel if he knew of the invitation or why it had been offered. She hadn't found much more than ten minutes alone with Daniel since two nights ago at the bathhouse, and the distant-yet-closer atmosphere surrounding them both had thrown Ida off-kilter. "Surely more girls will be coming in and we'll want some more socks set aside to welcome them with their own pair."

"I must admit I find the project most unusual," Mrs. Parker said as she added sugar to her cup and offered some to Ida. *Unusual* wasn't usually a word Ida associated with compliments or endorsements. Still, the woman's tone was congenial enough—for now.

Ida declined the sugar but picked up the cup. The tea smelled wonderful, exotic and floral. "But you saw how happy it made the children. They love the socks."

"They do. Daniel tells me he finds it a good program, and I trust my son's judgment."

Ida felt a twinge at her beloved socks being called a "program," but that would be a word Daniel would use. "I'm glad he is pleased with how it turned out."

Mrs. Parker sipped her own tea. "May I call you Ida, dear?"

That seemed a bit out of character for the formal Mrs. Parker, but Ida chose to see it as a step in the right direction. "Why, certainly. I'd be pleased if you would."

"Ida, I didn't really ask you here to discuss socks. Of course, I'll be agreeable to continue knitting for the orphans—I expect Isabelle would be on me in a minute if I didn't—but I have another matter I wish to discuss."

Ida felt the nervous buzzing in her stomach deepen into a rattle of suspicion. "Yes?"

"I'm very protective of my family, Ida. I take a great deal of pride in the Parker name. We've come through the war with some difficulty—as everyone has—and I consider the family future to be of vital importance."

Ida began to see where this might be heading, and why Amelia Parker chose to have this particular conversation in the privacy of her living room rather than calling on her at the Home. The rattle in her gut grew louder.

"More precisely, my son's future is of the utmost importance to me. He carries a great deal on his shoulders."

Ida put down her cup, any thirst or appetite dissipating in the glare of Mrs. Parker's eyes. Her eyes were dark and intense like Daniel's, but right now they held none of the warm glow she was so fond of in her son's gaze. The cool, polite tone of the meeting had turned decidedly cold. Ida didn't offer a response.

"I'm sure you can see my position. Daniel has sizable obligations to uphold, both to his family and to the Home. While my son has mastered the professional side of his role—" she placed her teacup down in so precise a manner that Ida felt the *clink* run like ice down her spine "—I fear he lacks a certain social sensibility at the moment."

I may be from the backwoods of West Virginia, but I'm no fool. I know what you're getting at, and I'm going to make you speak it plain to my face. Ida smiled as sweetly as she could, given the growing tension in the room. "Whatever do you mean?"

"Come now, Ida, let's do each other the courtesy of directness, shall we?" Mrs. Parker took a napkin and touched it to her lips. Her fingers glinted with a collection of fine rings. "Surely you don't think I'm blind to how you feel about my son."

"I admire your son and his work very much."

"His important work is precisely why we need to have this conversation." The older woman took up the teapot and began refreshing both cups even though they were still rather full. "I've always had some difficulty getting Daniel to understand the power of a suitable match. Up until now he simply couldn't be bothered with such things." She put the teapot down with the same cold precision as she had the cup. "I feel I may have done him a disservice by not insisting on it before it was too late."

Too late? "Your son is a grown man capable of making his own choices, isn't he?"

"Daniel is a fine doctor and a gifted administrator, like his father before him. But he is a man, and I find men to be…shall we say…easily *distracted* in certain matters."

"Distracted?" Ida did not bother to keep the edge from her voice.

"I know you are an unpolished girl, but I believe you to be clever. Clever enough, at least, to understand the consequences of whatever hopes you might harbor regarding my son."

Ida straightened in her chair. "Mrs. Parker—" and how telling was it that while she had asked to call her Ida, she had not invited Ida to call her Amelia? "—just what 'hopes' do you think I have?"

The woman's eyes took on an expression that said, *You are going to make me spell this out for you, poor child, aren't you?* Ida hoped the look she gave Mrs. Parker in reply spoke *Yes, I am* as loud as it could.

"If you were any other woman, I would say you're hoping I'll endorse my son's affections for you. That Daniel's momentary fascination with you could turn into something permanent."

Despite disliking being termed a "momentary fascination," Ida found Mrs. Parker's statement rather cryptic. "But you are saying I'm not any other woman?"

Mrs. Parker steepled her hands, a gesture Ida had seen Daniel do a thousand times. "I believe you care a great deal about the Home. I think you have genuine feelings for my son, and that you are not simply vying to raise your social standing."

"I'm glad to hear that, Mrs. Parker." Ida still felt as if the woman was speaking in circles. "It's all true."

"Then it would also be true that your affection for my son and for the children would lead you to want what's best for him and for the Home. You strike me as someone who can see the bigger picture. You've wits enough about you to catch that what you want might not be what's best in either case."

It wasn't until that moment that Ida truly understood the nature of her visit to Amelia Parker's front parlor. The cold truth washed through her so strongly, she almost shivered. "You want me to leave."

There was a long pause before Mrs. Parker said, "I want what's best for my son, and for the Parker family name. And I don't dislike you. I'm offering to help you find a better post so that Daniel will not be hurt."

Ida didn't hear the words so much as she felt them hit her. She drew up in her chair, the famous Landway stubborn nature roaring up inside her chest. "May I be perfectly frank, Mrs. Parker?"

"I think it's best."

"I think you have no right to make me the offer you just did. I think you must not love your son very much, because where I *come from*—" she emphasized the words "—love doesn't act that way. You're right, I do care a great deal about your son. Enough to let him run his own life and the Home as he sees fit." Ida stood up. "Enough to never tell him you even stooped to have this conversation with me."

Ida went to leave, but Mrs. Parker's voice stopped her halfway to the door. "Don't let your current success go to your head, Ida. I admit, you've charmed Isabelle Hooper, but even she won't be enough to keep the Home running if you make an enemy of me. Daniel thinks he can fund the Home on good deeds, but without my support, the patrons will dry up. Daniel needs his social standing to keep those donors. You know I am right. Are you selfish enough to doom those children's chances for something you know cannot last?"

Ida chose not to answer that last question even as it dug into her heart. She pushed through the parlor entrance, waved the maid off and let herself out the door to stand gulping air and near tears on the front steps.

Amelia Parker was wrong. Amelia Parker was right. Amelia Parker was an awful, loathsome mother. But was what Mrs. Parker had just done so much different from what Daniel had done in pressing Donna and Matthew to wait to marry? Hadn't she and Daniel urged the young couple to let long-term sense override their current passions?

Could she and Daniel last? Ida knew enough of how the world worked to know Daniel would indeed face social consequences if it was publicly known that he was courting her. There'd be talk, and talk could be the enemy of the charitable donations the Home so desperately needed. She'd be seen as a social climber no matter how genuine her feelings for Daniel. And no matter how many Isabelles Ida charmed, she'd still never equal the funds a wife of social standing could bring to the Home. Take Chelsea Hampton, the youngest of the Aunties. She was clearly taken with Daniel and the perfect age to be his bride. Ida knew Miss Hampton had already brought many sizable donations to the Home along with her knit socks.

"Love can't pay the bills." Hadn't she said that very thing to Donna?

Ida walked to the small public garden beside Daniel's

family home, dropping herself onto a bench and fighting back tears. She hated that Mrs. Parker was right about her hopes for approval—she'd had the very thought when the invitation came for tea this afternoon. She'd foolishly thought Daniel had spoken of his feelings for her to his mother, and that something wonderful might be in the works. *That proves it*, she told herself sourly. *I don't know how this world works. I've let myself believe the fairy tale.*

He cares for me. Ida knew that to be true. The way she felt in Daniel's arms made her ready to change the world, to face any obstacle. But Donna had said much the same thing about Matty, and even Ida could see that waiting was best for the young couple. Love was wonderful, but love had to live in the real world.

If she told Daniel what his mother had just done, he'd be furious. He'd reject his mother's meddling, and they'd fight. Amelia would threaten to withdraw her donations and most likely talk others into doing the same. She was a mother who believed her son was in danger—she'd do anything it took to save Daniel from what she saw as harm.

Daniel, in turn, would defy his mother and let her pull her funding rather than submit to such manipulations. While that was the honorable course, the Home would suffer—Ida didn't need to be an administrator to see that consequence coming.

Oh, Lord, Ida cried in prayer as she sat paralyzed on the bench even though she was due back at the Home. *It's all gone wrong. What am I to do?*

"Ida?" Daniel poked his head into Ida's rooms after knocking. She wasn't in the infirmary even though she was scheduled to be there an hour ago. She wasn't anywhere on the grounds that he could see. He was worried she might be ill—MacNeil had seen her leave earlier in the day, but that was all he knew.

Her rooms were just like her—colorful and a bit cluttered. Books sat open on various chairs and tables, and at least two different knitting projects lay in different stages of completion on each end table of her small settee. He ought to leave, seeing that she clearly was not here, but he couldn't stop himself from standing in the room and gazing at the evidence of her spirit that spilled all over the rooms.

Dozens of sketches were tacked onto every wall. Some were small, quickly done studies of flowers or buildings in charcoal or pencil. Others were larger, color-filled watercolors of scenes—the beehive, a corner of the bathhouse where some sort of flowering bush had been blooming, a particularly charming painting of Grimshaw reading on a bench in the yard. It was powerful to see the Home through her eyes.

Another wall held pencil studies of many of the children. She was especially gifted at this; he could see each child's personality so clearly in the sketches. The way Gwendolyn pursed her lips in her Gitch doubt, the set of Donna's eyes as she stared at Matthew, even an amusing sketch of Mrs. Smiley with her hand parked angrily on one ample hip. Ida had captured each of them with a talented eye for detail. He could tell, just by looking at the drawings, what charmed her about each child. Some of the sketches were black-and-white, but all of them had some burst of color added specific to the subject—as if she simply couldn't leave them without it. They were charming, every one of them. He'd proudly have hung any of them in his office.

The personal nature of her drawings made him feel guilty, a voyeur, for lingering in the room. *I ought not to be here*, he said to himself, and forced his feet to turn toward the door. What he saw on the far wall, tucked away behind the door—safe from entering eyes on purpose, perhaps?—stopped him cold.

There, tacked to the wall, were sketches of him. A pencil drawing of him at his desk, his forehead in one hand as he studied papers. Another of him standing in the yard, watching the children play, as he often did while drinking his coffee each afternoon. One that was just the detail of his eyes and hair, another of his face in laughter. Each one with the same emotional power as her drawings of the children. The detail and tone sank deep into his chest, swelling in a warmth behind his ribs that made it hard to breathe.

The two at the center nearly stopped his heart. One was a full-color painting of him as he lay sleeping on his couch, his head still in bandages. She must have done that one while she sat with him those first days home from the hospital. He felt studied, known, but not in a dark way. The drawing showed how much Ida knew him, how much she understood him. He reached out and touched the edge, somehow thinking he could feel her in the paper—her presence was that potent in the art.

The second drawing was a charcoal sketch of two hands. He knew instantly the moment she'd captured—that night at the bathhouse when he'd opened his hand for hers and she'd slipped her fingers against his. That moment had played over and over in his mind, and surely from this drawing the same had been true for her.

Ida had managed to show all the feeling in those two hands—they could not have belonged to any two other people in all the world. He knew her hands, could see the things that made them Ida's in her drawing. Daniel had the urge to take it from the wall and fold it into his pocket, keeping it close.

Of course, he could not do that. He should not have even seen this wall. And yet he was endlessly glad to have this glimpse into her heart. The heart he was quickly coming to need, to want—that he was willing to fight for if it came to that. How very wrong Mother had been in her assessment of what Ida would be to the Home. She was the farthest thing from a problem—she was the solution to every problem. How like her that her words had not shown that to him, but her art had told him in a way no one could dispute. *Ida belongs here. Ida belongs with me.*

Daniel took one last look around the room, drinking in the lines and colors and storing them in his memory. He apologized to God for invading her privacy, but thanked God for the gift of this vision at the same time.

As he turned to go, Daniel's eyes landed on a letter open on Ida's desk. The letterhead from Walter Reed Hospital in Washington, DC caught his eye. The heading, "Nursing Position," drew him in, reading even though he knew he should not. It stung to learn that Ida had been open to an offer from this other hospital, even though the particulars of the post seemed to suit Ida's skills. He'd thought she was happy here. Yes, her friend was headed off to Washington, but she'd been so open about feeling as if she belonged here at the Home. Some part of him was glad to note the letter predated their tender moments in the bathhouse Sunday night.

He could not have believed her to be looking elsewhere after what they had shared.

The signature, however, burned a black hole in the pit of his stomach: Dr. Terrence Bennet.

A friend of his father's. Or, more currently, a friend of his mother's.

Could Mother be behind this? She was certainly capable of such a thing, but he never thought her willing to stoop so low as to go behind his back like this. The more he considered it, however, the more certain he was that his suspicions were true. Near-perfect nursing positions combining art—and even knitting—and medical care did not appear out of nowhere. Bennet could have owed her a favor.

The more he thought about it, remembering her words, the easier it was to believe Mother had simply decided he was wrong not to send Ida away and taken her own action. Daniel ground his teeth and fisted his hands, anger growing every second. She'd always been domineering, and he'd tolerated it out of respect for all she had accomplished and pity for all the things she had lost. This latest scheme, however, he simply could not abide. Daniel's pulse roared in his ears. *Enough. I have been as kind as my soul will allow, Mother, but we are done. If you have hurt Ida...*

Ida. Could that have been where she was this morning? Would Mother be so cruel as to ask—no, demand—that Ida leave? Scheming behind his back was one thing, but cornering Ida in the way he now believed Mother to be capable of doing? That was quite another. Ida had changed the Home. Ida had made it a "home," not just a school or a house. That deserved praise and welcome, not orders to leave town.

Orders to leave *him*.

An icy point in his gut told him that was the true core of all this. Mother knew him well and was an uncanny judge of character. Had she sensed the growing attraction between him and Ida even before he'd fully realized it? It made sense; this was about more than the Home. This was about the possibility that he might ruffle feathers by bringing Ida into their social sphere. Or—even a more distasteful notion to Mother—bring her into the family.

Daniel wanted to grab the letter and tear it to pieces. He wanted to throw something, hit something, but he was in Ida's rooms and had no right to disturb anything. He would not stoop to Mother's tactics and take the letter. He would deal with this directly, openly, and with the honor Mother currently lacked.

But how? It would help if he confronted Mother first—he knew where to find her and he ought to confirm that she had indeed been behind this. He also needed to know if Mother had already made a demand to Ida before he did anything else. Still, the thought of Ida out there in the middle of this ridiculous battle twisted his heart. He wanted Ida to know—now and with certainty—that she belonged here, that he wanted her here, and that Mother's manipulation held no power over him. Every patron could walk from the Home and he would simply find another way to go on. Hadn't that been the single thought thrumming through his heart at the bathhouse? *I could do anything with you beside me.* For the first time in his life, Daniel cursed the Parker name as he closed Ida's door and turned toward the front gate.

Chapter Twenty

Ida held back the tears all the way to Leanne's house, but the moment she caught sight of her dear friend's face in the hallway, they came in a flood.

"Goodness, whatever is wrong?" Leanne took Ida's hand and pulled her into the front parlor.

Where to start? "I've…I've just come from a visit with Amelia Parker." Ida sank into a couch, the tears coming freely now.

Leanne pulled a handkerchief from her dress pocket and handed it to Ida. "Daniel's mother?"

"Daniel's horrible mother, yes." Ida wasn't given to calling people horrible, but she felt so belittled, so dismissed, that her heart burned in pain. "I actually thought…she was…coming to like me." It stung to realize how much she'd *wanted* the woman to like her. How much she'd let herself buy into the fantasy that she and Daniel could actually be together. "How could I have been so foolish?"

Leanne had every right to look confused. "I'll call for some tea. Take a few deep breaths while I do, and then try to tell me what happened."

The tea arrived, and Ida couldn't help but notice how very warm and comforting it felt. How could this be the same beverage over which Amelia Parker had been so cruel? Slowly, Ida let the story unfurl, beginning with the kiss at the bathhouse, which she'd not even had the opportunity to relate to anyone, up until now.

"Oh, Ida. How wonderful and awful at the same time. No wonder your head's in a spin—how could it not?"

"The tables are turned, aren't they?" Ida moaned. It was not that long ago that Leanne had cried to Ida about the wonderful and impossible nature of her love for John Gallows. They'd received a happy ending despite facing mortal dangers. How sad that Ida faced only societal traps, but felt much less sure she'd ever get the happy ending she desired.

"I wish I'd known how you feel about Daniel earlier." Leanne wrapped her hands around her teacup. "I might never have passed along the offer from Washington."

"No, I'm glad you did. I think it may be my saving grace." Ida fell back against the plush cushions, grateful for their softness in a world that felt all too sharp and cruel this morning. "I couldn't stay here now, not knowing how she despises me and all the harm I could do to the Home."

Leanne's back straightened and she set down her cup. "Now, you wait just a minute. You're not really thinking of letting Amelia Parker keep you and Daniel apart, are you?"

"If it were just about Daniel and me, maybe not. But Ida, she is right about the donors. They could choose to withdraw their support. She could *make* them withdraw it. Daniel is all the family she has left, and she'll do whatever it takes to keep his reputation unblemished." Ida put her hand to her forehead, reliving the oh-so-civil ruthlessness in Amelia Parker's eyes as she closed her own. "I could see it in her expression, Leanne. She'd stop at nothing to ensure I never came near Daniel again."

"And what of Daniel's view on this?"

"He loves his mother. I couldn't possibly tell him what she's done. He'd never speak to her again, I think. She's a beast, yes, but she's still his mother. If working at the Home has taught me anything, it's how you can never replace family."

"You don't think Daniel ought to know what his mother has tried to do?"

"What would be the point? It galls me to say it, but she may be right. She'd be scandalized if Daniel and I took up together. All those other donors—the ones the Home depends on—wouldn't they take the same view?"

Leanne shook her head. "All those women you've brought into the knitting circle—do you really think they'd look down their noses at you?"

"*You* brought them in, Leanne. You're one of them." When Leanne balked, she went on, "No, you're not *like* them, I know that, but they see you differently than they see me. I know how these things work, Leanne, and I know how they almost never change. Amelia Parker said it outright—I'm fine as a nurse but definitely not one to join the family. I'd just write her off as a stodgy old lady if…" She couldn't finish that thought.

"If it weren't for how you feel about Daniel," Leanne finished for her. "It's all over your face. I don't know why I didn't see it earlier." She put her hand on Ida's. "He's so perfect for you. And you for him."

"I'm not what he needs." Even as the words left her mouth, they echoed with sad truth in the hollow of her stomach. "I love the Home, and we're fine partners in working there, but Daniel Parker's wife needs to be able to move in all those fancy circles he was born to so the Home keeps its donors."

"I think you move just fine in those fancy circles," Leanne declared, picking up her teacup.

"I'm *tolerated* in those fancy circles. Let's not pretend it's anything else. And honestly, I'm fine with that. I couldn't care what those silly old ladies think of me as long as they help the Home." Ida looked down, feeling her heart already breaking. "But to stay here and watch Daniel, to fight back against all those feelings—Leanne, I just don't think I've got the spine to do it. I hate to let Amelia Parker win this one, but at least you and John have made a way for me to tuck tail and run before it hurts more."

Leanne set her cup down and stared into Ida's eyes. "Do you love him, Ida?"

There wasn't a harder question in the world right now. "Enough to want what's best for him."

"What if *you're* what's best for him?"

Daniel's words, "You're an absolute gift," sounded in her head. She'd already changed him, she'd already brought color to the Home. Perhaps that was all she'd be allowed to give. She'd finish the dining room mural as her final gift to Daniel and the children and move to Washington with John and Leanne. She'd try to be grateful God had handed her a way out and trust that He'd heal her broken heart in good time. "I'm not. Even I can see that. Can you help me write a reply to Dr. Bennet right now? I want to know it's on its way."

"If you're sure it's what you want."

"It's not what I want. But it's what's best, and that'll have to be close enough."

Ida could not be found anywhere on the compound. Daniel had searched every building and most of the grounds, asking after her with everyone he saw. It wasn't like Ida to disappear—this had to be Mother's doing. He burned at the thought of Mother skewering Ida with that demanding glare of hers. He'd been too busy to tamp out Mother's continual meddling in the Home's affairs, telling himself her decaying health would eventually lessen her need to interfere. But in the meantime, while he'd thought he'd been running the Home on his own, in truth he'd taken large decisions to her for approval, lying to himself that he was inviting the participation to keep her occupied.

He wanted to know Father would have sanctioned how he ran the Home, and with Father gone, Mother's approval was the only endorsement he had.

But he did have another Father to guide him. He had God the Father, and God had sent him exactly what he needed in Ida. Perhaps that was why she had ruffled him so at first—she woke up his own long-dormant independence.

She also woke up his long-numbed heart. Daniel had never felt this way about any of the social swans Mother paraded before him. Yes, many of those finely coiffed Charleston fillies would give him social access, but he already had that. Ida gave him what he desperately needed: Inspiration. Fire. The spirit to take on the world. The thoughts kept clarifying in his mind at such speed that Daniel felt he would burst if he didn't find Ida and tell her. Only where was she?

The final place he checked was the bathhouse. It was filled with children at this time of day, and he'd held off going there for fear his growing anger and panic would be apparent to them. Still, would she perhaps return to the place where their hearts found each other? The twin plunge pools were noisy and hectic, teeming with playing children, but no sign of Ida. He laid his hand on the spot where they had kissed up against the column, begging God to let him find her, asking Him to soothe her wounded heart until he could do so with his own words.

Daniel was just pushing off the column when the screech filled the bathhouse. A knot of children exploded in noise and shouting. It wasn't hard to guess that someone had slipped and fell—it happened so often that Daniel had been fighting the decision to close down the bathhouses for months. "Gitch!" someone yelled.

Daniel hoped the child had suffered a minor mishap until he saw the fear on the faces of the children looking up at him. He dashed over, parting them to let himself through.

Gwendolyn lay at the edge of the pool, her cheek and mouth dripping blood into the water. And worst of all, the child who never seemed to stop moving was utterly, frightfully still.

Chapter Twenty-One

Guilt consumed Daniel even as his clinical training kicked in. The twin plunge pools had been part of the compound of buildings before they became the Parker Home for Orphans, and he'd spent too long weighing the trouble of removing them against the relief they brought from the oppressive Charleston summer heat. Now Daniel was staring straight at his greatest fear: a child badly injured from slipping and striking his or her head against the mercilessly hard concrete.

He had known himself to be a worrier—it seemed to be a common trait among physicians—but he'd convinced himself, as his father had before him, that the good of the pools outweighed the dangers. Even the children recognized the baths to be a privilege and were uncharacteristically obedient of the stringent safety rules Daniel had in place for the pools. As such, in all his time at the Home, no one had ever been seriously hurt—before today.

That it was now, and that it was Gwendolyn, seemed to twist his gut in half while doubling his dread.

Her head hung at a ghastly angle over the edge of the

pool so that her hair dipped into the water, its beautiful blond streaked with red that seeped from her brow down her locks. He simultaneously hated and loved that he had gained Ida's eyes for color, even at this terrible moment.

As fast as was sensible, he ran assessing fingers down the child's neck and skull, checking for swelling and fractures. When it seemed safe to at least move her head to the edge, he whispered, "Come now, Lady Gwendolyn, come on back to us," and began sliding her neck and head back up level onto the stones. Daniel kept his hands on Gitch's good cheek—the other held a deep gash—stroking while he turned over his shoulder and said quietly yet firmly to the teaching assistant who had been serving as pool guard but now stood pale and frozen beside him, "Get the first-aid kit.

"Doris," he repeated, snapping his fingers impatiently in front of the young woman's face when she failed to move, "get the first-aid kit in the cabinet over there!" She blinked, and finally obeyed.

Daniel held out his hand for bathing towels from two of the children standing nearby, tucking one under Gwendolyn's head while pressing the other against the wound on her cheek and jaw. "You're going to be just fine, Miss Martin. You've just given yourself a good bump. Open your eyes for me now, okay, dear?"

When she failed to do so, one of the girls who had handed him a towel began to cry.

"Gitch?" Daniel tried the favorite nickname in the hopes of getting the girl to reply. He checked her pulse, glad to feel a solid, if skittish rhythm, as a second girl began to cry, as well. "Now, now, girls, she's not dead." He tried to imitate Ida's gift for warm tones in a crisis, wishing to Heaven the sweet nurse were beside him right now. Gwendolyn did indeed look alarmingly limp and still on the concrete, not to mention how bloody the whole scene appeared. "She's just knocked herself out." He prayed he'd kept the alarm from his voice, for in truth his own pulse had begun to thunder in his ears. He'd had little choice but to move Gwen's head, but in fact he did not know if a fracture was present. The unnatural angle of the child's swelling jaw could mean any number of things. *Father God, have mercy on this dear child. This may be beyond my skill. Spare her.*

The towel under his hand was rapidly turning red as someone pushed the white tin first aid box against his leg, now wet as he knelt on the poolside concrete. Daniel pressed harder, infinitely relieved to see the child's face register pain. Pain meant life and consciousness. *Thank You, Lord.* She wasn't out of the woods by a long shot, but if she could feel, she hadn't broken her neck in the fall.

The sound of boys' voices began to fill the room— the boys had evidently come in from their pool next door. "Donna?" Daniel called without taking his eyes from Gwendolyn, hoping the older girl was nearby.

"Yes, Dr. Parker?"

"Find Matt and clear the pools. Help Doris get the children out of here. Send someone to Mr. Grimshaw to call the ambulance. Have him tell them to come to the service entrance at the back gate. Tell the cook to send some ice. Can you do all that?" Donna didn't have Ida's experience—and where on earth was Ida right now?— but she was the best he had at the moment.

Daniel didn't even look up, but he could hear the tears in Donna's voice, hear her attempts to stay calm.

"Yes, Dr. Parker." Donna had a soft spot for Gwendolyn. Everyone had a soft spot for the gutsy little girl.

"That's my girl," Daniel said as much to Gwendolyn as to Donna. "Off you go. Everything will be all right. It looks worse than it is." *Please, Lord, let that be true.*

"Where's Nurse Ida?" one child cried behind Daniel as Donna, Doris and Matt herded the frightened children from the area. "Gitch needs Nurse Ida."

I need Nurse Ida. Why did this have to happen now? How could Daniel possibly hope to get word to Ida if he didn't know where she was?

It seemed forever before the bleeding began to slow, draining Gwendolyn's already pale complexion to a further pallidness that grew knots in Daniel's stomach. He found one of the older children to hold the towel firmly in place while he checked her neck and shoulders again for signs of fractures, grateful to find none and only minimal swelling. The cheek and jaw, however, were another story. He rolled her head to her good side to keep the blood from pooling in her mouth. She was still unconscious, but perhaps that was a blessing given that movement wasn't yet wise. Daniel opened her eyelids to check her pupils. She was breathing unsteadily, but she was breathing.

In the best case, she had a concussion and would sport a scar that might rival his own. In the worst case, she'd fractured her skull or jaw, or had bleeding on her brain that would require dangerous surgery. Daniel knew her treatment went beyond his skills, but he hated the thought of relinquishing her care to someone else. These were his children.

Mrs. Smiley's voice came over his shoulder. "In here, gentlemen." A pair of ambulance orderlies rushed to his

side. Daniel told them all he'd been able to assess and
stepped back, not wanting to retreat but knowing they
needed to do their jobs.

"And where is Miss Landway when she's needed?"
Mrs. Smiley's sharp tone startled Daniel. "She's not off
on Tuesdays, is she?"

"I beg your pardon?" Daniel turned to her.

"I know your mother was talking with her this morning, but that doesn't mean she can take the whole day
off."

Daniel struggled to pull his attention from Gwendolyn based on what he'd just heard. "So Miss Landway
was with my mother this morning?" He couldn't keep
his eyes on the orderlies shifting Gwen to a stretcher
and Mrs. Smiley's scowling expression at the same time.

"Well, someone had to have a talk with that woman.
She showed no signs of listening to me."

Daniel's head was spinning. "What are you talking about?"

"I'll come out and say it, then. If you won't look out
for your own affairs, Dr. Parker, someone's got to do
it for you."

Gwendolyn made a pained cry as the orderlies
hoisted the stretcher up. He checked to see that her
neck had been properly stabilized with canvas braces
before turning back to Mrs. Smiley. "You spoke to Mrs.
Parker—" right now he couldn't even bring himself to
call that woman his mother "—about Ida?"

Mrs. Smiley's eyes narrowed. Clearly, she took his
use of Ida's first name as confirmation of her suspicions.
"I spoke to your mother about Miss Landway, yes. And
I see I was right to do so. No respectable young woman

ought to be making sandwiches for you alone in the kitchen in the middle of the night."

The look in her eyes as he'd passed her in the hallway that night shot up into his memory. She'd been coming from the kitchen and knew Ida was there. Apparently, she'd thought him deliberately sneaking off to the kitchen not in search of a sandwich but in search of Ida. Suddenly the pieces of this whole disaster began falling into place.

"Mrs. Smiley," he said through gritted teeth, his years of frustration over the effective but persnickety matron boiling up beyond his control. He leaned in, keeping his voice as quiet as he could manage given that there still might be children in earshot. "You could not have been more wrong," he growled, gripping her shoulder. "How dare you go behind my back like that! How dare you make such assumptions! I'll deal with you later. But for right now, I'll thank you to lead the girls in prayers for Miss Martin's safety because it is *the children* who should be our concern, not petty gossip!"

With that, Daniel turned on his heels to follow the ambulance. At least now he had no need to visit his mother to see if she'd been behind Ida's offer—he had all the proof he needed. His impossible challenge now was to find Ida and see to Gwendolyn at the same time.

Ida lay slanted against Leanne's soft couch cushions, willing herself to find the energy to get up and return to the Home. She was dreadfully overdue, but her whole body felt fragile and hollow, as if she might shatter to pieces before she made it down Leanne's front steps. She'd always prided herself on being such a strong, unsinkable type. It threw her to know Mrs. Parker's clever manipulations could steal all that away.

What threw her most of all was how much she'd come to hope she would be considered worthy of Daniel Parker. "I'm a sensible sort," she said to Leanne. "I'm not given to fairy tales, much as I'm fond of the happy ending you and John ended up with. I thought I'd talked myself out of being with him. Until he kissed me, that is. That knocked the sense right out of me."

"Love does that, Ida." Leanne stared at Ida again. "Are you sure, *really* sure, leaving is what you want to do?"

"Yes. If Daniel and I lived all alone on a desert island, we could get our happy ending. But Daniel needs to live in Charleston society for the Home to survive. Even if he loves me—and he truly might—it's still about more than just the two of us." Ida put her hands over her eyes. "Glory, but I wish I could just walk right onto that train right now. The thought of going back there and looking into his eyes again, of facing that monster of a woman in Isabelle Hooper's parlor ever again… I think I'd rather go back to the army than to the Parker Home!"

Leanne sat up. "Maybe you can. If anyone could make it happen, John could. Do you want me to send word to his office?"

Ida managed a dark laugh. "Of course not. I'm just whining. But I love you for even taking up the notion." She slapped her knees, telling them to make her rise. "No, it's time for this old girl to get herself on back and show some of my legendary gumption. Besides, I'd never, ever leave those darling children without a proper goodbye."

Someone started abusing the front knocker of Leanne's house, rapping at it hard.

"Goodness," Leanne said, "what is going on?"

Before she could even make it to the salon door, Ida heard a commotion in the hallway and a familiar voice. Seconds later a sweaty, out-of-breath Donna Forley pushed through the doors. "Nurse Ida. You've got to come!"

"Donna!" A dozen questions buzzed in Ida's head. "How did you find me?"

Donna spilled words out in a waterfall of wheezes. "I heard Mrs. Smiley say she thought you were at Dr. Parker's mother's house and I didn't know where that was so I went to Mrs. Hooper's house and she knew Mrs. Parker was somewhere else so we thought about trying here so I ran here and you have to come now because Gitch is hurt badly, really badly—" Donna bent over and collapsed into the nearest chair.

Leanne sprung up and poured a glass of water. "Someone's hurt?"

Ida bolted up off the couch. "Gitch?"

Donna grabbed at the water, gulping it down between words. "She fell. At the bathing pool. Oh, Miss Ida, her head. It was all bloody. Dr. Parker was calling for the ambulance. She was all pale and still. Everyone was crying. It's terrible. She didn't wake up, Miss Ida. If she dies, I don't know what I'll do." Donna started crying herself.

Ida grabbed Donna's hand. "You clever girl for finding me. Donna, you never stop surprising me. Dr. Parker sent for the ambulance? To Roper Hospital?"

"I don't know. I suppose so."

Ida began gathering her things. The vision of Gitch

lying bloody on the bathing-house floor filled her head, the red color pooling like dread in her stomach as if she'd been there to see it herself. She could picture Daniel on his knees, assessing, trying to stay calm beside the pale, still child. *Gitch. Dear, sweet Gitch!* All her dread at returning to the Home was replaced by a desperate need to be back there, beside all those frightened children. Or at the hospital beside Daniel and Gitch—honestly, she couldn't say which urge was stronger.

Ida squeezed Donna's hand tight. "Do you know if Dr. Parker went with the ambulance?"

"He was shouting at Mrs. Smiley just before he left. I'm pretty sure he left with the ambulance, yes."

Daniel? Shouting at Mrs. Smiley? That wasn't like him, even in a crisis. That, combined with a quick calculation that Roper Hospital was closer than the Home, made her decision for her. "Donna," Ida said as calmly as she knew how, "here's what you're going to do. You're going to take Mrs. Gallows here and go back to Mrs. Hooper's house. Gather as many of the Aunties as you can, and bring them all back to the Home so that there are plenty of friendly adults to help keep the children calm."

"Okay." Donna sniffed. Leanne produced two more hankies, handing a fresh one to Ida—who'd gone through several—and one to Donna.

"I'm going to go to the hospital where Gitch is," Ida continued. "I promise I'll send word back as soon as I can, but you have to understand it may not be for several hours. It's time for you and Matthew to show us the adults you can be today. That means staying calm and in control. Help Mrs. Smiley and Mr. Grimshaw." She patted Donna's hand. "You can cry and let the little ones cry—we all want to cry—but you can't lose your nerve. Mrs. Gallows and Mrs. Hooper will help. I know for a fact they're good friends to have." Ida looked up at Leanne, then back at Donna. "You can count on them. And pray. Gitch needs our prayers. Dr. Parker does, too. God loves Gitch as much as we do, and we need to trust that today."

"Everyone was wondering where you were." Donna sniffed again. "Mrs. Smiley was shouting at Dr. Parker about you not being in the infirmary. Is something wrong?"

Ida sighed. "I had a little problem, but it's all sorted out now, so you don't have to worry about it. You tell everyone at the Home that I've gone to the hospital to be with Gitch and I'll be back just as soon as I can. Mrs. Gallows knows everything else and she can talk to the Aunties if they have any questions, but right now our hearts and minds need to be on Gitch, right?"

"Right."

All three of them stood. Leanne had already pinned her hat on and was handing Ida her own while she passed a damp napkin to Donna. "Press this to your face, child. It'll help. You've been through quite a dash and we don't need you to overheat." *That's my Leanne*, Ida thought. *Once a nurse always a nurse.*

While Donna pressed the cloth to her face, Leanne caught Ida's gaze. "Will you be all right at the hospital?"

Ida felt her resolve settle into place, that steely certainty she could always count on in a tight spot. "I'll be where I'm needed. The rest is up to God." After a quick hug, Ida added, "But I wouldn't mind a prayer or two, if you're asking."

"We'll be praying every second," Leanne said. "Won't we, Donna?"

"Yes, Mrs. Gallows."

Leanne smiled tenderly and wiped a wet tendril from the young woman's forehead. "Why don't you call me Leanne? Or better yet, Auntie Leanne?"

"That'd be a fine thing…Auntie Leanne." Ida was glad to see a slip of a smile return to the girl's face. What a harrowing day Donna had endured. And the day was far from over—Ida expected it would be a very long night before any word of Gitch's prognosis could be sent.

Just before they left the house, Leanne pulled Ida aside. "I think that I shall find some reason to ask Isabelle's assistance in keeping Amelia at the Home with us or at her own house. I don't think she'd go to the hospital, but you don't need her there."

Ida pushed out a breath. "I hadn't even thought of that. Thank you, Leanne. Daniel must be beside himself right now. I'm so thankful I can be there for him this one last time. Say nothing to Isabelle or the children about my plans for Washington. I'll find a way to tell them in my own time, but that certainly isn't now."

"Of course." Leanne gave her one last hug. "Oh, take care. I won't stop praying until I hear from you. We'll have every single one of the Aunties praying, as well."

"It will be enough," Ida said, hugging her friend back. "It has to be."

Ida hugged Donna once more, and watched Leanne and the girl turn left out the door while she squared her shoulders and turned right toward Roper Hospital and the fragile fate of Lady Gwendolyn Martin.

Chapter Twenty-Two

Doctors did not belong in waiting rooms. It was the cruelest of tortures to ban a physician from the surgery, to exclude him from participating in the care of someone he cared about. On the other hand, Daniel was glad they had taken Gwendolyn straight into X-ray and surgery in order to identify and treat her wounds.

Cranial fractures were held hostage by time, their damage made better or worse by how well swelling or bleeding was controlled right from the start. His own brain knew he was of no use in a surgery in this case, his own emotional state making him more liability than help should drastic measures be required. He'd called in Michael Hartwick—the doctor who'd worked on his own face—but that hadn't eased his panic one bit. Too much could still go wrong.

He walked down the hall to stare at the pediatric ward, finding the rows of metal hospital beds far too much like those at the Home.

Ida was right—too much about the Home was institutional. Identical and colorless, with no individuality. It was no "home" at all. The dormitories at the

Home should feel nothing like this ward, and yet Daniel could not help but think that only the change of the walls from gray to white would be Gwendolyn's clues that she was not at home.

Ida could change all that. Ida had already begun changing that.

Half of him yearned to bolt through the hospital doors and go find her. *I need her. The Home cannot be a home without her. You sent her to me, Lord, and I pledge to You as surely as I pledge to fight for Gwendolyn to heal, that I will fight for Ida to stay. I know what Mother is up to, and she will not win.* And yet he knew Ida was strong, while tiny Gwendolyn was weak. His heart was with Ida, but his duty was with Miss Martin. And so he found himself standing in the hall of the hospital, fists clenched, cursing the woman who had placed him in this loathsome war between two allegiances for the sake of some silly social contrivance that had never meant anything to him in the first place.

"Daniel!"

Daniel turned to see Ida rushing toward him down the hallway. He didn't bother with words. He didn't care who saw. He simply drew her to him so fiercely that a nurse farther down the hallway nearly dropped her files. Ida resisted for a moment, which told him all he needed to know about how successful his mother's tactics had been. But he would not let her keep her distance. Daniel held her close until her worry and the power of his care overrode her caution, and bit by bit she melted into his arms.

He knew the moment he had won her back, and it was as if his entire world stopped holding its breath. He had been as fearful—if not more so—of losing her as he had been of losing Gwendolyn. He gave silent thanks that she could still be his. He stroked her hair, breathing in and drawing strength from the particular precious scent that surrounded his Ida.

Her unruly hair was wild out of its braid and her eyes were puffy with tears as she looked up at him to ask, "Is she…?"

"We don't know much yet." He kept her hand in his as he walked her back toward the surgical waiting room.

"What do we know?"

"Concussion, that much is sure. They should be able to rule out cranial fracture soon, but I don't know the extent of the damage to the cheekbone and the jaw."

Ida's shoulders fell in relief, and she let out a breath. Daniel had pretty much done the same when the surgeon had sent word out of that good news. "Thank Heaven. I've been praying with every step I ran over here."

"There are no signs of bleeding on the brain yet, but they have to keep watch. What we do know," he went on, running his thumb across the back of Ida's palm, "is that there is some kind of fracture of the jawbone, with two broken molars. Hartwick has a procedure he learned from the war that he's doing—wiring her jaw shut until it heals. I expect he's doing that right now."

"You called in the doctor who worked on you?"

"I wanted the best man for her. It's her face, after all." He felt his own voice near to breaking.

"Her jaw wired shut," Ida said with a burst of nervous laughter at the procedure even Daniel had to admit sounded a bit gruesome. "Oh, she won't like that."

"She will live," Daniel said, infusing the words with all the certainty he could. "It will give her the best chance at healing. From what we know right now, unless something new springs up, I believe she will make a full recovery." He hated what he had to add. "But some things will never be the same."

"I know."

"I will never get the sight of that blood on the cement and in the water out of my head as long as I live."

Ida touched his cheek. "Oh, Daniel, it must have been horrifying. The children—they must be so frightened. We have to tell them Gitch will be okay."

Daniel took a deep breath. "I'm having the bathing pools filled in starting tomorrow."

"Are you really sure that's necessary?"

"I've made a decision."

She looked at his eyes, and silenced whatever reply she was readying.

"I've made another decision. My mother is never to speak to you outside of my presence ever again."

Ida's eyes flew wide open, her face showing a flurry of emotions before her gaze went to the floor. "You know."

"I learned only moments before the ambulance arrived, or I would have been out looking for you. Mrs. Smiley let it slip that she'd approached my mother about the impropriety of us being found alone in the kitchen after midnight."

Ida's brows bent and her lips pursed. "Mrs. Smiley? Your mother never mentioned her, or even that they'd spoken. And here I thought I'd won that woman over."

"I've half a mind to fire her for going behind my back like that. And I won't discuss in your company what I feel about my mother right now for whatever it is she said to you." He took Ida's arm in his. "I saw the letter from Walter Reed, Ida. Don't go. Don't you dare leave me."

"John found out about the position and I thought…"

Daniel held his hand up. It galled him to admit the depth of his mother's actions to Ida. "Dr. Bennet is a friend of the family. My mother made sure John Gallows heard about that position. She pushed Bennet to mention it to Leanne's husband while suggesting that I should arrange for you to leave."

"Even before the socks?" Ida had every right to look shocked.

Daniel hated to make it worse. "Actually, it was even more devious than that. I believe she put the whole thing in motion before she even tried to convince me to send you packing. I believe she only viewed my consent to give you up—consent which I would not give, by the way, consent I would never, *ever* give—as an unnecessary luxury."

Ida pulled her hand from his, turning her head to look out the hallway window they happened to stand beside. "It wasn't God." Her tone was half question, half statement.

"Pardon?"

She turned back to him. "You read the letter. The post at Walter Reed involved art and knitting as accepted parts of the treatment protocols. Art and knitting, Daniel—it seemed so perfect, but I didn't think I wanted to leave. And then, when we…" She flushed. "I knew I'd never want to leave."

"Ida…"

"But your mother," Ida went on, grabbing his hand. "When she told me if I really cared about the children and the Home that I had to leave or she would ensure that the Home would lose its donors, I wondered if God hadn't been kind enough to make a way for me to leave." She squeezed his hand. "I couldn't stay here and not be with you."

Daniel was glad his mother wasn't anywhere nearby. The words he would speak to her right now would far overstep the bounds of a respectful son. They would overstep the bounds of any respect at all. He touched Ida's cheek, needing to feel her skin to stem the tide of rage boiling up inside him. "There is no reason at all for you to leave. I want you to stay, and I want you to be with me."

Ida closed her eyes for a moment, breathing deeply. "Daniel, she's not all wrong." Her eyes opened again. "Oh, believe me, lots of her is dead wrong, but there are plenty of people in Charleston who think the same way she does, and plenty of those people donate to the Home."

"I don't care." Daniel wanted to defy the world, to kiss Ida right here in the hospital hallway and declare to the sterile walls that Gwendolyn Martin would not be permitted anything less than a complete recovery.

Ida placed her hand on top of his, smiling. "You need to care. I'm not saying we need to cow to your mama's conniving, but we need to figure out how to fight it. I know her kind. You can't defy her without a battle plan." Her voice softened a bit. "But Daniel, are you sure this is a war you want to wage? Think of the children. The Home. I'd hate to think your mama would use them as pawns, but—"

"—but we both know she would. Hasn't she already, trying to take you from them? They care for you." He pulled her close. "*I* care for you. I realized I cannot build the Home the way it needs to be without you. If you really want what's best for the children, you must stay."

Ida pressed her cheek into his hand, and his heart cinched as he watched a tear spill over to meet his palm. Her eyes gave him the answer no words ever could.

"Daniel?"

Hartwick stood in front of the doors of the operating theater, pulling the mask from his face. "We've finished treating your Miss Martin."

Ida could barely stand how small and frail Gitch looked all bound up and braced in that enormous hospital bed. The way Daniel had described the fall, Ida said a prayer of thanksgiving that Gitch was even alive. She'd seen enough battle injuries to know the damage a neck fracture could do, seen what skull fractures could do to the fragile human brain. She'd seen grown men laid low and feeble by such falls, and Gitch was such a tiny little thing.

Still, she breathed. She moved, reminding Ida that paralysis was not an issue. Daniel had told her that, but Ida had to keep seeing it for herself. Hardest yet happiest of all, Gitch showed signs of pain. Pain meant awareness and mental capacity, even if it meant loss of comfort. Every time Gitch moaned, Ida stroked the parts of the child's face that she could touch, talking to her in soft tones, praying peace and comfort over the girl.

Daniel seemed especially troubled by Gitch's highly bandaged face, and it wasn't hard to guess why. "Wrapped up like that, the injuries look far too much like my own, and I remember how much those hurt. They throbbed and stung miserably, and I'm a grown man." He stroked her hair with a tenderness Ida had never seen before in him. "She's so small, so young."

"She's a fighter, though." Ida took Daniel's hand and gave it a squeeze. "I wouldn't be surprised if she gives you no end of grief for shutting down the pools. Once she can talk, that is."

Daniel leaned up against the high metal foot of the bed. "You weren't going to tell me what my mother did to you, were you?"

Ida ran one hand across the bed railing, feeling it cool under her fingers even in the early-evening heat. The day felt ten years long. "No. I didn't see what it would help."

"You would just have left?" Hurt singed Daniel's words.

"Never. I would have said goodbye to the children." She swallowed hard. "And to you." *But it would have torn my heart into a million pieces*, she added silently.

"You would have let her win?"

Ida laid her chin on the high metal frame. "I would not have let the children become her battlefield."

Daniel moved his hand to cover hers as it sat perched on the railing. "You are an astounding woman, Ida Lee Landway. You are worth more to me than every dollar every donor could give. The donors who see your worth are the donors I want to keep. Those Mother could sway, well, they're not worth keeping."

Gitch moaned.

"Shh," Ida said. "None of that now. Right now our thoughts are with dear Lady Gwendolyn here. I think she's waking up, and we're going to have to do all the talking for a while. I expect she won't take kindly to that, so we'd best be ready." Ida stepped over to lean close to Gitch's puffy, pale face, taking the child's hand in hers. She was grateful her army hospital training gave her skills for this situation. "Gitch, honey, can you hear me? If you can, you just squeeze my hand once."

Tiny fingers gave her hand a small squeeze, and Ida felt relief flood her chest. She looked up and nodded at Daniel, watching his own shoulders lose the tension they'd held since she'd arrived.

"You've been hurt badly, but you're going to be just fine after you've had a bit of a rest. You won't be able to open your mouth for a while, so no trying to talk, okay? You just answer yes or no by squeezing my hand and we'll get along just fine. Do you hurt?"

Squeeze.

"One squeeze for lots, two for only a little."

One squeeze.

Ida felt her heart twist as she held up one finger, and Daniel sucked in a breath. "I know it hurts now, but we're going to do our best to make it better real soon. Dr. Parker is right here."

At the mention of Daniel's name, Gitch's eyes fluttered and opened for a moment. She began looking drowsily around the room for Daniel, and he immediately stooped and shifted his face into her view. His expression when he caught her gaze raised such a lump in Ida's throat that she thought she might start sobbing and never stop. How could she have ever thought this man rigid and uncaring? His heart was so full of care for these children—and she hoped for her—that it would have been the worst of mistakes to leave him.

"I'm right here, Gitch," he said, his voice thick with emotion. She noticed he used her nickname—the first time she'd heard him say it. "I'll always be here for you. You're going to be okay. I know it hurts now, but just close your eyes and go to sleep." He glanced over to Ida with glistening eyes. "Remember Nurse Ida's trick? We'll do it together—I'll say the words for you, you think them in your head. Genesis, Exodus, Leviticus, Numbers, Deuteronomy, Joshua..." He pressed his fingers to his forehead, his memory failing him in the emotion of the moment. He knew it now—she'd helped him to learn the entire list during his own recovery.

"Judges, Ruth, First and Second Samuel," she said, feeling Gitch's fingers relax against her hand. Daniel stroked Gitch's shoulder, and she heard the girl's breathing lengthen out from the pained gasps she had made earlier. "First and Second Kings, First and Second Chronicles." She nodded to Daniel to continue.

"Ezra, Nehemiah, Esther, Job, I love you."

Ida blinked and looked up, startled by the declaration at the end of Daniel's list. His hand slipped over Gitch to take hers, making a perfect circle of caring hands—hers to Gitch to Daniel and back to her. Of course he loved her. She loved him. It ought to be shocking, but it wasn't at all. She'd been fighting the truth that she loved him for days, maybe weeks now. Why wasn't now the perfect time to admit it?

"I love you." She smiled as she whispered, feeling as if her skin could not contain the swells of care and hope surging inside. Surely, she would break open in sparkling happy colors any second, turning the pristine white hospital into a riotous rainbow. "Psalms, Proverbs, Ecclesiastes, Song of Solomon..." She stopped the list, and instead quoted from that last book, "I found him whom my soul loveth."

Daniel squeezed her hand—once for yes. Gitch's

slow, even breaths signaled the girl had lapsed back into sleep, and Ida gave a prayer of thanks. Daniel was right—what obstacle of small-minded judgment could overcome the power of the love in this room at the moment? She and Daniel were capable of so much more together than they were apart.

They sat in two chairs next to Gitch's bed for the next pair of hours, holding hands, holding vigil over Gitch's sleeping form, stringing tougher the bonds that would hold them through the struggle to come. Ida felt as if the hours were holy, healing to all three of them in particular ways. As they talked and sat and prayed, Daniel shed some of his guilt over the bathing pools. He still insisted they be closed, but he came to understand Gitch's fall for the accident it was. Ida's sting over Amelia's judgment softened, and while she never would agree with the tactic, she saw it for what it was: a mother who thought she was protecting her son. Gitch received pain medicine, and while she repeatedly reached out for Ida's or Daniel's hand, she managed a fitful rest.

By seven o'clock, Daniel rose. "I'm going to go back to the Home for a short bit. I'll return with some dinner for you. I want the children to know Gitch will be okay, and I want a few words with Mrs. Smiley." His tone brooked no argument, nor did Ida wish to give him one.

"Of course. I'll be praying for you, Daniel."

He took her hand and kissed it. "Thank you."

He leaned over and left a light kiss on the part of Gitch's brow that was exposed. His sigh was sweet and piercing. "She loves you," Ida said softly. "We both do."

She watched Daniel fix that truth strongly against his heart in the moments before he walked from the room. The Daniel Parker who returned to the Home tonight would be a different man from the one who left the institution this afternoon. Ida looked after the door where Daniel had departed and prayed. *You've begun such a good work in him, Lord, now stay with him—and us—until it is completed.*

She hadn't even realized she had nodded off until Daniel's hand on her shoulder gently prodded her awake what seemed only moments later. The clock on the ward wall and the full dark outside told her that more than an hour had passed. Gitch was still sound asleep, even though Ida noticed ugly bruises had begun to darken at her surgery sites and her bandages had begun to stain. The crisis of injury was for the most part over, giving way now to the long, steep road of healing.

Daniel's eyes looked raw and tired, his face lined with weary creases. He held two bags. "Supper," he said, lifting one, "and knitting," he added, and Ida wondered why she hadn't even been awake enough to recognize her own knitting bag. His thoughtfulness stole her heart all over again, making her sniff back a teary smile. "If I didn't already love you…"

He managed a grin. "Had I only known…"

It was the closest to a joke she'd seen from him in days. He really was a changed man. She waited for him to sit down, but he remained standing. It took her only a moment to work out why.

"You're going to see her, aren't you?"

"Yes."

"Wouldn't it be better to wait until morning?"

His voice was iced with determination when he said, "No."

"You'll come back here?"

"I think I'll need to." She heard the *I'll need you* in

his voice, and was glad for the hundredth time she was not on a train to Washington.

"I'll be here."

Chapter Twenty-Three

Amelia Parker swept into her front parlor. "Daniel, whatever are you doing here at so late an hour?"

Daniel saw no point in pleasantries. "You arranged for Ida Landway to leave."

She sat down carefully in her accustomed chair, barely even flinching at his direct statement. He'd almost forgotten how very good she was at this brand of civilized warfare. "I suggested she ought to be removed, yes."

"That's not what I said. You arranged for her to go. Even before you spoke to me, you had Bennet suggest the post to John Gallows."

She opened her mouth to deny it, but he held up a hand. "Save the denials, Mother. I saw Bennet's letter. And I saw the date on the letter. Tell me, did the post actually exist, or did you have to call in extra favors to have one made up?"

Her eyes burned at him. "Mind your tongue, Daniel Parker," she snapped. "I am still your mother."

"Oh, I have held my tongue for years, Mother. Out of respect for all you do for the Home and for who you are, I have let you play queen and be your grand self. I have listened to your lectures and your endless opinions. I have swallowed my fill of arguments for the good of the Home and for Father's sake—even for the sake of his memory. But I am done."

Mother's fingers wrapped their way around the ends of her chair arms. "How dare you! Don't tell me you're going to let that no-good army nurse sway your—"

Daniel stormed over to her. "Do you know where I have been today?"

"Of course I don't know where you've been." She said it as if she had no interest in keeping tabs on his whereabouts—a ridiculous argument given the nature of their current conflict. There were times Mother knew about Home events even before he did.

"I've been at Roper watching an eight-year-old girl get her broken jaw pinned shut. I've been washing her blood off my shirt and hoping she wouldn't bear the scars of her accident the rest of her life. I've been sitting at that girl's bedside with a woman who loves that girl and all the children not as *a cause*, but as children. She cares for them in marvelous, creative ways that change their lives, Mother. That 'no-good army nurse' is the best thing to happen to the Home since Father founded it, and not only won't you see it, you've tried to send her away."

"Because she is after you!"

Did Mother really see love only in terms of acquisition? Could a woman who had done so much in the name of charity be that blind to the selfless nature of real love? "She was ready to get on a train to Washington not because she wanted to go or because she was afraid of you—although I'm sure you tried your best to intimidate her—but because she couldn't bear to see the children hurt by what you'd do in retaliation if she stayed. Now, tell me, Mother, who is the villain here?"

"She's twisted your mind, has her hooks already into you. The Parker Home exists on the reputation of our family, a reputation you are about to sully for… for a backwoods hussy. This is exactly what I feared would happen if I let this infatuation go any longer," she hissed, rising out of the chair. The graceful exterior had peeled away, leaving a woman Daniel cringed to see. His anger boiled just barely under his control. If he ever learned that she'd called Ida "hussy" to her face, Daniel was sure he couldn't be held responsible for what he'd do.

Dear, sweet Ida. Her only crime was to care. With all her heart, with exactly who she was. And the children had—as children do—responded to her authenticity with deep affection and emotional growth. Not ever, for as long as she lived, would she even be capable of the cold cruelty he saw in his mother now. Daniel pictured Mother threatening Ida with the vicious eyes he saw before him, and his gut seared. People often said he had his mother's eyes, but at this moment he wished that nothing was further from the truth. He found himself glad his father had not lived to see such ugliness.

The more Mother glared at him—her eyes silently shouting "See? See what she's done?"—the more Daniel's rage hardened and settled into an icy, immovable determination. It was almost sad—she could not see that the strength of her protest merely doubled his resolve. She went on talking, but Daniel didn't hear the words. In her desperate attempt to manipulate him, she'd removed the last hold of any sense of duty or loyalty she'd had over him. Some oddly detached part of him wondered why it had taken this long.

Daniel let her stalk angrily around the room, waiting until he could speak with absolute calm. In a moment of surprise, he realized that his stance—feet slightly apart, shoulders square, hands clasped behind his back—was that of his father's. He'd aged a decade since this morning, but the years settled on him with confidence rather than with weariness. He spoke slowly, very clearly and without raising his voice. "I am of my own mind on this. Ida stays."

Mother wheeled on him, hands flying in the air. "Is she 'Ida' to you now? Oh, if only Jane Smiley had come to me earlier." She was half panicked mother, half cordial predator as she grappled with the realization that her usual tactics would not work here. She moved toward him and put a hand on his lapel. It was all he could do not to flinch from the contact. "This can still be fixed, Daniel. You would not be the first man to have his head turned by a pretty conniver. The position for her in Washington is genuine and…"

He took his mother's hand by the wrist and removed it from his chest. Her eyes showed a mixture of hurt, anger and confusion. "Ida stays," he repeated, giving the words more force this time. "It is Jane Smiley who will be leaving. I'll not have staff going behind my back, especially to collude with you."

"You can't run the Home without Jane Smiley."

"She'll be missed." Mother was right that Mrs. Smiley's removal would be a huge loss, but one he was ready to bear. "But I assure you we will get by. We always do."

"If you persist in this nonsense, I'll withdraw from

the board and take patrons with me. I'll not be associated with such scandalous behavior."

Daniel had been waiting for that. He'd known it was in the offing since the moment he chose to come here. Perhaps he'd been waiting months—years, even—for whatever offense would eventually drive Mother off. It should be terrifying, but Daniel found the only emotion he felt was a hollow, weary relief.

"And we will suffer your loss as well—but we will survive it." Somewhere, from a place he was sure could have come only from God's supernatural mercy, Daniel heard himself say, "End this, Mother. Ida is not your enemy. We are all we have, you and I. This is not what Father would have wanted."

"Don't you dare bring your father into this. It's enough I had to ship away one of *his* pretty little underlings and sit there smiling about it. I will not stand for it in my son."

His father? Someone from the Home? "You're lying."

"Am I? How do you think I was able to accomplish this so quickly? I've done it before, Daniel. I know how. I wasn't talking about Shepler before. I was talking about your father and one of the teachers. I'd hoped to spare you this, but since you now seem to take after him in every regard…"

"Stop that!"

"Stop what? Aren't we telling the truth now? Isn't that what you want?"

Daniel felt the air turn to dust in his lungs. The sterling reputation of Harold Parker, the man whose character Daniel strove every day to emulate? A man who did so much good in the world that Daniel woke up every morning feeling the weight of his name press down on his conscience?

"No, it wasn't pleasant, but this is what married women must do to protect our families. Your father came to thank me for what I was able to do, and in time I was able to forgive him for what he'd done."

Even as she said the words Daniel could see she had not ever forgiven him. How easily a cold marriage could hide in a civil society. It made him yearn for Ida's warmth all the more.

"I'm going to marry her, Mother, if she'll have me." He hadn't even settled on the idea until this very instant, but it made perfect, immediate sense the moment the words hit the air. Daniel wished he could have turned and proposed to Ida right then; the urge was that profound and irrefutable.

"If she'll have you?" Mother nearly spat the words out. "You are Daniel Parker! You cannot marry some wild mountain woman like that."

"I can indeed. And I shall, if she says yes, which I expect she will. I'll be happy, Mother. Does that mean anything at all to you?"

She looked at him as though he were a lost cause. One of her projects now beyond hope. Whatever the expression was, it wasn't anything he would classify as the kind of look a mother ought to give a son. There seemed to be no love in it at all, just a pale wash of long-suffering disappointment. "You are just like your father."

"I hope in many ways that's true." In all the good ways, that is. For what man is without fault? And who could even know where the truth stood in whatever

Mother told him tonight, or ever, now? He could only aspire to the character he knew and follow where God led.

And God led him to Ida.

As he looked at his mother, he felt the final snap of their long-strained relationship, the burst of a man coming into his own true identity out from behind a shadow he hadn't even realized was there.

It was done.

It had been a tortuously long day, but Daniel felt weightless, scrubbed clean of an obligation that no longer made sense. He hoped that someday he might find a way to repair the relationship to the point of civility, but he was grateful the obligation to Amelia Parker was forever severed. Too many children depended on Daniel Parker for it to stand as it was.

It was time to go home.

Her life was in tangles. Ida was used to causing trouble, but not to making enemies. The thought of Jane Smiley and Amelia Parker—two women she had actually thought were coming to like her—plotting her removal was hard to bear. She felt her own heart was as beaten and bruised as Gitch's jaw. Then again, that same heart was so full of love and wonder over Daniel, it was hard to believe the day had gone so far in opposite directions. Such happiness in the midst of such sadness—how was it life could come up with such a clash all at once?

In the darkened ward, listening to Gitch's breathing, Ida groped for stillness and balance one stitch at a time. The ward had a dozen or so children in it, and it struck her how wounds came in visible and invisible forms. The boys and girls at the Home came from lost, missing, broken or embittered families. What was to become of Daniel's family tonight? Could God somehow save the relationship between Daniel and Amelia Parker? Or was Daniel about to become a different kind of orphan?

I can't see Your plan, Ida prayed as she sat knitting in the dim light, her eyes not even seeing the stitches, her fingers working the yarn by sheer touch, as she'd seen the Catholic nuns at the army hospital worry at their rosaries. *Will the Home survive? Can Daniel and I have a life together? Have I truly helped or just made a terrible mess of things?*

She couldn't know. She couldn't move the obstacles surrounding her. She could only be who she was, where she was. She could tend to Gitch, she could love Daniel, and perhaps knit an ounce of peace and stillness into the growing darkness.

All the rest would have to be God's territory.

Chapter Twenty-Four

Daniel felt like a different person as he made his way into the hospital ward. It was past midnight, and while he should have been exhausted, he felt an energized peace, as if he'd just woken up from a long sleep. In many ways, he had.

Ida was beautiful as she slept, her head tucked onto a free corner of Gitch's bed, the child's hand still grasped in hers. The low lights of the hospital ward cast long shadows over the scene, mixing with the blue-white of the moonlight that came through the windows. He couldn't help but see the world in Ida's colors now; the flush of Gitch's wounded lips against the pale of her skin and the way Ida's hair made cascades of red-gold circles around her temples.

Ida had changed him. Ida had changed everything. *I'm so grateful, Father God*, he breathed into the night air. *I'll trust You with what You have planned for us next, but I don't mind saying it's a rather frightening affair*. He smiled, thinking Ida would laugh at the honesty in his prayer.

"Dr. Parker?" the night nurse whispered and tapped on his shoulder, curling one finger to call him aside.

"How is she?"

"Frightened, uncomfortable, but I don't think we could expect much more given her injury. Miss Landway said you would be returning, so Dr. Hartwick told me to tell you he feels it may be eight to ten weeks before the wires can be removed."

Eight to ten weeks. That would seem like forever to someone Gitch's age. "And after that?"

"Difficult to say, but Dr. Hartwick did say her speech will most likely be impaired. There's some question about the vision in the right eye, but it's too early to tell. I'm sure you know that."

Daniel turned to look at poor Gitch, his heart swelling with concern. He wanted to do something, but there wasn't anything to do. "She's been wonderful," the older nurse said, nodding to Ida. "She drew pictures for all the other children when Miss Gwen was asleep."

Daniel looked around and saw that, indeed, there were small pictures tacked up over the beds of the other children in the ward. He recognized her drawings instantly. Three decorated the wall over Gitch's headboard.

"What I wouldn't give for more like her around here," the nurse said as she closed her notes. "You're fortunate to have her at the Home."

Daniel felt his throat tighten. "You've no idea how much."

He moved over to sit quietly beside Ida's sleeping form. The knitting lay at the foot of the bed, the ball of yarn on the floor where it had rolled from the covers. Daniel picked up the yarn and placed it back on the bed. The motion roused Ida, who woke to blink at him with sleepy eyes.

"You're back."

He loved her to distraction at that moment. He knew with absolute certainty that he belonged with her, and she with him. *So this is what all those poems are about*, he thought, amused. *They were right.*

"You're smiling?" She yawned the question as she straightened up.

"I was thinking how much I love you." The words were lush and close, whispered so soft in the low light.

"Well, that's mighty nice to hear." She gently slid her fingers from Gitch's grasp, and the child murmured and settled deeper into her pillows. Ida's face grew serious as she woke further. "How was it?"

The unpleasant details seemed too sharp for this tender place. "Over. Done. Nothing that needs recounting now."

She looked at him, puzzled. "How?"

Daniel merely shook his head.

Ida took his hand. "Daniel, she's your mother."

"She's a mean, conniving old woman trying to take something that cannot be hers. She won't be a bother to us anymore."

"I know she's terrible, but…"

"Marry me."

Ida blinked. "What?"

"Marry me. The Parker Home needs a Mrs. Parker. *I* need a Mrs. Parker. I know it's the middle of the night, but I don't need another hour to think about it. I know. Marry me."

Ida smiled. "I thought *I* was the impulsive one."

"Well, evidently you are contagious."

She leaned toward him. "How delightful. Yes. I will absolutely marry you, Daniel Parker."

Wide awake, Daniel kissed her until the ward nurse gave a warning tap on her clipboard, smiling even as she *tsk*ed and shook her finger.

Ida woke in her bed at the Home weary and disoriented. The sun was already high in the sky—she'd not come back from Roper until nearly two in the morning when Daniel had sent for MacNeil to come and take her home. Evidently the groundskeeper had told the staff to let her sleep.

It felt as if years had been stuffed into the past twenty-four hours. Yesterday's sun had risen on a normal Home day until the summons to Amelia Parker's parlor had begun the chaotic chain of events still unfolding. Ida drew in a deep breath and touched the battered spine of her Bible as it lay open on her bedside table. She'd thought herself too wound up to sleep and had opened the Psalms for comfort last night, but hadn't lasted two pages before nodding off. *I know none of yesterday came as a surprise to You, Father*, Ida prayed, *but it sure did to me. Watch over Gitch. Watch over Daniel while he's still there with her. Watch over all of us.*

She'd wanted to stay with him, but Daniel was right—the children needed her presence. Her gifts to calm and distract might be the best resources they had today as things continued to tilt and whirl. She'd slept through too much of the day as it was.

Ida made quick work of washing and dressing. Her shoulders ached from the long hours in the metal hospital chair, and she needed a gallon of coffee. She wrestled her hair into a bun, but declared the dark circles under her eyes beyond repair. "It'll have to do," she told her reflection in the mirror, feeling nowhere near strong enough to face the day.

Ah, but there was one amazing, powerful thing a week of sleepless nights couldn't undo: Daniel had asked her to marry him. Ida put her hands to her beating heart, amazed again that her cautious, thoughtful Daniel had made such a bold move. She stared at the letter from Dr. Bennet at Walter Reed, a rush of gratitude filling her. *To think I was ready to leave. Oh Father, how You've hemmed me in when I was ready to run away.*

The shift in Daniel's life, in the Home's life, would be hard. Starting today—starting this hour, when she walked out of this room. *Hard never stopped me before.* Ida walked to the window and peered out, listening for the sounds of children. Until the busy, serious quiet of the hospital, she hadn't even realized how much the growing chatter of the Home had become an encouragement to her. The noise was life, and she loved her life here.

She tied her nurse's apron in a strong, declarative knot and headed for the door. Just before opening it, she stopped and closed her eyes. *Lord, if ever there was a day I needed a guard on my tongue... Send me all the grace and mercy You can. I don't know what I'll do when I see Jane Smiley, but I'll try to make sure it honors You.*

After finding a large cup of coffee in the kitchen, Ida went to find Mr. MacNeil. She located him out in the yard.

He leaned on his shovel and mopped the sweat from his brow. "How are you faring this morning?"

"A bit worse for wear, but I'll survive, thank you."

"In all the rumpus, I neglected to offer my congratulations last night." His eyes gleamed. "Dr. Parker looked as though he was burstin' to tell someone. I found it rather funny that it ended up being me."

Ida shared his grin. "And why not you?" She gestured around the compound. "This is his family."

"You're right there, lass. But if you'd like to avoid a 'family argument,' I'd steer wide of Mrs. Smiley. She's a fierce one on a good day, aye? And this is far from a good day, if you ken my meaning."

"Daniel told her to leave, didn't he?" She could still hardly believe Mrs. Smiley had gone to Amelia Parker the way she had. She'd truly thought she and the schoolmistress were getting along—well, as "along" as anyone got with Jane Smiley.

"I've never heard him use such a tone, ever. He stopped classes, made Grimshaw take them all outside, marched her into his office and closed the door. Even behind two closed doors, I heard him. It's a wonder she didn't stomp off right then. I think, if she had somewhere else to go, she would have."

"I can't *not* see her."

MacNeil sent his shovel into the sandy soil. "Well, I'd just be terrible careful about how you do, then. Not anywhere near the young ones." He looked up at her. "They need to see you. They were all scared when poor Gitch was hurt and you weren't here."

Ida put her hand to her forehead. "How on earth am I supposed to see the children and yet avoid Mrs. Smiley?"

MacNeil took out his pocket watch and checked the time. Of course! "Lunch duty!" The group charged with setting the lunch tables would be down in the dining room while Mrs. Smiley and the rest were still in classes. Ida startled MacNeil with a quick peck to the cheek before she hurried off. "It won't be all of them, but it will be a start." After that, she could impose on Fritz Grimshaw to let her into the boys' classes to say hello later. This wasn't so impossible after all.

Ida dearly hoped it was Donna's turn on lunch duty, and was grateful to pull the young woman into a fierce hug as she entered the dining room. "Thank you for all you did to help me yesterday, Donna."

"How is Gitch? Will she be okay?"

Ida held both of Donna's hands. "She has lots of recovering ahead of her, but you know our Gitch. She won't let this keep her down for long." Ida looked up at the collection of Daniel's cards still gracing the staff dining room doors. "I think it's time we got everyone started on cards for Gitch, don't you?"

Donna smiled. "I already did. No one could sleep, so I went and got your pastels and papers out." The teen's eyes grew very serious, and she pulled in close. "I'm sorry I went into your rooms like that, but I tried to think what you would do. And I'm sorry to admit that I saw the letter on your desk—I didn't mean to snoop, honest, but it was just lying there. Tell me you aren't leaving us, Nurse Ida. I couldn't stand it if you left."

"I'm not going anywhere, Donna. I promise. You and I will have a long talk about that later. As for the papers and pastels, you did the right thing. We'll just need to make sure the Home has an art room from now on in, don't you think?"

The other students at the far end of the room had noticed Ida's presence now and came rushing up to her. A dozen questions from "Where were you?" to "Is Gitch dead?" flew at her in a matter of seconds.

"Whoa, there!" Ida exclaimed, grabbing as many of the outstretched hands as she could. "Gitch is alive and well but rather banged up, I'm afraid. She'll have lots of recovering to do—much more than Dr. Parker did—so she'll need our support."

"I drew her flowers," one girl said. "Blue ones because she likes blue."

Ida touched the child's long brown braids, thinking of Gitch's matted hair underneath the ghastly bandages. "She'll like that."

"I drew her cookies because she likes those," another girl offered.

"That may be the only kind of cookies she can enjoy for a while." Ida sat down on one of the dining table benches and gathered the girls around her. "Her jaw," she explained, pointing to the bone Gitch had fractured, "broke when she fell, and they can't put a cast on it like an arm or a leg. So they have to wire it shut to help it stay still."

The youngest girl winced and gasped.

"I know it sounds like it hurts, but mostly the hardest part is that Gitch can't talk or chew or eat like you and I for many weeks. She'll need lots of love from us, and help keeping her spirits up."

"She'll get it," Donna said, taking the hand of the small girl. What leadership young Miss Forley had shown in the crisis of the past hours. Ida was so very proud of her. "From all of us."

"Of that, I have no doubt," came Daniel's voice from

the other end of the room. Ida hadn't even realized he was on the compound. Had his appearance really changed so, or was it just how much the world had tilted in the past twenty-four hours that altered her view of him? He stood taller and stronger and even more settled.

"Dr. Parker!" The herd of children rushed from her side to his. Even the way he bent down to answer little Audrey's question seemed transformed. It kindled such a warm glow in her chest that Ida felt she could face a dozen Jane Smileys and not lose hope.

"I have a job for you girls," he said tenderly. "Run upstairs and tell all the classes that lunch will be one half hour early today."

"That's in fifteen minutes," Donna said, looking around the room. "We're not finished setting."

"We'll manage. I want everyone downstairs. Everyone needs to hear how our Gwendolyn is faring—" he caught Ida's eyes above the group of upturned faces "—and Miss Landway and I have important news to share."

Chapter Twenty-Five

T he girls needed no more encouragement than that to scurry upstairs and leave Daniel and Ida in the empty dining hall.

She rushed to his side, and a surge of happiness coursed through his weary body when she took his hands. Would it always be like this? He dearly hoped so. A man felt he could conquer the whole world with such a boost of spirits. Daniel longed to kiss her—soundly and more than once—but decided holding her hand might be shocking enough for anyone from the now-frantic kitchen staff who might happen into the room.

"Here? Now?" Ida asked. He enjoyed that the blissful sparkle of her eyes showed the same love-struck quality that had carried him all morning.

"Can you think of a better time or place?"

She laughed. "I was just telling Mr. MacNeil that the people here really are your family."

Daniel joined in her laughter. "You should have seen his surprise when I told him. I believe you've improved his estimation of me considerably."

She squeezed his hand. "He is so very fond of you, you know." Her face grew serious. "I'm sure I can't say the same of Mrs. Smiley. MacNeil warned me to stay away from her today. Do you really want her to hear it like this?"

"Believe it or not, I think it's the best way. She'll know there's no going back on our plans, and she wouldn't dare make a scene in front of the children. If she's as smart as I hope she is, she will use it as an excuse for a quiet exit."

"Gracious, you're absolutely right. I declare, what a very clever man I'm going to marry." He watched as the words struck her with delight, feeling it, as well. "I'm going to marry Dr. Daniel Parker." She whispered it like the grandest of news. It was, wasn't it?

"Gitch was awake this morning. I talked her through everything that had happened and that will happen. She was very brave."

"Donna went and found my pastels and already has the girls making cards." She took one of Daniel's hands in both of hers. "I don't think we should make her and Matty wait, Daniel. They're ready. When they graduate, they should marry. I know I couldn't stand the thought of waiting now, and Donna has been so mature in all this."

Daniel took off his glasses and pinched the bridge of his nose. "I have to admit I was thinking the very same thing." Her eyes were so warm and intense. "I'd marry you this afternoon if I thought I could manage a free hour."

"Goodness," she declared with a laugh, "I really have infected you, haven't I?"

"A happy contagion to be sure."

* * *

The unmistakable sound of fifty-seven pairs of excited feet filled the hallway, and Daniel led Ida to the front of the dining hall to greet the children and staff. Ida felt his hand solidly around hers, and she felt her stomach give a small flip as one or two of the older students noticed their clasped hands.

The staff mostly looked curious—some of them looked alarmed, worried that Dr. Parker had gathered them to hear grim news. Ida could watch their faces fill with relief as they entered the room, so it must have been obvious by her and Daniel's expressions that good news was about to be delivered. She watched the children file into their table groupings, her heart lightening further with the chatter. So much had changed since her first visit to this room and its unnerving quiet. It was still orderly—or as orderly as hungry and excited children could achieve—but it was a happy, hopeful kind of efficiency. The kind of a busy kitchen or a bustling home. *Thank You, Father, for all You have done here. For the children, for Daniel and for me.*

Ida felt Daniel give her hand one final squeeze before clearing his throat loudly and raising his hands to quiet the children.

"We've had a difficult time since last night, but I want to say I am proud of all of you for handling it as well as you have. You all have shown Parker Home to be the family it is, both in taking care of each other and in showing care for Miss Martin."

"Is Gitch all right?" a thin voice, pitched high with concern, piped up from one side of the room.

Daniel clasped his hands behind his back. "Gitch will make a good recovery, yes." Ida gave no outward sign of how she recognized that reply for the merciful doctor's answer that it was. Every nurse knew that "making a good recovery" was not the same thing as being "all right," but now was a time for reassurances. Daniel had confided that Gitch might never speak as clearly as she had before the accident, and that she had a long road to getting better.

Ida knew, however, that Gitch had the vital advantages of a hearty spirit and lots of support. Already she'd seen more fight in the small girl than in some hardened soldiers with half her wounds. Whatever life lay ahead for Gitch, she would embrace it. Ida felt a glow in her heart from the knowledge that she would be here at the Home to help make that happen.

"Gitch will be in the hospital for a month or so, and then we hope to bring her back to us to finish her recovery. I'm confident all of you will do whatever it takes to help Gitch heal. And I'll make sure the cards you made her last night get delivered to her as soon as possible."

Ida felt Daniel's demeanor stiffen a little and she looked up to see Mrs. Smiley walk slowly into the room with a narrow-eyed glare.

"I have other news that I want to share." She heard him take a deep breath, and it struck her further what an enormous leap this was for Daniel to be taking on her behalf. On behalf of both of them, really. She held her own breath, and turned her eyes to watch Daniel rather than to do battle with the steely stare of Jane Smiley.

"We have all come to think of Nurse Landway as part of our family here." He faltered, making Ida think he was in the process of discarding whatever carefully worded speech he had prepared. She wanted to take his hand, but knew the moment must be his to command.

"I know you all join me in feeling that the Parker Home is a far better place for her...unique and colorful contributions.

"The truth of the matter is that she's become very special—to all of us. And to me especially. And, so..." He coughed, a flush coming to his face, and Ida felt a hundred pounds lighter when he simply reached for her hand before continuing. "And so I wanted you all to be the first to know that Miss Landway and I will be married just as soon as we can make arrangements."

Squeals—really, there was no other word for the sound—erupted from the girls' tables while the boys gaped in shock. The room seemed equally divided into those who couldn't be more thrilled and/or shocked, and those who nodded to each other in an "I told you they were sweet on each other" fashion. All semblance of order was lost for a boisterous bit of time, with girls tumbling out of their seats to come up and give Ida a hug and staff members, including a grinning Fritz Grimshaw, shaking Daniel's hand in congratulations.

"I knew it!" Donna said as she crushed Ida in an enthusiastic hug. "Martha said I was imagining things, but I knew it! Now you won't be leaving."

Ida felt such a surge of near-maternal affection for the young woman that she found herself choking back tears. "I'm not ever leaving, Donna. This is my home now. And you were a big part in making it that way."

"Who'd have thought you'd beat me to the altar?" Donna said, her smile enormous and stuffed with happiness.

"Well, let's just see about that." Ida winked, nodded toward Daniel and gave the girl another big squeeze before a trio of smaller girls grabbed at her nursing apron and began pulling her away.

She managed, as she was being tugged toward a table filled with well-wishers, to look up toward the back of the room. Jane Smiley's eyes were alternating between popping wide in astonishment and squinting narrow in rage. As if she had two-dozen reactions to what had happened and couldn't decide which awful one to feel first. As wounded as she had been by Mrs. Smiley's betrayal, Ida now found herself too full of happiness not to find a tiny portion of pity for the woman.

"Oh, lass," said Mr. MacNeil, who had just ducked in the kitchen door to catch the end of the announcement, "I'm so happy for the pair of you. You've been a good thing for Daniel, and he's a smart enough man to know it, aye?" He winked. "Don't you worry about her," he added softly, following Ida's gaze out the door Mrs. Smiley had just stormed through like a round, black raincloud. "She'll make noise and fuss, but she knows better than to make too much trouble. And I'm not so sure Mrs. Parker wouldn't have done what she did with or without Smiley's help. She had it out for you all along, I'm sad to say." He gave Ida's hands a squeeze. "But like I said, Daniel's a smart man and knows a good thing's worth fighting for. You'll be grand together, I'm sure of that."

Daniel felt he had just leaped off a terribly high cliff, and had barely been able to eat with all the fuss at lunch. He had only a few minutes to spare before he would be forced to attack the mountain of paperwork at his desk, but he wasn't at all sure his brain would focus after a day like today.

Ida came up behind him as he stood at the doorway of his study, and together they looked out over the mass of children as they took their outside recreation after lunch. She looked as happy and as spent as he felt.

"Thank you," she said, her hand resting on his chest.

"For what?"

"For all of it. For here, and for all you've done." She inhaled deeply before adding, "And for the fight ahead of you. Ahead of us."

"It's only a fight if you think you can't win. If you know you will win, then it's only a struggle. You know, my father said that to me. I think today I understand it better than I ever have before."

"Well then, it's a struggle you won't have to face alone." She drew herself up. "I hear tell the future Mrs. Daniel Parker is a very stubborn sort."

His arm slipped around her waist. "Impulsive, even."

"Decisive," she corrected.

"Beautiful," he added, letting one finger wander through the waves of her hair that had already escaped her bun.

"And rather smitten," she said, smiling up at him.

How had he grown even more handsome? The authority had always been there, but now the severity that used to darken his eyes was gone, replaced with a warm glow. Daniel was capable of such tremendous care—it made her feel as if she sparkled like sunlight to know he loved her.

She stood on tiptoe and kissed him, not caring that they were right there in the window where the children could see. Children ought to see love every day—most especially these children. "It's one of God's best gifts, you know," she said as she leaned her head against his shoulder.

"A kiss? I admit, I agree." She could hear the broad smile in his voice as he murmured into her hair.

Ida swatted his chest gently. "No, silly—love. My mama said love never took love away, only made more love. That's why you can never use it up." She looked up at him, wanting to see his eyes as she tried to get the fullness of her heart into words. "I love these children. And I love you. One only gives more to the other, not less. It's like it doubles itself because both are there. I have more love to give because I give more love." She pursed her lips, unsatisfied with the description. "Does that make any sense?"

"As much as colored socks do in an orphanage." His words teased, but Daniel's eyes told her he understood completely. His arms tightened around her. They gave her strength, his arms. She'd never felt more sure this was where she belonged.

"Colored socks make loads of sense in this orphanage," she declared. "I want it to always be that way."

Daniel made a face as if he were committing the command to memory. "Parker Home children shall have colored socks until further notice."

"Knit by Mrs. Daniel Parker and her friends." Ida sighed. "Mrs. Daniel Parker. I do like the sound of that."

Daniel kissed her forehead. "Mrs. Daniel Parker," he echoed. A ball bounced by the window, sending one of the children scurrying after it. The girl picked up the ball, but not before stopping to offer a giggling wave at the two of them through the glass. Ida thought her heart must be spilling so much happiness, even Mama in West Virginia could surely feel it.

"Will you still be Nurse Ida to the children?" Daniel asked.

"Of course!" she replied instantly, then thought about that for a moment. "Can't I? Is there some sort of rule about that kind of thing?"

Daniel pulled away just enough to look her in the eye. "When have you cared about the rules?"

She shrugged. "Will I have to start caring about them as Mrs. Daniel Parker?" She was ready to, if it came to that. She knew she'd have to make some changes to help shoulder the social expectations Daniel dealt with in order to keep the Home up and running. Ida dearly hoped Isabelle Hooper would help her with that, as well as John and Leanne.

His eyes gleamed. "In time, but there's no reason to start now. We've broken half a dozen in the last twenty-four hours alone." He nodded toward the window. "And look how happy those children are." He pulled her closer. "I'm better for you being here, Ida. We all are."

Ida wrapped her arms around Daniel as tight as she could. "Oh, it's good to be home."

Epilogue

June 1930

Dear Auntie Isabelle,
Thank you so much for the graduation present.
Turning eighteen feels like such a grand thing!
I'm very excited to be going off to nursing school
in the fall, and especially glad I will be nearer to
you. I'll be ever so thankful to have you to intro-
duce me to a much bigger city like Atlanta. I can't
wait to see your new dog as well—Chester was so
loved here at the Home, the little ones cried when
you moved and still talk about him.

I'm sure all the other Aunties have kept you
up to date on the big party we are having to cel-
ebrate Dr. and Mrs. Parker's tenth anniversary.
Little Hal is five now, toddling around the Home
and just beginning to understand how he's come
to have so many "brothers and sisters." He is giving poor Mrs. Ida a terrible time, tired as she is
with the new baby coming. Much as Hal loves
the distraction, I think Dr. Parker is regretting

the puppy—he is a wild thing. They named him "Chessie"—after your wonderful dog, I'm sure. Mrs. Ida says it's a blessing she has lots of us "nannies" all ready to help out, and I agree. We are all hoping for a girl, as is Mrs. Ida, I think (she'll never say such a thing of course, but I notice she's been knitting far more little pink socks than little blue ones).

The new nurse—another one from the army base, too—is very nice and has been here since March. I think she fits in well, but I continue to go and find Mrs. Ida when my jaw hurts on rainy days. I still think of the silly faces she made back during all those dreadful speech exercises. I hope I become as fine a nurse as Mrs. Ida. I cannot draw like she can, but I've discovered how much I love writing. I have rather a decent singing voice, too—and I hardly ever lisp when I sing!

I knit my first sweater this month. You would be so proud—it turned out quite nicely, and was just the thing for the red cotton yarn you gave me for Christmas. I've taught several of the younger ones to knit socks, just like you taught me. It's funny to watch Dr. Parker explain to visitors why all the girls here have such wonderful, brightly colored socks. We've had lots of visitors with the new wing being built. Can you imagine the Parker Home with over a hundred children? I'm sure I'll barely recognize it when I come for visits when school is out.

"Auntie Donna" heads up a whole other group of "Aunties" now, although they are more big sisters than wonderful, wise Aunties like you. She and "Uncle Matthew"—we certainly couldn't keep calling him "Matty" when he became a father and opened his own brickyard, could we?— are expecting their third baby in November. We see them a lot because Donna runs the volunteers who keep up the gardens and Matthew's firm is handling all the bricks for the new wing.

I must go and finish studying for my last exam—the girls' matron is very strict about study halls! I promise to send word the day my feet land in Atlanta and dearly look forward to being able to visit you much more. God bless you and keep you, dear Auntie!

Love,

Gitch

PS: I've decided to go by "Gwen" in school—what do you think? No matter what, I trust I will always be "Gitch" to you and all my Parker family.

* * * * *

Dear Reader,

Each of us brings special gifts to the world around us. Sometimes they are easy to see, other times they appear "odd" to others. Our uniqueness is part of God's perfectly woven tapestry, and can always be trusted. I hope Ida and Daniel's story has helped you see what particular gifts you bring to the world around you. If you haven't yet read *Homefront Hero* (Love Inspired Historical, May 2012), you can go back and discover how Ida and Leanne became friends and read Leanne and John's dramatic love story.

The Charleston Orphan House was a much larger institution than my fictitious Parker Home for Orphans, but straining from the same dire need presented by what the Great War had done to children and families. The plunge baths were actually a part of the Charleston Orphan House, odd as it may sound. Children were indeed indentured into communities—often with frightening results. The Aunties are based on real women who became pen pals with Charleston Orphan House children—but the sock knitting is of my own devising. As for treatment philosophies, conventional wisdom at the time was just coming around to the shift from an institutional atmosphere to something known as the "cottage plan"—a change depicted by Ida's sensibilities in this book. Tight finances and scarce resources, however, were true realities at both orphanages in Charleston—the Charleston Orphan House for white children and the Jenkins Orphanage for black children (still in existence today as the Jenkins Institute). Both institutions enjoyed broad public support and donations, but always the need outpaced charitable giving. Many orphans went on to live long, happy lives with close relationships to fellow students serving as stand-in "relations." Proof that a family is indeed where you find love, genetics notwithstanding.

I love to hear from readers—knitters and nonknitters alike—so please visit my website at www.alliepleiter. com, email me at allie@alliepleiter.com, stop by my Facebook page at www.facebook.com/alliepleiter or write me at PO Box 7026 Villa Park, IL 60181. I'm eager to hear from you!

Warmly,

COMING NEXT MONTH FROM
Love Inspired® Historical

Available May 5, 2015

WAGON TRAIN SWEETHEART
Journey West
by Lacy Williams
The hazards of the wagon train frighten Emma Hewitt even *before* she's asked to nurse enigmatic Nathan Reed. Yet the loner hides a kind, protective nature she could learn to love... if not for the groom-to-be awaiting her in Oregon.

SECOND CHANCE HERO
Texas Grooms
by Winnie Griggs
When Nate Cooper saves a little girl from a runaway wagon, the child's single mother is beyond grateful. But can Nate ever let go of his troubled past to forge a future with Verity Leggett?

LOVE BY DESIGN
The Dressmaker's Daughters
by Christine Johnson
Former stunt pilot Dan Wagner has already taken Jen Fox's seat on a rare expedition, and—despite their mutual interest—she's not about to offer him a spot in her guarded heart.

A FAMILY FOUND
by Laura Abbot
As a single father, Tate Lockwood has his hands full with two inquisitive sons. But maybe their headstrong—and beautiful—tutor, Sophie Montgomery, can fill the missing piece in their motherless family...

LIHCNM0415

REQUEST YOUR FREE BOOKS!

2 FREE INSPIRATIONAL NOVELS
PLUS 2
FREE
MYSTERY GIFTS

Love Inspired
HISTORICAL
INSPIRATIONAL HISTORICAL ROMANCE

YES! Please send me 2 FREE Love Inspired® Historical novels and my 2 FREE mystery gifts (gifts are worth about $10). After receiving them, if I don't wish to receive any more books, I can return the shipping statement marked "cancel." If I don't cancel, I will receive 4 brand-new novels every month and be billed just $4.74 per book in the U.S. or $5.24 per book in Canada. That's a saving of at least 21% off the cover price. It's quite a bargain! Shipping and handling is just 50¢ per book in the U.S. and 75¢ per book in Canada.* I understand that accepting the 2 free books and gifts places me under no obligation to buy anything. I can always return a shipment and cancel at any time. Even if I never buy another book, the two free books and gifts are mine to keep forever.

102/302 IDN F5CN

Name	(PLEASE PRINT)	

Address		Apt. #

City	State/Prov.	Zip/Postal Code

Signature (if under 18, a parent or guardian must sign)

Mail to the Harlequin® Reader Service:
IN U.S.A.: P.O. Box 1867, Buffalo, NY 14240-1867
IN CANADA: P.O. Box 609, Fort Erie, Ontario L2A 5X3

Want to try two free books from another series?
Call 1-800-873-8635 or visit www.ReaderService.com.

* Terms and prices subject to change without notice. Prices do not include applicable taxes. Sales tax applicable in N.Y. Canadian residents will be charged applicable taxes. Offer not valid in Quebec. This offer is limited to one order per household. Not valid for current subscribers to Love Inspired Historical books. All orders subject to credit approval. Credit or debit balances in a customer's account(s) may be offset by any other outstanding balance owed by or to the customer. Please allow 4 to 6 weeks for delivery. Offer available while quantities last.

LIHI3R

Emma went looking for Nathan.

He stood in the shadows behind the wagon. Alone, just as he'd been since he'd come into their caravan to drive for the Binghams. He watched her approach without speaking.

But there was something in the expression on his face. A wish...

Maybe the same wish that was in her heart.

Stunned that he'd allowed her to see it, he who was usually so closed off, she swallowed hard.

"I need you, Nathan," she said softly, reaching out a hand for him.

He jolted, as if her words had physically touched him.

"The children are restless. Come and tell a story. Please. At least until supper."

And he came.

He settled near the fire, but far enough away to be out of her way. His surprise was evident in the vulnerable cast of his expression when Sam crawled into his lap and rested his back against Nathan's chest.

As she worked with Millie to cook the stew and some pan biscuits, he told of tracking a cougar on a weeklong hunt. Of the winter that another trapper had stolen furs out of Nathan's traps until he'd figured out what was happening. Of losing a favorite horse and having to pack out a season's worth of furs by himself.

"Your beau is so brave, going on so many adventures," Millie said softly at one point, as they began ladling the stew into bowls for the children. "And not bad to look at, either."

Emma looked up to find Nathan's eyes on her. Had he heard Millie? She couldn't tell.

She didn't think quite the same about Nathan's stories of life in the wilderness. Each adventure sounded...*lonely*. His stories reflected that he was alone most of the time.

The isolation would have driven her crazy, she was sure. Not having someone to talk to, to listen to her joys and sorrows...

She regretted the resentment she'd held for her siblings over the trip West. She'd been at fault for not expressing her fears and desire to stay back home. She was thankful she'd come, or she never would have faced her fears.

But more than that, she wanted to give that to Nathan. Family.

Would he let her? Would he let her in?

Don't miss
WAGON TRAIN SWEETHEART
by Lacy Williams,
available May 2015 wherever
Love Inspired® Historical books and ebooks are sold.

When the truth comes to light about Oregon Jeffries's daughter, will Duke Martin ever be the same again?

Read on for a sneak preview of
THE RANCHER TAKES A BRIDE,
the next book in
Brenda Minton's
miniseries **MARTIN'S CROSSING**.

"So, Oregon Jeffries. Tell me everything," Duke said.

"I think you know."

"Enlighten me."

"When I first came to Martin's Crossing, I thought you'd recognize me. But you didn't. I was just the mother of the girl who swept the porch of your diner. You didn't remember me." She shrugged, waiting for him to say something.

He shook his head. "I'm afraid to admit I have a few blank spots in my memory. You probably know that already."

"It's become clear since I got to town and you didn't recognize me."

"Or my daughter?"

His words froze her heart. Oregon trembled and she didn't want to be weak. Not today. Today she needed strength and the truth. Some people thought the truth could set her free. She worried it would only mean losing her daughter to this man who had already made himself a hero to Lilly.

"She's my daughter." He repeated it again, his voice soft with wonder.

"Yes, she's your daughter," she whispered.

"Why didn't you try to contact me?" He sat down, stretching his long legs in front of him. "Did you think I wouldn't want to know?"

"I heard from friends that you had an alcohol problem. And then I found out you joined the army. Duke, I was used to my mother hooking up with men who were abusive and alcoholic. I didn't want that for my daughter."

"You should have told me," Duke stormed in a quiet voice. Looks could be deceiving. He looked like Goliath. But beneath his large exterior, he was good and kind.

"You've been in town over a year. You should have told me sooner," he repeated.

"Maybe I should have, but I needed to know you, to be sure about you before I put you in my daughter's life."

"You kept her from me," he said in a quieter voice.

"I was eighteen and alone and making stupid decisions. And now I'm a mom who has to make sure her daughter isn't going to be hurt."

He studied her for a few seconds. "Why did you change your mind and decide to bring her to Martin's Crossing?"

"I knew she needed you."

Don't miss
THE RANCHER TAKES A BRIDE
by Brenda Minton,
available May 2015 wherever
Love Inspired® books and ebooks are sold.

LIEXP0415